DRIVEN BY AMBITION

GAMBLE RACING
BOOK 3

RENÉE DAHLIA

DRIVEN BY AMBITION

RENÉE DAHLIA

Two men in the spotlight with too much chemistry...

Media personality and retired driver Freddy Hiptonstall knows one thing. Getting involved with someone in the S1 paddock only leads to disaster, so why can't he stay away from Gamble Racing's new Team Principal?

Suddenly promoted to Team Principal, Jaxxon Loharani-Jones has a lot to prove. He's always been ambitious, but now he needs to step up and run Gamble Racing as the second youngest Team Principal in S1 history. The last thing he needs is a distraction.

The chemistry between them results in kisses, but will the intimate nature of their work be too much for their burgeoning relationship with all the pressures of their jobs?

ABOUT THE AUTHOR

An avid reader, Renée Dahlia writes contemporary and historical queer romance. Renée is a bisexual cis woman who is fascinated by people and loves to explore human relationships, with a side of humour, through her writing. Renée has a degree in physics and mathematics, using this to write data-based magazine articles for the horse racing industry. Her love of horses often shines through in her fiction, and she loves a good intrigue and to escape the real world in the pages of a book. When she isn't reading or writing, Renée spends her time with her four children, usually watching them play cricket.

FOREWORD

Welcome to DRIVEN BY AMBITION, the third book in the Gamble Racing series.

If you love gay sports romance with a rivals to lovers theme, workplace tension, and a little mystery thrown in, Driven by Passion is the book for you. This series contains a few mystery plots that continue between each book; however, I have tried to make each book a standalone read.

Please note this book contains a car crash causing disability, alcoholism, medical debt, stalking.

This book is written in Australian English and some spelling and phrases may be unfamiliar to American readers.

If you are keen to keep up to date on new releases and, more importantly, sales, I recommend you sign up to my newsletter at reneedahlia.com or follow me on social media.

I hope you enjoy reading this book!

Renée

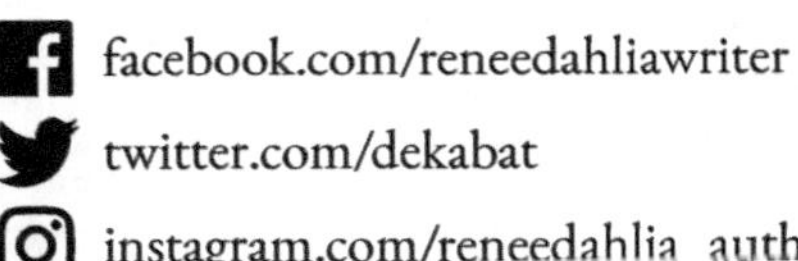

facebook.com/reneedahliawriter

twitter.com/dekabat

instagram.com/reneedahlia_author

bookbub.com/authors/renee-dahlia

patreon.com/reneedahlia

CHAPTER 1

"Fucking boring." Freddy closed his eyes and leaned back with his hands behind his head. The big boss, Mr Inoue, whose company Inoue Media owned the broadcasting rights for Series One—the pinnacle of motorsport—had personally requested he write this detailed introduction to Gamble Racing's surprise new Team Principal. Freddy wanted it to be good, interesting, for his own pride in his work—he didn't need this job but he loved everything about it—and therefore he wasn't going to submit the tedious piece of junk writing that he'd produced so far. He rubbed his temples. With his education and background, a feature article like this should be easy. He'd certainly done plenty of interviews in this style on television and his producer Carol Wisterman said he was good at it. He breathed out roughly. He shouldn't need the fucking validation from anyone. He had this.

"Okay. Gamble Racing's announcement of a new Team Principal, Jaxxon Loharani-Jones, is a surprise—" Freddy groaned as he read aloud. "Surprise is an understatement."

Team Principal's tended to have a lot more years under their belts and more actual engineering experience. Freddy rubbed his eyes and deleted the last three words. Maybe he should ring Socrates again. Why wasn't the owner of Gamble Racing answering his phone? Mike, Socrates' husband, wasn't answering either.

There was something going on at Gamble, and Freddy couldn't help but wonder if it didn't have to do with the recent sabotage drama. He'd flown to Gamble Racing after a desperate phone call from Socrates during the off-season and had been the first one to break the scandal a month ago. The story had made Mr Inoue notice him, and now bloody Socrates wasn't answering his calls.

"Damn it." Fucking everyone already knew that Jaxxon had been appointed Team Principal. Nothing spread as fast as exciting, verified, gossip in S1; someone had once described S1 as Gossip Girls on Wheels, and the love of chatter was always described rather favourably as politics. This article wasn't news, it was a profile. He deleted everything.

If there was one constant in S1, it was that Socrates Drayton would always be Team Principal for Gamble Racing, the team he founded and co-owned with his husband Mike Patel. Everyone, it seems, was wrong. Gamble Racing have done the unthinkable and appointed Jaxxon...

Freddy paused. He couldn't imply that Jaxxon was an unthinkable choice, although picking a race engineer for the role, and someone relatively young, was a bold choice. He deleted a few words and had another crack.

...Gamble Racing have done the unexpected and appointed a new Team Principal—Jaxxon Loharani-Jones.

Who is the surprise He deleted surprise. Too repetitive. Who is Loharani-Jones?

Freddy re-read the text so far. It was a little casual in tone, but much less boring. He wasn't quite sure what to write next. Who was Jaxxon? People already knew him, or thought they did, since he was Ondrej D'Grieg's race engineer and sat on the pit wall for every race. It was Jaxxon's voice that people heard when they broadcasted the radio calls with D'Grieg. Jaxxon was an imposing presence on the pit wall too, a tall Black Englishman with a swoony voice, who was athletic in the same way that baseball players were. He carried a good amount of bulk and it added to his presence and his general attractiveness. Imagine being pressed against a wall by Jaxxon with that voice whispering desires in his ear...

Okay, Freddy couldn't really write that. The man was irresistibly competent and utterly gorgeous... The man had such gravitas, like a damned sun with everyone pulled towards him, that it made sense—if not on paper—to promote him into Socrates' role. Freddy found Jaxxon distracting, and so he had spent most of the last four seasons keeping his distance, easily achieved as he didn't have to interview the race engineers very often. It would be much more difficult now. Every race weekend, he tried to interview all ten Team Principals, so he would need to figure out how to focus on the work, and not stare at Jaxxon's dark brown eyes, or his broad shoulders and wonder what it would be like to have Jaxxon's weight on him. He swallowed.

Freddy stood up and paced around his apartment for a while, then stared out at the view across London. He loved this apartment and was thankful there was only one other apartment on the same level as him. It was nice and private. His PA, Georgie, had had it decorated by D&Y Designs, whose owner, Elle, was a friend of his only neighbour on this level, Reiko Inoue, daughter of Mr Inoue, his big boss. Small world. He sat down at his laptop again and wrote the last sentence of his piece.

Socrates Drayton was not available for comment.

And why not? Socrates was a huge personality and always available to the media. The change in Team Principal had to be connected to the off-season dramas. For years, Gamble Racing's Chief Engineer had been Reggie White-hall, who'd been the engine designer and technical lead when Socrates had been the World Champion driver back in the day. But over the last few seasons, Whitehall's designs had become increasingly slower, and when rookie driver, Paulo Sanchez, had joined Gamble Racing last season, he'd brought massive sponsorship for the team, resulting in the sacking of Whitehall and the appointment of Victor Tsui into the Chief Engineer role. Unlike the appointment of Loharani-Jones, Sanchez had been no surprise at all, not with the vast amounts of money he brought with him. Money always talked in this sport.

Freddy leaned against the glass, the coolness against his forehead, for a while mulling it all over. Okay. Back to work. He rolled his head on his shoulders and sat down to type.

Gamble Racing has a track record of unexpected picks, having promoted Victor Tsui from an assistant Technical Engineering position in S3 directly into their Chief Engineer role last season, with spectacular results. Tsui's design propelled Gamble Racing from the rear of the grid into the mid-field, and they had been battling for fourth place in the constructor's title during the majority of last season when a spate of reliability issues impacted the end of their season. The reason behind those reliability problems has been well-documented.

They could add links to his other articles here. This was an article about Jaxxon, not the whole team. What was he going to write about Jaxxon that was palatable and yet still interesting?

Loharani-Jones has worked for Gamble Racing for— Freddy looked down at his notes—*four years as a race engineer, most recently for Ondrej D'Grieg.*

With the successful appointment of Tsui, perhaps the promotion of Loharani-Jones aligns with the way that Drayton and Patel run Gamble Racing. Drayton took brave risks as a driver, with skills that propelled him into World Championship victories in 1988 and 1989. If it were not for his accident, and the resulting partial loss of vision, many racing aficionados believe Drayton would've gained at least another Championship. Drayton's boldness is written all over the appointment of Loharani-Jones into such a key role at Gamble Racing.

Not much is known about the early life of Loharani-Jones. He was born in Liverpool, England, and gained a scholarship to the prestigious Oxford University where he took a double degree in mechanical engineering and commerce.

Loharani-Jones, an ambitious man No, he couldn't write that. It smacked of jealousy. The problem was that he didn't know Jaxxon very well at all and it was a deliberate choice. Jaxxon was exactly the type of man Freddy thirsted over; highly intelligent, big, and confident without ego or arrogance. Actually, he didn't know if the latter was true, he only assumed because he'd listened to all his radio comms with D'Grieg over the past couple of years. Freddy could have anyone in the world—and had indeed had many—and his favourite type of lover was someone who knew their own worth on an equitable basis with him. He didn't have much of a preference for physical type, the variety of humanity fascinated him. He rubbed his eyes. A little inconvenient lust for Jaxxon couldn't get in the way of his work.

Immediately on graduation, Loharani-Jones gained a position with automotive company Subaru in their World Rally Championship division, initially on the engine design team, and then working as a team strategist. After ten years with the WRC team, Loharani-Jones spent a year working as part of the Research and Development Engineering team for a potential shift by Subaru into S1, but when this didn't come to fruition, Loharani-Jones accepted a job with Gamble Racing as one of their race engineers. He has been with Gamble Racing for four seasons now, and for the last two seasons, he has been the race engineer for Gamble Racing's Ondrej D'Grieg. D'Grieg thrived last season with Tsui's new car design and many believe that a similar season this year will propel Gamble Racing into the top three teams on the grid.

Freddy nodded as he read it back to himself. It was still a little boring, but not too bad, and filled with the bare facts. The leaps in Jaxxon's career were unusual and Freddy knew there must be more to the story than this. With one exception, people didn't become Team Principals when they were so young—Jaxxon was only thirty-eight—and they were usually lead engineers and designers, not race engineers. He needed to know more. But mostly he needed to know why Socrates wasn't answering his phone.

Fuck it. He flicked through the contacts on his phone.

Freddy
Ondrej, do a fellow driver a favour and send me Jaxxon's number.

Ondrej
I was wondering when I'd hear from you

Freddy typed out a question about Socrates, then deleted it. Getting Jaxxon's contact details was a better long-term option to resolve his curiosity. He could kill two birds with one stone or whatever by getting a quote from Jaxxon and finding out why Socrates wasn't answering his calls.

Freddy
I need a quote from him for Inoue Media

Ondrej sent him a thumbs up emoji and Jaxxon's number.

Freddy
Appreciate that. I'll buy you a drink at pre-season testing

Ondrej
I'll hold you to that

Freddy chuckled. No one actually spent money on buying drinks during pre-season testing or on race weekends, as each team supplied enough hospitality for all their staff and the media who dropped by to spread any gossip a team wanted out in the media. Freddy hadn't bought himself a drink for years, not in the paddock, anyway. Freddy added Jaxxon's contacts to his phone and called him, making sure he was recording the call for notes later.

"Hello?"

"Jaxxon. It's Freddy Hiptonstall. Congratulations on the promotion."

"Thanks."

"Is now a good time to have a quick chat?"

"Of course." Damn, that voice rumbling in his ear was delicious and he sank into the shiver that travelled down his spine.

"How many people have asked you if you are too young for this role?"

Jaxxon chuckled. "No one has been so blunt yet, Freddy. I'm hardly the youngest person to be promoted to Team Principal in S1." No, there had been one person younger than Jaxxon. One.

"No, but you also aren't a retired driver or have family money." Unlike himself, but as much as he loved his sport, he didn't want the pressure of being a Team Principal. The stress of that job aged people quickly. He'd carried enough stress when he'd been a driver; young and invincible; and now he had the best job, getting to be involved at every race, talking to all the drivers and Team Principals. Being involved, knowing all the gossip, travelling with everyone. It was the ideal life. He loved S1 more than anything else.

"The job of a Team Principal is to run the team, not drive the cars, or bring financial connections into the team." If Jaxxon believed that, he was going to have a difficult time of it. The entire point of being Team Principal was to make sure they had enough money.

"In that case, what do you bring to the role?" Freddy didn't have to ask why Jaxxon was different from any other Team Principal, that much was implied in his question.

"Motorsport can be an orgy of elitism, and S1 is the most expensive, most high profile of all motorsports. As many people say, it's the pinnacle of engineering and speed and consequently, it takes a lot of money to run a team."

Freddy loved that quote—an orgy of elitism—brilliant. "Yes?"

"There are very few people who have come from a middle class, or poorer, background with only a passion for motorsport to then succeed in this sport. It is no secret that connections and money open doors here. I didn't have—" Jaxxon paused. "I don't have either connections or money, and this gives me a different perspective, and one that Gamble Racing believe will be advantageous for the team's performance."

"Are you implying that you had to work harder than anyone else to get where you are because you lack the advantages others in your role have?" Freddy wished this interview was face-to-face, because he really wanted to see Jaxxon's reaction to his question.

"Yes and no. Everyone who succeeds in this sport, in any role, has to work incredibly hard. I would never suggest that I have worked harder; only that I don't have some of the advantages that many of the colleagues bring to their team and their role."

"It is hard to avoid the implication though."

"There are, quite literally, thousands of people who have money and connections and are vying for only ten Team Principal jobs. People also need talent and hard work to succeed. By asking about my workload, you miss my point."

"Which is?" He wasn't quite sure what Jaxxon was saying as it was hard to avoid the implication that he had more talent than those who had connections or money. His rise through motorsport could only have been possible with a well-endowed dose of intellectual capability. Shit. The last thing he needed to ponder—during an interview—was Jaxxon's endowment. He gripped his phone tighter, then slowly breathed out, hoping that Jaxxon couldn't hear the tremble in his breath through the phone.

"The thing about power, in any form, is that it stops people from seeing the whole picture. Humans are not very good at seeing their own privilege. With my background, I bring a different strategic approach because I can see the sport from a perspective that is rare."

"Unique?"

"No. There have been others before me, like Louis Kingston whose rise from nothing into a multiple World Champion has been well recorded." The subtext was that Jaxxon might be daring Freddy not to mention that both himself and Kingston were Black. He avoided the temptation to make the comparison.

"There have been several other drivers whose parents were mechanics, or owned go-kart tracks and worked hard to give their children opportunities. Team Principals, too, who've worked hard as mechanical engineers and risen through the ranks." Freddy knew this and he could name each and every one of them. He wouldn't be on that list. He had been handed everything he wanted, and he'd still had to work bloody hard to rise above the many other competitors who had also been given every chance. Perhaps that was Jaxxon's point. Freddy was one of the few who'd made it to the pinnacle as an S1 driver. He tried not to find it condescending when Jaxxon mentioned that humans weren't good at seeing their own privilege but quickly pushed that uncomfortable prickle across the back of his neck away. Jaxxon was correct. He knew he had a ton of privilege and his reaction against acknowledging that was also a learned response and one he had to work to unlearn.

"Yes. It's a path that has been trodden before, among drivers and among Team Principals. Not often, which can be an advantage and a disadvantage. I would never claim to be the first of anything, as everyone stands on the shoulders of those who have come before." The sincerity in Jaxxon's voice made Freddy pause. It was so fucking admirable, but Jesus, he was going to get eaten up by the other Team Principals. Did Jaxxon have enough fight in him to survive this cut-throat world?

"Tell me about the disadvantages."

"I am unwilling to give my competitors an advantage by outlining that on the record." Jaxxon's quick retort made Freddy smile. He was going to enjoy verbally sparring him with this season.

"You have a business degree. Is that correct?"

Jaxxon's puff of breath seemed loud in his ear. "Yes.

Mechanical engineering and commerce, double degree from Oxford. Full scholarship."

"Impressive."

"Thank you. My career pathway has been written about before. Personally, I would rather discuss my more recent roles, including the integral part I played in the recent improvements at Gamble Racing."

Freddy's fingers twitched. "Are you referring to the bold decision to employ Victor Tsui as the Chief Engineer?"

"I was an integral part of the selection process, yes. With the Sanchez Shipping sponsorship, we had an opportunity to invest in new personnel, and together with our stable of drivers and engineers, I assisted Socrates and Mike in collating a potential list of candidates."

"Why Tsui?"

"He was obviously a star on the rise in the engineering ranks in the lower grades of racing. Yes, the promotion we gave him put him under a lot of pressure, but I think it's easy to say that he has thrived with the opportunity. We are very excited about this season's car; his second design for us. It is showing plenty of promise in the wind tunnel."

"Socrates Drayton has given you a big responsibility now that he has ... retired." Freddy paused, trying to draw out more information, but Jaxxon didn't take the bait.

"This job is a responsibility that I take incredibly seriously. Socrates has built a fantastic team at Gamble Racing, and this season is about building on our strong history to take this team to the top of the mid-field, and perhaps even to push the top teams." Oh, he was good. Slippery in just the right way that was required for this role, while also sending out a warning to the other mid-field teams. Freddy smiled into his phone. He needn't have worried that Jaxxon wasn't equipped to deal with the politics and game-playing of S1.

"Thank you for your time, Jaxxon. I'll see at pre-season testing." He didn't have enough details, but he didn't want to linger on this phone call for a minute longer, listening to Jaxxon's beautiful tones. He would write about Jaxxon's passion and his obvious love for cars and their sport. He'd make it work, and then when he was done, he'd close his eyes and dream of Jaxxon's rumbling voice. Freddy shook his head. It wasn't like him to want more from someone he couldn't have. He didn't mix pleasure with work for a fucking good reason.

CHAPTER 2

Breaking News: The 1988 and 1989 World Championship S1 Trophies are missing, allegedly stolen. Gamble Racing's new car, the GR-S390, was revealed to the public by S1 drivers Ondrej D'Grieg and Paulo Sanchez tonight. The trophies, won by Socrates Drayton, were to be part of the Gamble Racing car reveal for this season but weren't there. No further information is available at this stage.

Jaxxon approved the press release—a controlled moment in this bloody disaster—and it was put on all of Gamble Racing's social media immediately. The marketing team ought to have been sharing videos of tonight's event; not this. This wasn't exactly how he wanted to launch his first car as Team Principal. He really didn't want to go down in history as the Team Principal who'd lost Socrates' trophies. He'd worked too fucking hard to get here for some asshole to, literally, steal his moment of glory.

The entire place was in an uproar, with both the Gamble Racing staff and Socrates' house staff searching frantically for the missing trophies. Mike's face had been ashen when they'd first noticed they were missing, and he hadn't improved since.

Skye was reviewing the security footage. They hadn't been overly hopeful since most of Socrates' house wasn't under surveillance, only the trophy room. Jaxxon had taken the trophies out of the cabinets himself for tonight's car reveal, so the footage wasn't going to tell them anything he didn't already know. The stress stuck in his throat, and he wanted to punch something—don't act angry—or cower in a corner—he wasn't a coward—or fucking don't react at all because he was the boss and people needed leadership. His emotions had to wait until he found the trophies and could throttle whoever was responsible. This couldn't be the way he began the job he'd worked so hard to get.

"No one is talking about the car." One of S1's highest profile retired drivers and journalists, Freddy Hiptonstall, looked up from his phone as he stated the fucking obvious. Jaxxon wanted people to talk about the car. He'd only talked to Freddy once before, when he'd done an interview with Freddy about his promotion a few weeks ago, although he'd seen him around the paddock for years. Freddy made Jaxxon curious ... But he couldn't do anything about his unwilling desire for a handsome face so he lifted his chin and did his damned job instead.

"I'm not giving you a quote, Freddy."

"Off the record?"

Jaxxon knew he needed to build a relationship with the media, so he swallowed his irritation. Freddy was only doing his job, after all, just as he was.

"Sure."

"Why wasn't Socrates here tonight? He's never missed a car launch." Freddy's reputation for astute observation gave Jaxxon pause. Who else had noticed?

"Has he run off with his trophies?" Freddy's taunt was probably designed to draw information from Jaxxon, so he just shrugged.

"Off the record. Socrates is dealing with a personal matter." It was the reason Jaxxon had been given his promotion, because Socrates didn't know how long he'd be away from the team and Gamble Racing needed a Team Principal. The season was about to begin. Jaxxon had been positioning himself as the obvious successor to Socrates for over a year now. The promotion itself wasn't a shock to him; the timing of it was as he'd assumed Socrates would be in the role for several more years yet. The only other viable option for Team Principal was their Chief Engineer Victor Tsui who was even younger and more inexperienced than Jaxxon, while none of the other options had the engineering experience either of them had. And with Socrates wanting to keep his reasons for stepping away from leading his racing team private, they'd kept the promotion internal to avoid any unnecessary press.

"What sort of personal matter?"

"Freddy." Jaxxon put a warning tone in his voice. "It's a medical issue. Please respect Socrates and keep it completely off the record."

"Oh. I'm so sorry to hear that." Freddy's tone changed to one of empathy. "Everyone in the paddock adores Socrates. Please give him my best."

"Thanks." Jaxxon didn't have the capacity to deal with

any rumours about Socrates' health on top of everything. "I can give you something. I personally removed the trophies from their secure cabinet and placed them on the stage. We had our own security for them, and the broadcasting team also had security measures in place." Skye was reviewing the footage of the stage to try and work out when the trophies had been removed and switched out for an empty box.

"Did you expect there to be a problem? That seems like a lot of effort for a couple of old trophies."

Jaxxon shrugged. "They matter to Socrates."

"And because he is sick..." Freddy's voice trailed off and Jaxxon recognised the technique. He wasn't going to finish the sentence or fill the space for Freddy.

"Anything about Socrates is off the record. You can talk about our security procedures and what we are doing to find the trophies, but not about him."

"Are you always this defensive?"

"Excuse me?"

"In our interview the other day, you spent a lot of time defending Gamble Racing's choice to select you for Team Principal. If you want some advice, you should own the job."

"You want me to take advice from you?"

Freddy's shrug shouldn't bug him this much. The man was far too handsome for his own good; like how bloody blessed could one person be? Not only was he a retired S1 driver, but he had a face for television and a fucking posh accent with a voice that could seduce anyone. Jaxxon had worked too hard to get here to be seduced into a mistake by a ... pretty face. If he could frame Freddy as pretty it might help him maintain some distance, rather than stare for a second too long at Freddy's lips. A kiss ... No, he shoved that thought to the dark recesses of his mind and it could bloody stay there, out of the way, never to bother him again.

"Yes. I've been in the paddock for longer than you."

"Fine, old man. Give me your advice."

Freddy's grin lit up the room and did absolutely zero to stop Jaxxon from staring at his mouth. His smile was obscene; perfect teeth and lips combined with the glint of enjoyment in Freddy's gaze was a little too much. Jaxxon wanted to kiss that smile right off Freddy's face. Fuck. He swallowed. He wanted to make Freddy smile like that again too.

"That's more like it. Show us your snark and your personality."

"Is that your advice?" He hadn't expected that.

"Yes. Sport is entertainment. S1 is entertainment."

He conceded the point. "It's also about selling cars and innovation."

"None of that is possible without first entertaining your fans. With all the television coverage you have an opportunity and if you want to succeed, you'll need entertain people. Let them see your sassiness and personality. You need the people to see you." Freddy's emphasis on 'you' was sinfully attractive.

"And when I do?" He loaded the question with sarcasm because Freddy was only reiterating what Jaxxon already knew. He'd purposefully built a following online as Ondrej's race engineer as part of his long term plan for get this job, and he aimed to build on it now.

"And when you do, you'll achieve the dream life." Dream life? Freddy wasn't wrong about the entertainment angle. It wouldn't be enough to be great at leading Gamble Racing or winning races, a huge part of his job would be using the media for strategy.

"How long have you been living this dream life, Freddy?"

"Never long enough."

Jaxxon smiled. "This sport really gets in your blood and becomes an obsession."

"You've been with Gamble for four years now? Which is your favourite track?"

He shook his head. "Which one is yours?" He turned the question back onto Freddy and deliberately raised one eyebrow.

"Imola." Freddy didn't hesitate.

"Makes sense. It was your first win." Jaxxon had always had a good head for retaining data.

"You follow my career?"

Jaxxon rolled his eyes. "I follow everyone. My uncle Lorenzo took me to Silverstone when I was twelve, and I fell in love with S1."

Freddy leaned slightly closer, his gaze intensifying.

"Yes, you can put this on record. My parents ran a bakery in Liverpool. They didn't have much time or money to take me to anything." He wondered if Freddy would notice that he'd said ran not owned. His parents worked as employees for the bakery owner on a salary. They never benefitted from any profits they generated through their hard work. With this promotion, he had been able to buy the bakery for them and that alone made the promotion to Team Principal hugely satisfying.

"One morning, very early, Uncle Lorenzo arrived and he said he had a surprise for me. We got in his car and we drove for hours until we arrived at Silverstone. The noise, the people. Ahh, the cars." Later, Lorenzo had told him that his parents were so proud of him and the grades he was getting at school, but they couldn't afford the time away from the shop to take him on a vacation, and Lorenzo had stepped in to give him a day of fun. Lorenzo wasn't the most consistent of people, but that one day had put Jaxxon on this path, and for that, he'd forgive all the times Lorenzo promised a day out and never showed. His parents had given him the gift of confidence and a belief in hard work, and Lorenzo had shown him the world he wanted to inhabit.

"It's a bug that burrows into your heart and stays there."

Jaxxon raised one eyebrow. "Such a poet, Freddy."

"And now you have the bug too."

Jaxxon shook his head. "You make it sound like an STI."

"Gross." They both stared at each other for a moment until Jaxxon wanted to scrub the awkwardness off his skin.

"So, the trophies? Any clues?" Freddy reminded him of the most pressing matter in his realm. A pretty face and easy conversation shouldn't have distracted him from the task of finding Socrates' trophies.

"It's too early to know anything much. Our team is going over the footage to see if we have any clues, and obviously we have the local police involved for due process."

Freddy squinted. "There is a decent trade in S1 memorabilia. I could have a talk to a few people who collect and see what they think."

"You'd help us? Or is this the journalist in you wanting to solve a puzzle."

"Always, but it's also personal. I love S1, and I think it's horrific that this could happen."

Jaxxon unclenched his teeth and forced himself to pause. The theft of two trophies wasn't exactly a horror on a global scale; recovering them might make his boss—a rich old white man—feel better, but it was nothing like the long string of human rights abuses happening around the world. Some of which were happening in countries where they raced.

"Interesting word choice."

"Excuse me?" Freddy asked.

"This is a frustrating expensive theft, but it's hardly a horror."

"It's not a harmless crime either."

Jaxxon blinked. "Is there such a thing as a harmless crime?"

"Are we going to debate semantics while a thief wanders around?"

"You think they are still on the grounds?" He had assumed the thief would have bolted as soon as they had the trophies in their possession.

"Leaving immediately would garner suspicion, don't you think? Is everyone on the invite list still here? What about the staff?"

There was one thing Jaxxon hated the most and it was feeling like a fool. He was a strategic expert, good at planning and foreseeing things that others couldn't, and yet, the stolen trophies, the knowledge that he was the last person to be known to touch them, and the pressure of this being his first big event as Team Principal, had fried his ability to think rationally about this. He was responsible for the trophies going missing and he needed to focus on finding them. He shouldn't be wasting time chatting to a reporter about semantics and word choices.

"I hate to say this, but off the record, the timing is terrible for you."

Jaxxon's chest squeezed tight. "I know. Socrates is … away. I've been promoted into his job without the usual rumour mill pre-announcing it. And I was the last person to touch the trophies."

"You were?"

"I told you that already. I took them out of their secure cabinet and placed them on the stage into another secure cabinet. I covered the cabinet with a sheet, ready for the car reveal. Damn it, I made the decision to have them hidden when I could've left them on display without the drama of a reveal. Mike and I planned tonight's car reveal to be a celebration of Socrates' career and life in S1." It'd been designed to help Socrates, and now everything was worse.

"It's an audacious theft to take them from the stage with so many people milling around."

"That's why I thought they'd be safe." He'd discussed the whole procedure with his security staff, and they'd signed off on each step. Socrates' car from his first ever S1 win was on the stage too, borrowed from the big manufacturer that he'd driven for, and the security around that was even tighter. When they'd wheeled both the old car onto the stage and then parked this year's car beside it, Jaxxon hadn't been able to stop grinning. The development that had happened over almost forty years was incredible.

"With so many people moving on the stage during the set up, it probably provides cover for a thief rather than protection against it."

Jaxxon couldn't hold back a scoff. "You've been watching too many heist movies."

Freddy's spontaneous grin was a delight. "Perhaps."

"I have one of our IT people going over all the footage. Skye's expertise in that area was instrumental in solving the sabotage issue last season. I trust them."

Freddy nodded. "I met them a few months ago. They are highly competent."

Jaxxon hadn't had much to do with the sabotage issue; it had affected him as the race engineer for Ondrej, whose car had been tampered with twice, while Paulo's car had suffered three sabotage failures. Until a month ago, being Team Principal had only been a dream; one he'd believed was still a decade away.

"We have an excellent team here. If anyone can find the trophies, it is our people."

"Good luck." Freddy stuck out his hand and Jaxxon shook it. The tiny tingle that meandered up his arm had to be his imagination.

"Call me when you find something from your collector friend."

"I will."

Jaxxon nodded once, then walked away from the intriguing Freddy Hiptonstall before he did something daft like invite him to help with their investigation. Getting a high profile media personality involved was the height of ridiculousness. He swallowed down a sigh; Freddy was already helping by asking his collector friends for information. Could Jaxxon trust him to come to him with the information first, or would he learn it as part of a breaking news story?

CHAPTER 3

Freddy high-fived Georgia's hand and chalk dust puffed into the air. His PA had been the one to introduce him to bouldering a few years ago, and now he came as often as he could before the season started. Bouldering was great for his fitness and coordination as well as being a good mental challenge. Now that he was ... fuck ... nearly forty-five, it took more work to keep his body fit. Back when he was a driver, he'd spent so much time focusing on his fitness and he'd taken it for granted that he'd always be an athlete, always be able to do anything without worrying that he might pull his hamstring or twinge his left ankle.

"That was a tricky one, boss."

Freddy grinned. "How many times have I told you to stop calling me boss."

"I imagine it's better than the alternative.

"Yes." He really didn't want to be addressed by his formal title. His father insisted on it, calling him Beautravers whenever he visited the family pile, but Freddy wasn't his father and didn't need to impress anyone with all that nonsense. It wasn't a secret—he was literally in Debretts—but he didn't like flashing it around. His life was impressive enough without needing to flaunt the one thing he'd been gifted at birth and did nothing to earn.

His phone rang and he grabbed it from the little pile at the edge of the mat. Jaxxon's name flashed on screen and for half a second, he contemplated ignoring the call.

"Freddy speaking."

"Hi, it's Jaxxon Loharani-Jones."

"Yes, my phone told me that. What's up?" He hadn't expected a call from Jaxxon, especially with only a week until pre-season testing. Most of the media was filled with the usual invented bullshit where people tried to drum up excitement for the season without any basis for truth. He ignored it; his real job would start as soon as the cameras turned on in Bahrain.

"There's a rumour that the 1962 championship trophy has been stolen."

"Graham Montblanc?"

"Yes."

"Only his first win, not 1968 as well? It makes no sense. Both trophies are still held by the Montblanc family."

"It's a rumour."

Freddy breathed in. "Probably total bullshit." Logically, if he were to go to all the effort of stealing a trophy from a dual world champion's house, he'd take both, not one.

"Yes. Did you hear from your contact?"

Freddy choked back a laugh. "This isn't a spy movie."

"And Socrates had a bad week, so I'd like to be able to give him some news." The tension in Jaxxon's voice tugged at Freddy's heart. Everyone in the paddock loved the old fucker, and the news that Socrates was struggling—in his mystery illness—made Freddy square his shoulders and step up to help. "I can call him."

"Thanks."

"See you at pre-season testing." Freddy hung up before Jaxxon could say anything else.

"Everything okay, boss?"

"Yeah, just the usual rumours and nonsense at work." He swallowed, evading Georgia's real question. "Want to come to pre-season testing with me?"

Georgia shook her head. "I can't. It's my week with the kids." They were with her ex-wife today, hence the bouldering session. She always put a note in his calendar for when she had her kids and when she didn't.

"Bring them."

"I'm not taking them out of school on a whim for you." She narrowed her eyes and peered at him for a while. "Who was on that phone call? Is it someone you want to avoid and you want me to run interference on?"

Damn, she was astute, but then, that was why he'd employed her. He cleared his throat.

"It is," she laughed and pointed her finger at him. "What did you do?"

He tapped his chest. "Nothing. Why do you assume I did something?" He pretended to be upset but Georgia saw through all that with a little frown.

"Then it's someone you fancy. ... Hold up a second. It's not like you to be interested in someone in the paddock."

"Don't worry about it." His cheeks were hotter than

he'd like, and he could hardly blame the physical exertion from climbing either.

Georgia grinned. "Oh my god! It's true. You have the hots for the person you were just talking to, don't you? Who? Who?" She reached for his phone, and he batted her hand away.

"The hots? It isn't the nineties anymore." He tried to distract her with nonsense.

"Tell me who you want to fuck." It didn't work. She saw right through his basic strategy.

"Fuck, Georgia. Don't you have any boundaries? I'm your boss."

She cackled. "Now you want to use the boss card."

"Yes. Definitely. This is me using the boss card and telling you not to continue this line of questioning."

Georgia bowed, a sardonic expression on her face. "And he confirms the rumour by avoiding talking about it."

Fuck. "It's nothing."

"Really?" Georgia's eyebrows flew upwards.

"Yes, really." He didn't need to explain himself. Not to anyone, except this was Georgia who'd saved his ass on more than one occasion. "Fine. But only because you are a decent friend."

"Go on, tell your friend everything. I want all the little details."

Freddy rubbed his forehead. "I need a drink for this."

"I think we are done here. Let's head next door to the pub." Georgia grabbed her things and marched off to the change room. He followed. At least this would give him a few minutes to figure out what the heck he was going to say. Jaxxon was incredibly hot—physically and oozing with confidence—and after talking him for the sum total of twice, he wanted to fuck him. It broke all his rules about not hooking up with anyone from work. It was just a crush. Damn it. He didn't even know if Jaxxon was queer, although, he was Team Principal for the most openly queer team on the grid, so at least he'd be kind about it if Freddy did do the unthinkable and flirt with him. Shit. What a tangle.

Half an hour later, Freddy slid into a booth at the pub and passed Georgia one of the two pints he'd purchased. The pub next to the bouldering place was an old dive that smelled of beer-soaked carpets and bad decisions, but during the quiet afternoons only three old bar flies sat spread out around the bar, deliberately seated so each person was definitely and defiantly alone.

"Time to tell Aunty Georgia everything."

"Fuck off." He rolled his eyes. "There's nothing to tell."

"Sure. Why are we here then?"

Freddy sipped his beer. "There really is nothing to tell." It was mostly his imagination and a healthy dose of fear of repeating the past.

"Come on. You can bullshit yourself, but me?" Georgia tapped her chest.

"Fine." He wouldn't have come to the pub unless he wanted to talk about this, so he may as well admit it out loud. "I think I have a crush on someone who is—"

"Out of bounds?"

"Impossibly so."

"In what way? Are they straight?"

Freddy drank more of his beer. "If I had to guess, I'd say no, but it's not like you can tell by looking at someone."

"So why do you guess that?" Georgia's question was exactly what he wanted because it shifted the discussion away from why he couldn't flirt with a Team Principal.

"Just a hunch."

Georgia rolled her eyes. "Freddy."

"Fine. He works for Gamble Racing."

She nodded. "Right. So if he ... He?"

"Yes, he's a cis man."

"If he works for Gamble Racing, then if he's not straight, he's at least not a bigot." Georgia nailed the summary. After more than five years of working for him, she couldn't help but know all the teams. He waited and yes, there it was, the moment of understanding.

"Back up a second. You. You have a crush ... on someone who works for Gamble Racing?" Georgia spoke slowly, over-enunciating each word.

"Now you see the problem."

She shrugged. "I always thought your rule about not banging anyone in the paddock was a silly one. It's not going to happen again." She'd been there during the Chester disaster, but her curious glance made him hope that he could avoid talking about it.

"Yeah, it's not that." It was. "It's more that there's a high potential for long term awkwardness. We all travel together all year." Freddy worked with these people. The season was its own weird bubble with ten teams competing in the same space, staying the same hotels, and using the same planes to get between tracks. He had a reputation for being likable and easy to get along with. He didn't want to wreck that by creating potentially awkward situations; and sometimes ex-lovers could be pretty fucking weird, especially when they figured out the implications that followed from knowing who his father was. Especially then.

"Okay. I can see how that might be a problem. But if he's cute?" Georgia wrinkled her nose with a little grin and a tilt of her head.

"Come on, you remember Chester Ormsby." He didn't want to bring this up. Like ever, except it was reason number one why he'd never get involved with someone from the paddock again.

Georgia scrunched up her face. "Oh God. What a fucking disaster that was." She hadn't worked for him when Chester had been around and hadn't met him when they'd been together. Freddy had employed her to help him tidy up the messy aftermath.

"Yes."

"How long ago was that?"

He realised that he'd never told her the whole story, only the bits that she needed to know to do her job. Back then, he'd been surviving the drama and then he'd avoided talking about it as much as possible. "I met him seven years ago, in my last season as a driver."

"I never asked you about this. How did you meet him?" She waved her hands in the air. "I assume he's the reason you won't get involved with someone in the paddock. Yeah?" She made the connection quickly.

"Yes. He worked for my team, part of the social media team who travelled to each race. He did a lot of the graphic design."

"You saw him around the paddock a lot?"

Freddy winced. "Not really. I didn't interact with them

much, just Sonia who was the boss of all that social media stuff."

"Did he seek you out?" She knew Chester well enough to ask the right questions.

"Back then, I didn't realise it, but yeah. After Kerrigan's crash, I needed to get away from everyone, and he comforted me. Having someone queer in that moment of dread … well, my therapist says that I latched onto him."

"Makes sense. You'd just seen something awful, and he took advantage. Of course you weren't going to see what he was back then." Georgia knew what Chester had become; they'd just never talked about how it'd been before it all went to shit.

"Thanks. It took me a long time to forgive myself and not look at it with a pile of self-judgement."

Georgia nodded. "I remember what a mess you were." She held up one finger.

"What?"

"If you met Chester seven years ago, and I've only worked for you five and a half years, did that mean he stalked you for eighteen months before you asked for help?"

Freddy winced. "Not exactly. After I announced my retirement, he wanted to know if I was going to work for my father—"

"Did he think you, the second son, seventh in line, would become a Duke?"

"I think so?" He shook his head. "No. I know he thought that. I broke up with him because he hinted that I should arrange to have my brother killed so I'd be next in line for the Dukedom." He still couldn't believe the audacity that someone would suggest killing one's own brother for gain. It was gross then and still gross now.

Georgia gasped, covering her mouth with her hands. "You never told me that. Just that you had an ex who was stalking you."

"Technically true. I needed your help to get him out of my life. New emails, new address, etc." Obviously, Chester could find him if he really wanted to. Freddy was literally on television doing a job with a very public schedule, but it was the private ways to contact him that he'd changed. Georgia had helped set up restraining orders and all the legal stuff too. She'd probably done a bunch of things that he wasn't even aware of—wasn't capable of processing—to keep Chester away from him. She booked all Freddy's travel. She must have talked to all the security teams across S1 too.

They sat in silence for a while.

"It does seem unlikely that you'd be unlucky enough to get a second stalker." Georgia drank some beer. "Look, I understand your reticence and you've needed to ... fuck your way through the rest of the world who don't care about cars to compensate for all that mess, but is that really a life?"

He raised one eyebrow. "That's rich coming from you."

"My relationship lasted ten years before we chose to end it." Georgia was still good friends with her ex, Jennifer, and as far as Freddy could tell, their breakup had been mutual and they were able to be fairly pleasant to each other. Unlike his experience.

"Before Chester turned into stalker extraordinaire, I thought we were in a relationship. I was going to retire and grow old with him." Never again. He didn't need that type of drama in his life. He was better off living his life this way, alone but on his terms.

"Aren't we just a pair of cynical old fucks then?"

Laughter burst out of him. "Georgie."

"Well? It's true."

He stared at his PA for a while, eventually shaking his head. "It doesn't matter. It's just a crush. It'll pass."

"After pre-season testing, you will have moved on to someone else."

"Yeah, probably." It didn't sound satisfying though. Would this be his life forever more? He'd always imagined he'd have a husband one day after he retired from driving. He'd assumed Chester would be that person, and instead Chester's bad choices had put him off the idea for a long time, and no amount of therapy could get rid of the combined fear of being alone and also that being in a relationship was bad for him. It left him stuck in this place of endless hook ups, temporarily satisfying.

"What's the matter?"

"Maybe I shouldn't let one stalker stop me from trying again? If I pick someone who isn't from the paddock and who understands that I'm seventh in line for the Dukedom and will never be a Duke. No delusions of grandeur." He held his breath.

"Freddy?"

He winced. "Yeah?"

"Good for you. I want to see you happy."

"But not for yourself."

"It's not the same. I'm still co-parenting, so I'm never lonely. I can chat to my kids anytime, and besides, it'd be a little mean to bring someone into my messy situation. Not every new lover wants to accept that I'm still good friends with my ex."

"I have a different type of messiness. Who would want to be in a relationship with me? I spend most of the year travelling and talking about cars. Like..."

Georgia's eyes sparkled, giving him a fraction of a second's warning. "Perhaps you could try to have a relationship with someone who also spends all year traveling with the S1 circus?" Georgia's emphasis on 'also' wasn't as annoying as it should be.

"Georgia."

"Does that tone mean that you think it's not a circus?"

He shook his head indulgently. "You know I meant that I don't want to mix a relationship with my work. Never again."

"You don't like my solution?"

"I could sack you." He was kidding. She ran his whole life, organised fucking everything, so he just had to go where she sent him. The look on her face, absolute enjoyment in his discomfort, told him that she knew he would never do it.

"Fine. I would never."

"Sack me, or chase your crush?"

He rolled his eyes. "He can chase me." It was a joke, a way to obscure the truth, and judging by the grin on Georgia's face, he'd failed at hiding anything.

"Let me know how that goes."

"You know that I tell you everything."

Georgia's grin widened. "If I wasn't a lesbian, we'd make the perfect couple."

"No, we wouldn't. I'd take advantage of your practicality and eventually you'd resent me. This way, you are paid for your excellent organisational ability."

"And I get to gossip with you as a friend."

"To friendship."

It wasn't until a few hours later that he wondered if there wasn't something she'd been trying to say with her joke. He'd selfishly unloaded all his worries about Jaxxon onto her and not taken the time to listen to her. He flicked her a text.

> **Freddy**
> You'd tell me if you weren't happy,
> wouldn't you?

> **Georgia**
> Yep

When his phone stayed silent, he decided to park that concern until he saw her next. He'd better get some sleep because he had a date at his club tomorrow with his favourite couple.

> **Georgia**
> I'll be late tomorrow. Date is going well.

Freddy breathed out. He'd been all worried about nothing.

> **Freddy**
> Stay safe.

She sent him a thumbs up emoji. He wasn't ready to go to sleep yet, so he jumped on his old simulator and drove for a while. The focus always helped slow his brain. He didn't really miss driving competitively—the frustration of not being as good as he had been when his reflexes were at a peak was enough to stop him, not to mention Kerrigan's crash had reminded him of the inherent risks—but he found the process calming because he was in control behind the wheel. Growing up, it had been the one place where he'd had choice over his life, and now it was a passion and perhaps a habit.

CHAPTER 4

BARCELONA

Jaxxon straightened the collar of his Gamble Racing uniform polo shirt for the third time in ten minutes. His first pre-season testing as Team Principal was about to begin and he wanted everything to be perfect. The odds were that it would go better than the car reveal—mostly because it couldn't go worse—but he absolutely wasn't going to jinx the next few days by thinking about that. In an hour, the cars would be on track, and they'd see if their car was going to be competitive this year. Wind tunnel tests only went so far and if they'd improved twelve percent but if their competitors had improved by twenty percent, they'd be screwed. They were about to discover if they would be fast enough to stay in the mid-field, or if they'd be relegated back to the back of the grid again.

"Theron, are you ready?" Jaxxon knew the answer would be yes. Theron Gagneux came from one of the big manufacturing teams as a factory-based strategy engineer before his promotion into Jaxxon's old job as Ondrej's race engineer. His strategic planning skills was one of the key reasons Jaxxon had employed him, as he'd bring excellent insights to the pit wall. Paulo's race engineer Monica brought racing instincts to the team as a retired World Rally Champion. It should be a great combination.

"I can't wait. I'm actually here ... in the paddock." Theron reminded Jaxxon of his first day in Series One, bursting with enthusiasm. He had the same buzz buried somewhere under the nerves of his new job. Fucking hell, he was the Team Principal. He'd worked so hard for this and here he was ... he'd craved this for so long, ever since his first engineering job out of university. He was only thirty-eight and he'd achieved his dream almost a decade before he'd planned. His hard work—paved with a healthy dose of good luck—had paid off.

They walked to the pit wall together. Jaxxon automatically slid into his usual seat on the pit wall. Theron coughed.

"Right. Sorry." They had only five people on their pit wall—a lean operation—with each race engineer at the far ends of the wall. Seating them at either end meant they could see the track easily as well as not distract each other as they communicated with their drivers. He sat in the middle, in Socrates' old seat, next to Aurora Romano who was the Track Director and managed all the pit stops and mechanics. On his other side sat Victor, their Chief Engineer, who helped Jaxxon with overall race strategy during the race. Some of the richer teams had up to seven or eight people on their pit wall, which seemed like it would be a lot of additional communication to manage. Sometimes during the race the radio between the five of them could get quite intense, and it used to be his job to communicate the strategic decisions to his driver. He leaned forward on his elbows and closed his eyes, remembering the role Socrates used to do during races. It was a new role for him, being in the centre of all the communications, to lead the whole pit wall. They'd done a few practice races in the last couple of weeks, sitting on the pit wall at Socrates' test track while running old data through their system. Skye had set up several different scenarios so they could practise communication. He was ready—as ready as he could ever be.

"Jaxxon."

He spun in his chair at his name to discover Freddy shoving a microphone in his face. One of his camera crew stood behind him with a huge camera perched on his shoulder and several others were grouped around too.

"A few words before testing gets underway?"

Jaxxon nodded.

Freddy turned to his camera. "We are here at the Gamble Racing pit wall with new Team Principal Jaxxon Loharani-Jones, who has big shoes to fill as he takes over from team owner Socrates Drayton."

"Hi." Damn it, where was his usual charm? Hi. How inane. At least he didn't wave.

"Every Series One fan wants to know; where is Socrates?" Trust Freddy to go for the jugular on camera when Jaxxon couldn't back out of it. He'd told him about Socrates in confidence and didn't expect to have that stripped away so easily, but in a weird way it helped as all his anxiety about his job disappeared and he breathed out slowly. Freddy was only asking the question that everyone in S1 had been asking quietly under their breaths. He'd been able to feel the whispers from the moment he'd arrived in the paddock two days ago, so in a way Freddy had done him a favour by launching into it.

"Socrates Drayton is dealing with a medical matter." It was a well-rehearsed answer that had both Socrates and Mike's approval.

Freddy feigned shock quite well. "I'm so sorry to hear that. Will he be okay?"

"We all hope so." Jaxxon wasn't even going to think about Socrates' health in case he accidentally said something he shouldn't. Nerves made it hard to trust himself.

"I'm sure I can speak for the whole paddock when I say that we all adore Socrates and we all wish him the very best." Freddy dealt with that very well. Jaxxon couldn't decide if Freddy had gone for the jugular by throwing this at him, or if it'd been a kindness to get the main topic of gossip out of the way. If he was a betting man, he'd give evens on either option.

"Thank you. Socrates would want us to focus on Gamble Racing and on pre-season testing. We will have Ondrej D'Grieg driving the first session, and Paulo Sanchez will drive the afternoon session. Tomorrow, they will swap, and we will decide the order for the final day based on the needs of the team."

"No surprises, then?"

"Not here." The actual surprise would be at the next testing session in Bahrain, where Lucien Grenville would'd drive one of the sessions, as a gift from his boyfriend, Chief Engineer Victor Tsui. Lucien was driving for the Series E team this weekend and it would take some coordination to get him to Bahrain for a test drive, given his own racing schedule. Socrates wanted it—the old sap loved love—so it would happen regardless of whether it suited Jaxxon's plans for the team.

"Not here. Are you implying that you have a surprise for us at Bahrain?"

"Yes." Jaxxon let himself smile a little, aiming it directly at the camera

"There's nothing S1 fans love more than a surprise. Will you hold us in suspense until then?"

Jaxxon winked at the camera. "Absolutely. I can't show all my cards before we've even seen any cars on the track."

"With all the cameras around, nothing can be hidden at pre-season testing. If you can keep this surprise under wraps until the third day, I will be impressed."

"I live to impress you."

Freddy flushed, just a tiny bit, and his throat shifted as he swallowed. "Last season was the first season with Victor Tsui as your Chief Engineer and frankly, Gamble Racing achieved a huge improvement from the season prior with his design."

"Yes." Jaxxon paused. "Do you have a question?"

"Can we expect to see the same amount of improvement again this season?"

"I certainly hope so. In percentage terms, that would catapult us to the top of the grid consistently."

"And you think you can compete with the biggest teams?"

"Optimistically speaking, I'd like to think so. You know as well as anyone that everyone is bringing a new car today and until we see each other's cars, we aren't going to be able to accurately make any predictions. Of course we want to be fast and reliable. So does everyone. This is a competitive sport and it is always hard work no matter where you are on the grid. All we can do is focus on our own work and ensure that we work as a team and put in the best performances we can."

"In—" Freddy glanced at his watch, "in less than an hour, we will get the first hints."

"Yes. I'm looking forward to seeing what everyone else has."

"We all are, Jaxxon. There's nothing like the anticipation in the air before pre-season testing."

He shrugged, aiming for casual. "I prefer the first race of the season. This week will be a lot of posturing, especially from the teams who were in the top three last season. It's not until the first race when everyone reveals themselves completely."

"Is that a hint that Gamble Racing won't be pushing the car this week?"

"We have our plans for what we want to achieve at pre-season testing this week. Whether that includes a speed test or not, remains to be seen." Jaxxon knew what they were going to do; they'd spent several weeks putting together a plan with the factory team before they'd even put the cars onto containers for shipping here.

"Thank you for your time, Jaxxon." Freddy turned to the camera person, who pointed the lens at the ground. He leaned forward and whispered. "I'm impressed with the way you handled that."

"Thanks." He didn't need the compliment, from anyone. Socrates believed in him and so did Mike, and more than that, he believed he should be here as Team Principal. When the trophies had gone missing, he'd doubted himself and it still nagged at him, although he had no doubts over his ability to do the core parts of his new job.

"Let's have a drink together tonight."

"Okay." Jaxxon should say no. There were a million reasons why he shouldn't have a drink with the media after the first day of testing, and especially not while he was carrying Socrates' secret and they had had zero traction on the search for the missing trophies. "Yes. We need to talk about your collector friend."

"I'll text you." Freddy walked away and his entourage followed.

The first day of testing had been a success. Jaxxon stood under the shower in his hotel room and ran through the summary data. Ondrej's session had gone well with nearly 50 laps in the four-hour period. They'd gathered a lot of data and the car had been fast and responsive, and most importantly, they hadn't pushed it yet. Maybe tomorrow. Paulo had settled into the new car quickly and completed his session satisfactorily too to put Gamble Racing at the higher end of the lap count with 116 laps for the day. Paulo had done well enough in his rookie season last year with two podium finishes, although the end of the season had been marred by the fucking saboteur. His composure during this testing session showed he'd matured over the break. He'd put in a lot of work over the break and looked fitter and leaner too.

Jaxxon jumped out of the shower to discover a text

from Freddy. He made a quick reply that he'd be down soon. They needed to decide; public or private. Being seen in the hotel bar would definitely spark speculation about Gamble Racing, because why else would the Team Principal be chatting to one of the most famous members of the media pack unless there was some gossip to be had. On the other hand, going somewhere private had two major sticking points; if they were seen, it would blow up as a scandal with everyone in the paddock making up all manner of reasons for why they might want to talk in secret. It would be speculation and gossip gone nuclear. The other problem was the temptation of being in the same space as Freddy, and Jaxxon preferred a public spot where the presence of others would help him keep his distance.

He scrubbed his short hair with the towel. It was fucking embarrassing to find Freddy sexy. Yes, he was conventionally attractive; a white Englishman with gorgeous bone structure and hazel eyes that changed shades between brown and green depending on the light. The real problem—for Jaxxon—was that Freddy was a white man with a shit ton of privilege. He was literally an aristocrat, a retired S1 driver, who worked for fun and didn't need the money. Pretty much the direct opposite of Jaxxon. The only thing they shared was a passion for their sport. It was an addiction in many ways, the way S1 took all your attention and time and drew you in and never let go. And yet, even though he wasn't going to try and impress Freddy, he still put on his nicest shirt and a pair of pants that made his ass look great, before he made his way down to the bar.

"Jaxxon. What will you have?"

"A beer."

"Any preference?"

"No, a standard lager is fine." He refused to be embarrassed by his upbringing. He was proud of his parents and how hard they'd worked to give him the chance to have a better life. Freddy didn't blink, just strode to the bar and ordered. It wasn't long until he placed Jaxxon's beer and a bright red sickly-looking liqueur in a martini glass on the table.

"What is that?" The fancy looking drink made him wonder if he'd chosen the correct thing by sticking with a basic beer. When he'd been Ondrej's race engineer, he'd always socialised with the team during the season. As Team Principal, he was going to have to mingle more with the media and with other Team Principals, and there would be a whole new set of rules to learn, a whole new game. Should he find himself a new signature drink? One that said, 'I belong in this group with all your wealth and privilege and connections and the rules you've all made to determine if someone belongs here.' It was a little like code switching but for class; class switching?

"Pacharán. It's a local sloe gin." Freddy slid into his seat with the ease of a retired athlete. He'd kept himself in shape, probably because he was always on screen and had to look good. Jaxxon wasn't going to dwell on Freddy's body or his exercise routine or anything distracting like the crow's feet at the corners of Freddy's eyes when he smiled.

"Sloe?"

"You know those little plums on blackthorns. It's related to roses or something."

"Are you an expert in weird alcohols?" Leaning on

sarcasm was a good defence mechanism when he was on the back foot in a situation.

Freddy laughed with his head tilted slightly backwards. "No. I like to drink whatever the locals drink. It's one of the best parts of this life where we travel the world all the time. I get to explore places and have new experiences."

"Are you judging me for my boring beer?"

"What? This isn't Twitter where me saying I like something automatically means I'm targeting you and saying something negative about you. I just like adventures with my travel. Full stop. Zero judgement on other people's choices."

"Perhaps I'm judging myself for the boring beer."

"Are you?"

Only if it made it obvious that he'd grown up poor. "I've worked so hard to be a part of S1 that I haven't really spent any time thinking about life outside of work."

"Your passion and knowledge of the sport is impressive." Was Freddy flirting with him? His mouth dried out and he drank some of his beer. Freddy couldn't know that, given they'd only had three proper conversations, and two of those had been formal interviews.

"Can I taste some of your drink?"

Freddy's eyes sparkled. "Did I just taunt you into broadening your horizons?"

"No. Fuck off." He grinned and Freddy grinned back at him.

"Here. Try it. It's quite good. Sweet but not too sickly, so quite pleasant. Mostly anise flavoured with a hint of bay leaves and something earthy, perhaps coffee?" Fucking hell, Freddy couldn't help being a bloody aristocratic snob, could he? It was good reminder to keep his distance and not wonder about what Freddy's skin would feel like under his fingertips.

"Fancy." He picked up the glass and sipped. It was a lot sweeter than he preferred; he liked his pastries sweet, not his drinks. "It's not dreadful."

"Not dreadful. What a stunning endorsement. You'd best stick to your beer."

He couldn't look away from Freddy's mouth and the urge to kiss him continued to grow. Damn it. The chatter of groups of people sitting around the bar filtered into the silence. He glanced around, it was a nice bar, similar to so many hotels with modern art on the walls to add colour to a mostly black and grey space. He could've been anywhere in the world, and perhaps that was Freddy's point with his bright red drink?

"Tell me, Freddy, as a retired driver, do you put any stock in the saying that athletes die twice?"

"We do?"

"Yeah." Jaxxon winked to cover up how inane his question was. "Once on retirement and again at the end of their life."

Freddy stared unblinking at him with those hazel eyes and Jaxxon could see that he'd surprised him. It sent a little thrill down his spine.

"What a fascinating idea. I think for me—" Freddy sucked his bottom lip into his mouth, then released it. Jaxxon tried not to stare. "—For me, I decided to retire before Silverstone, so for the rest of my final season, I was just marking time. If retirement was forced onto me, then I think it would feel like death. Yeah, that saying makes sense depending on the circumstance."

"Silverstone was very early in the season to make the decision." Jaxxon was surprised by the revelation. He hadn't worked in S1 back then, but he'd been a fan and he couldn't remember any rumours so early in the season about Freddy.

"Yes, well. The car was slow, and it was frustrating to spend so much time following others. I'd always preferred to be the hunted, not the hunter, when driving." Freddy's line felt like the standard statement to the press, not the real truth. Jaxxon wasn't sure why his gut told him that, just something in the way Freddy's eyes became guarded as he recited the reason.

"You liked being quickest and setting the pace, daring others to catch you?"

Freddy nodded. "Absolutely. If I'd been younger, I might've signed for another team for the next season, but I realised I didn't have the fight in me anymore."

"You were thirty-five." It wasn't old, although the average age for the drivers on the grid was usually around 25. Only a handful of drivers in the modern era had been still driving in their forties.

"Age wasn't a factor. I'd lost that edge, that ability to push a car to the limit. For a while I blamed the car, but it wasn't that."

"If I recall correctly—" And he did because he was good at data, "—you and your teammate were equal at the end of the season."

"Yes, if you don't count DNFs, I beat him ten times and he beat me ten times."

"Hardly a result for concern."

"I knew." The hard stare on Freddy's face told him to back off.

He agreed with a small nod. "It's the only thing that counts. No driver will succeed in this pressure cooker unless they want it more than anything."

"More than life itself." Now the truth came out. Freddy's expression opened up momentarily into something honest. What was behind the statement? Curiosity was going to cause problems because Jaxxon really wanted to know more.

"Yes, I suppose that is true." He kept to a bland answer to help maintain some space between them. His own driver Ondrej had that killer instinct where he would put himself in danger and take extraordinary risks to beat another driver. It was what it took to succeed at this level. They fell into an unsteady silence again and Jaxxon leaned back in his chair. Over at the elevators, an elderly white man was attempting to get his luggage in the lift. The staff quickly intervened, and the drama disappeared.

"Are you going to ask me about my collector friend?"

Jaxxon shrugged. "I assume you have no news since it's taken you all day to mention anything."

"All day?"

"You mentioned it this morning before testing started. And you've said nothing since."

Freddy raised one eyebrow. "Maybe I wanted to surprise you?"

"Okay, but why would you do that?"

"I wouldn't. And yes, you are right. The rumour around Graham Montblanc's trophy was false and Cliff hadn't heard anything about your trophies, although there are rumours that there is a new collector who has been quietly buying up memorabilia."

"Like what?"

"Obviously cars are a big ticket item, but anything that a driver has worn and can be authenticated."

"So Ondrej and Paulo could sell their racing boots and people would buy them."

Freddy grinned. "Cliff said that a Ricky Dee shoe-y racing boot from one of his wins would fetch over a hundred thousand pounds, maybe more because he's so iconic with that big grin."

"For an old boot soaked in champagne?" People with money spent it on stuff that made no sense to him. When he'd saved up enough, he had bought his parents their bakery business. They'd been so proud when his career as an engineer had allowed him to buy himself an apartment, a steppingstone into the housing market and he'd been so grateful to be able to afford to get off the rental wagon wheel.

"Helmets are big too, especially race winning helmets."

"And trophies."

"Yes, although they carry such sentimental value for the person who won them and so they hardly ever come up for sale. Only—" Freddy paused for long enough that Jaxxon filled the space.

"After a long-ago retired driver has died and their family needs money?" He had guessed correctly judging by the sorrowful nod from Freddy.

"Yes. It's shameful that families just sell off hard earned trophies. Why not donate to a museum?"

"Is that what you will do?"

"Probably." A flicker of something crossed Freddy's face.

"What does that mean?"

Freddy traced his finger around the top of his glass. "My family wish to create a trophy cabinet in the portrait gallery and preserve them as part of my…" He sighed. "Quote my family's rich history unquote."

"I see?" He didn't see. His parents still had his 'most improved player' award from U13s soccer. Why did Freddy make his family's wish sound so unreasonable and snarky?

"You don't, though, do you?"

He shook his head. "No. Not at all."

"Are your parents proud of you?" Freddy's question carried a sad note. Curious.

"Of course they are. Aren't yours?"

"If they are, they haven't told me."

Jaxxon's chest tightened. "If they aren't proud of you, then they are fools."

"Thank you. My father is an old man now, set in his ways."

"And those ways mean he can't be impressed by his son winning races on the world's toughest racing circuit?"

"Driving a car? No, it's not like I became Prime Minister or did anything important with my life."

Jaxxon shook his head. "Fucking hell. That was the expectation?"

"Yes." Freddy stated it without question, which only created a long list of more questions for Jaxxon. "But enough about me and my parents. I'm almost middle aged now. Their opinion shouldn't matter to me anymore." Freddy's dismissal had that tone of someone who cared deeply and didn't want to admit it. Jaxxon let that one slide by—silent empathy was hopefully better than platitudes—and he simply waited for Freddy to continue.

"Did your parents give you expectations?"

"Yes. Get an education. It'll give me options. They told me I was worth more than labouring like they did. They believe that children should improve on the life of the parents. They believed in me." It was a huge gift. One he'd held tight as he'd worked two jobs while studying, and the core confidence they'd taught him had formed a great basis for the work he did now. He owed everything to them.

CHAPTER 5

Freddy was jealous. He couldn't deny it. It seethed in his stomach like a fishtailing trailer about to jack-knife. Jaxxon had such confidence in himself and the easy way he talked of his parents and how proud they were of him made him grieve for the distant way he'd been brought up. The second son of a Duke with all the privilege and expectation and none of the love. He didn't need love when he had everything else, apparently.

"I don't expect you to feel sorry for me."

"Why would I?"

Right, because he hadn't actually told Jaxxon anything. "I am the spare. And now that my older brother has five children, I'm unnecessary, only tolerated in my family because I'm not an embarrassment." Although that was likely debatable depending on which family member anyone asked. If Chester had managed to realise that Freddy was now seventh in succession for the Dukedom, the whole stalking business could've been avoided. The fact that Chester hadn't understood the rules had added a cruel irony to the mess, or maybe it wouldn't have mattered because Chester's self-centred need to be in proximity to the Dukedom overrode reality or common sense.

Jaxxon blinked slowly. "How cruel to let a child know that."

"It's ingrained in them, unfortunately. When the system depends on being born to the right parents in the right order, then everything else is secondary." He sipped his drink, annoyed at the way his hand trembled. "Look, don't feel sorry for me. I went to the best schools. All my karting and early racing was paid for. I never had to think about money while competing in an extremely expensive sport. You know how it is."

"Talent will get you so far, but money will get you to the top."

"And ironically, talent is what gets you to the very top again."

"Excuse me?"

"Money gets drivers onto the grid. It comes back to individual driver skill to take someone from the grid to champion. Look at your Sanchez." Relief at being able to change the subject away from his family flowed down his spine like a reviving juice, giving him impetus.

"Okay?" Jaxxon had a wary expression which was fair given the way fans had been quite negative about Sanchez buying his seat last year. The lack of respect for drivers with billionaire fathers always amazed him, because it ignored the fact that every other driver came with sponsorship too. Just in less obvious ways; some were related to past champions and could utilise their name to get money for the team, others had the support of billionaires through political connections or otherwise. Very few made it into S1 without sponsorship, and those few were usually aligned with big car manufacturers who scouted for the extremely talented youngsters at karting races which was just a different form of sponsorship.

"Sanchez is fast. Almost as fast as Grenville was. He's still learning the other skills, like tyre management, and that will increase his race craft and overall performance."

Jaxxon nodded. "I agree. His rookie season showed promise, but he made too many mistakes and wasn't consistent enough. He followed instructions better today and I hope he's matured over the break."

"And of course, his father is a major sponsor, so he'll be given the time to mature. S1 is less forgiving of those who don't bring big dollars with them."

"Yes." Jaxxon's eyes narrowed. "Back up a second. Tell me about Grenville. Why do you say he was fast?"

"You can't look at his results, or lack of results, to be honest, in S1, to make that judgement. He drove a terrible car. Look at when he won at Spa in S3, he did it through pure pace. His race craft was always a bit lacking, he was too aggressive, but he was wicked fast." The notion of a driver being seen as fast in car racing wasn't about the way they handled the car, or how fast their car was. It was purely about reaction time.

"Socrates sent him to anger management therapy and he's found a good place in our Series E team."

"I've been watching. He's worked hard on improving his broader skills and it's paying off. I think electric cars would suit his driving style better too. They have so much torque and acceleration, they suit someone as quick as him."

"Yes, he didn't really have the ability to nurse an S1 car through the length of a race."

Freddy nodded. It was true; he'd always prided himself on having good driving skill and the ability to manage the tyres between pit stops well.

"Have you seen his tattoo?" he asked. Lucien Grenville had a large steam punk style cat, a panther or a cheetah, as a sleeve tattoo with the words 'wicked fast' written along the spine of the animal. The paw of the cat was reaching out and had scratched across Grenville's chest, exposing a mechanical heart underneath. It was stunning artistic work, and Freddy loved the concept of Grenville being a machine under his skin.

"I would ask if you were admitting to seeing one of our drivers naked, but everyone in the paddock has seen Lucien's tattoo. When he first got it, in his rookie season, he spent considerable time with his shirt off!" Jaxxon's lips curled upwards and he flashed his teeth as he grinned.

Freddy ignored the shiver that sliced down his spine and grinned back. "Did you know it's a quote of mine?"

"No."

"It's true. Lucien Grenville has my words tattooed on his body."

"That's a big claim."

Freddy loved this moment and he leaned forward slightly. "It says 'wicked fast'. I said that about him after his S3 win at Spa and he got the tattoo soon afterwards. Ergo, his tattoo quotes me."

Jaxxon laughed with a hint of scorn in the sound. "That's hardly an attributed quote."

"Let my ego have this one." Freddy grinned to let Jaxxon know he was kidding.

"He'll be at Bahrain. I'll ask him."

"He will?"

Jaxxon's lips twisted slightly. "He's going to drive a session for us at pre-season testing."

"I thought he drove Series E. Are you hinting at a return to Series One?" If it was true, it would be some of the biggest gossip since the silly season last year. Freddy wanted to know if they were planning for D'Grieg's retirement, or if Sanchez was going to get replaced.

Jaxxon chuckled. "Nothing that exciting. He's Victor Tsui's boyfriend and it's a little gift from Socrates to give Lucien a drive in Victor's latest car."

"I knew they were together." He'd guessed after seeing them together and he was glad they'd worked it all out.

"You did?"

"Yeah. Isn't that so typical of Socrates? He can't be that ill if he can make a declaration that upsets all your plans and yet is so adorable that you couldn't possibly say no."

Jaxxon made a rueful expression as he nodded. "That about sums it up. How did you know about Lucien and Victor? They haven't announced anything because it's no one's business, although it's not a secret."

"The powers of being the press."

"I didn't think they'd done a press release?"

Freddy shook his head once. "Like you said, it's not a secret. I can't imagine them doing the whole coming out story like D'Grieg did."

"They wouldn't need to. Lucien has been openly gay since his karting days. Where did you hear about Victor and Lucien?"

"I suspected they were together a while back. I was the one who broke the sabotage news story. Socrates invited me to his house the night when they discovered that it was Reggie's son who'd done all that mess, and Grenville had punched him. Not Socrates, the son."

"I heard that Lucien had done that."

"You heard?"

"I was Ondrej's race engineer then. Like most of our team, we didn't know until the news broke and we had a team meeting the next day."

Freddy frowned. "Your promotion really was quite sudden?"

"Yes."

"Yes. That's it?"

"Yes. My loyalty is to Socrates and the team."

Freddy's frown deepened. "You can trust me with the information."

"Says the media shark whose job it is to ferret out secrets."

"In confidence, off the record."

Jaxxon didn't bite, simply shaking his head slowly. "It's not my story to tell."

"But you benefited from his absence." He didn't intend it to be a question and when Jaxxon half-stood, then sat down again, he had that warm wash of satisfaction at having provoked someone into giving him information. It was one of his favourite parts of interviewing people.

"How dare you. No one wants Socrates to be ill. We are

all worried about him." Jaxxon's controlled anger was probably designed to be intimidating, not stunningly enticing and sexy.

"Therefore your job is temporary?" Freddy went for the jugular because he wanted more of Jaxxon's intensity aimed at him. A foolish game that would only end in trouble as lust blossomed in Freddy's mind, torso, and cock.

"Again, that is not anyone's business but mine and Socrates."

"Fine. I won't ask again." He admired the way Jaxxon rallied around his boss and gave no hint for why Socrates had suddenly stepped away from the team he'd started. "I admire you, you know."

Jaxxon raised his eyebrows. "Excuse me?"

Okay, so he probably shouldn't have blurted that out. He could fudge it, like he would with anyone else, but he wouldn't have said that to anyone else either. "It's true."

"Why would you say it though?"

"You think I have an ulterior motive?"

Jaxxon shrugged, an exaggerated move that had to be deliberate. "You are press. I am Team Principal. Your job is to get information out of me, and if you have to butter me up to get that, I wouldn't be surprised."

"It would make sense for you to think that way."

"You believe that I shouldn't?"

"Socrates trusted me to break the sabotage story. I would think that should be a good starting point for a working relationship." Freddy implored Jaxxon to trust him, holding his gaze. Heat bloomed and the air crackled as he waited, listening to Jaxxon's breathing, loud and intimate over the background noise of the bar.

"And you thought that saying you admire me was a good way to achieve trust between us?"

"It is true; although perhaps I should not have said it quite so bluntly."

Jaxxon sipped his beer for a while; those dark eyes of his focused intently on Freddy, thinking, thinking, but he didn't speak.

"People say that I've been given everything in life, and I can see why they say that." He wasn't sure why he needed to explain this to Jaxxon, who just tipped his head slightly to one side for a second. "It's the core tenant of privilege. I have had, by most standards, an easy life, yet not everything has been easy. The privilege of my life is that there are many things that have not made my life harder."

"Being rich, white, and a talented driver?"

"Yes. You have the whole of it. Essentially that's why I admire you. You've made it to the top of a very competitive sport at a relatively young age through sheer brilliance and hard work, without any of those advantages."

"Thank you. I'm surprised that you mention that I'm Black with such alacrity."

"You are?" He cringed. He'd meant that Jaxxon was surprised because obviously Jaxxon was Black, but to explain now was going to be a mess of overthinking.

"People go to a lot of effort to talk around it without stating the obvious."

"Isn't that what I just did? And doesn't that mean that they are trying not to make a big deal of it?"

Jaxxon raised those eyebrows again. "But it is a big deal, is it not? I'm likely the first Black Team Principal."

"Yes, most likely. It is a very European sport." As soon

as he said it, he knew from Jaxxon's expression that he'd said something wrong, he just didn't know what it was.

"Black people have existed in Europe for centuries, Freddy."

"I'm sorry." He wanted to hide under the table, ashamed of his own ignorance.

Jaxxon's face stayed still, expressionless. "Yes. And it is the essence of why I don't trust you, not completely, given the relative … motivations of our jobs."

"You don't trust me because my privilege in life means I can't understand what hurdles you've had to overcome to be here?"

"That about sums it up." Jaxxon sipped his beer and Freddy waited for him, trying to ignore the way his stomach squirmed with discomfort. He wanted Jaxxon to trust him, and he needed to understand his perspective and life to achieve that.

"Look, it's a good start that you understand your own privilege, but it doesn't give you the gift of seeing the world through my eyes."

"I don't think it's possible for me to ever see that, to be honest. I can try, but I will always be the second son of Duke who doesn't need to work, who only does this job because I love it."

Jaxxon smiled, a soft smile that charmed Freddy more than it ought. "I also love this job. I've worked very hard to have it and I intend to enjoy it completely."

"Then we agree on one thing."

"And what is that?"

"We have a whole season ahead of us. We love our jobs, and I'm sure we can find ways to help each other."

Jaxxon laughed, a strong booming joyful sound that drew the attention of several people in the bar. "And now we finally get to the core of your motivation for meeting tonight."

"Do you think I'm so calculating?" It wasn't quite the right question and it came out too whingey, making him want to swallow the tone right back into his mouth and try again. He was never this awkward with people. Damn, lust was really making normal interaction difficult.

Jaxxon's face relaxed a little more, with the ghost of that soft smile still apparent. "Calculating? No, I don't think you are purposefully calculating. I think you are so accustomed to getting what you want that it comes naturally. There is also the experience factor; you've spent so long in the paddock playing the games that everyone plays, and now it's all you know." It was a fair assessment and did nothing to remove the urge to kiss Jaxxon.

"I do enjoy the push and pull of trying to encourage people to give me information."

"I can see that."

"It's fun. Let me have fun with you." He gulped and hoped Jaxxon took it as a joke, because it really skirted far too closely to the truth. He wanted Jaxxon in his bed, much more than he ought. His self-preservation instincts fled whenever he stared into those dark brown eyes, although the cynicism in Jaxxon's expression was probably earned.

"Freddy?"

"Oh God. Not like that." His face blazed hot. Damn it, he wasn't usually this awkward. He swallowed. "Unless of course you can't resist how suave I am." He'd already fucked this up, why not go all in?

"Incredibly suave." Jaxxon raised his eyebrows and god, Freddy wanted to be kissed by this man. His heart fluttered, and he was keen to throw away reason and chase his lust for Jaxxon with no regard for the future. Hell.

After another long pause, Jaxxon stood up and stuck out his hand. "Well, keep me informed if your collector friend comes up with anything useful."

Freddy shook it and ignored the tingle that shot up his arm and into his chest. "I'll see you around the paddock, then." Yeah, Freddy, so bloody suave. Hell. He needed Georgia to metaphorically slap him around the face before he embarrassed himself more.

CHAPTER 6

BAHRAIN

Freddy couldn't get the weird conversation with Jaxxon out of his head. They'd ignored each other for the whole of pre-season testing but he couldn't avoid Jaxxon forever. He'd interviewed Grenville after his testing session and spent the whole time ignoring the surge of envy as Grenville thanked his lover for the chance to drive a properly fast S1 car. Now the first race of the season was over and Gamble Racing had achieved points for both cars in Jaxxon's first race as Team Principal. He needed to interview Jaxxon for professional reasons, so he painted his most neutral expression on his face and walked up to Jaxxon who almost smiled at him. Freddy didn't think he'd imagined the little curve at the corner of Jaxxon's mouth.

"Jaxxon Loharani-Jones. You must be thrilled with today's result." Freddy pointed his microphone in the direction of Jaxxon's handsome visage.

"Yes. Ondrej drove an excellent race and only just missed out on a podium."

"The official gap between third and fourth was one point two."

Jaxxon nodded in a way that communicated that he knew the data. "And Paulo Sanchez finished in seventh, after being caught up in the tangle at the start. The work he's put in over the break showed dividends today."

"The car looks a lot more stable in racing conditions than last year."

"We will have to look at the data and get more feedback from our drivers before I make a definitive statement. The result today is very pleasing and gives Gamble Racing a good base to build on. It's a long season ahead." Jaxxon's expression gave nothing away. Today he wore the Gamble Racing jacket over a polo shirt that was loose over his rounded stomach, and blue jeans that clung to his muscular thighs; not the Freddy was looking. He was absolutely not looking.

"It is. Give my thoughts to Socrates. We all miss him in the paddock."

"Thank you. He'll be watching. He may not be able to make it to the races at the moment, but Socrates would never miss a race."

He smiled at the camera. "The team has given him something to smile about today, that's for sure."

"Yes. Now we need to get back to work and make certain that we can get points consistently." Jaxxon smiled for the camera, then walked over to Paulo who had just finished being interviewed by Freddy's colleague, Alicia Blasi.

"Jaxxon." He pushed through the crowd of journalists to follow him along, not wanting to end the interview just yet and so he took the opportunity to ask Jaxxon about his driver now that he stood beside Paulo Sanchez. "I was very impressed with Sanchez's tyre management today after that enforced early stop."

Jaxxon turned back towards him. "It certainly was an excellent job in tough circumstances. Being a driver who can consistently score points is about being able to deal with the pressure of plans going wrong and respond positively. Paulo is a quick learner and I'm looking forward to seeing him build from today's race for the rest of the season."

Freddy stared at him for a split second with his mouth gaping open before he composed himself. "Paulo, it sounds like your team boss is putting a lot of faith in you. How will you repay that?"

Paulo's face was carefully neutral. "I will continue to work hard, to learn as much as I can, and I hope that my efforts will pay off on the track."

Freddy didn't have anything to say to such a perfectly scripted media answer. People always teased sports reporters for asking the same obvious questions, while athletes responded with the same boring answers. It made him want to blurt out something absurd—well, no, not quite—more likely, he wanted to impress Jaxxon with an unexpected question. His crush hadn't gone away in the couple of weeks since their circular conversation in the hotel bar in Barcelona. Suave. Yeah, right.

"Freddy." His producer called his name through his

earpiece. A welcome reprieve. "We have some breaking news. Wrap it up." Carol's urgency rang clear in her tone.

"That's great, Paulo. Good luck with the rest of the season." He spun on his heel and rushed off, waiting until he was out of earshot before he pressed his earpiece.

"Carol. I'm ready."

"Freddy."

"What happened and where do you need me to be?"

She mentioned one of the big teams, his old team. "If you can get to their pitlane first, you should be able to break this one. The 2010 world championship trophy has been stolen."

"Fuck." Seb's trophy. Freddy had come fourth in the driver's championship that year and his teammate, Sebastian Damiamo, had won.

Carol's voice was terse. "Just get the story."

He waved to Maddock, his cameraman, and jogged towards the pitlane. Nothing in the world beat the thrill of driving an S1 car, although chasing down a story came close. As he ran, he pulled out his phone and tried to send a text to Jaxxon.

"Jesus, Freddy. Stop running." Maddock laughed as he jogged beside him. The huge Lebanese man spent most of his day lugging about a massive camera and walking backwards when Freddy walked forwards and was probably fitter than Freddy.

"Fine." He stopped for a second and quickly sent the text.

Freddy
Trophy news. Meet at pitlane. My old
team.

He tucked his phone back in his pocket and ran again until he stood at the bottom of the stairs leading up into the truck they used as team offices during a race weekend. The whole office could be packed up and driven to the next race easily.

Sonia walked down the stairs towards him, a deep frown on her face as she glanced over at Maddock.

"Sonia. Tell me."

"No cameras." Sonia had worked for the team for decades, rising through the ranks until she was the Sponsorship Manager. From northern Italy, she was a white woman with striking blond hair, the proportions of a swimsuit model, and was incredibly intelligent. Sonia knew exactly how to talk to rich people to get them to sponsor the team. Her wife Alana was a lawyer; a real power couple. He waved at Maddock who shrugged and waited outside as Freddy followed Sonia inside.

"We had the trophy here—"

Freddy's phone dinged. "Hold up a second."

Jaxxon
Am here

"Sonia, I want someone else to join us."

"Who?"

"Jaxxon Loharani-Jones."

"The new Team Principal at Gamble Racing?"

"You've met?"

"Not yet. Why him?"

"Two of Gamble Racing's trophies were stolen last month."

Sonia shrugged. "Yes, I do recall that press release. Fine. Good idea." She probably could recite the entire press release. There wasn't much in the paddock that she missed.

"I have been known to have them sometimes."

"But no tours."

He smiled. "Sonia. I remember the rules." It might have been several years since he drove competitively, but he still remembered the sanctity of the team's highly guarded data. He jumped up and went to the door to let Jaxxon inside.

"Come in, but don't be nosy. No poking around looking for team secrets. You don't want to get on the wrong side of Sonia."

"I heard that."

"It's true."

Jaxxon's mouth quirked up at the corners. "Consider me well warned. What did your rather cryptic text mean?"

"Come in. Close the door."

Jaxxon did as he was asked, then turned to face Freddy. More than his physical size—a few inches taller than Freddy and much broader—Jaxxon had such presence that he filled the room. Perhaps that was just lust talking. Jesus, he usually had better control than this. He threw himself into a chair before anyone noticed the swelling in his pants.

Sonia held out her hand. "Sonia Como. Yes, like the lake. Sponsorship Manager."

"Jaxxon Loharani-Jones. Team Principal, Gamble Racing." He shook her hand and everyone sat down.

"Sonia has some trophy news." Freddy repeated his text, loving the way Jaxxon's already sharp expression focused. His PA Georgia had called it a crush, and he believed it because his chest tightened and his breathing sped up at the intense intelligence in Jaxxon's eyes. He could lose himself in those dark eyes. He wanted to get closer to him so he could see all the variations of the brown, all the nuances of colour in his irises. Shit. He was so fucking screwed.

She shook her head. "I'm impressed that you know about this already. Fucking press."

"My producer told me."

Sonia checked her watch. "News travels fast in this sport. Twenty minutes ago, one of our engineers noticed the trophy was missing. We think it disappeared during the race while we were all occupied."

"Isn't the truck locked?" Jaxxon asked.

"No, it's always occupied. We are going through the security footage."

"Have the police been informed?" Jaxxon asked.

Sonia shook her head. "Not yet. I have talked to our security team and the S1 security team, so they'll be checking everyone when they leave the paddock tonight."

"I doubt there's much the local police can do, but it is handy to have the theft on a record somewhere. The other theft happened in England." Freddy's brother, AA, might have a Scotland Yard contact through White's or one of his other clubs, and he'd rather talk to him than his bloody father. It was likely an inside job by someone who had access to the truck. But how would that connect to the Gamble Racing trophy theft? He kept his attention on

Sonia and Jaxxon. There would be time for speculation later.

"We do have a liaison in our local police for our case, and it would be good to connect the two, even if the police may not be able to do much. It's always good to have something official if it ever gets to the point of going to court." Jaxxon's cynicism was reflected on Sonia's face.

"This is probably beyond the capabilities of most local police forces."

"Yes." Jaxxon nodded. "We have one of our technicians, Skye, going over the footage at Gamble Racing, both of the night the trophies were stolen, and for the preceding month. I can give you Skye's number and you can liaise with them to see if any similarities can be spotted between the two events." Jaxxon picked up his phone. "Skye has an excellent track record for this type of thing. They have a very good eye for details."

"Thank you, I appreciate it." Sonia gave Jaxxon her number and his thumbs shifted over the screen of his phone. Like everything he did, it was quick and efficient. Freddy needed to get the bones of the story, to do his job, not stare at Jaxxon and the way he was so competent. This was his old team and Sonia's hard gaze told him where she expected his loyalties to lie. Not with the press, that's for sure, even though he hadn't technically been invited to join this conversation and was trying to stay quiet so they'd forget he was here, except he was curious about one thing.

"Why was Seb's trophy at the race?" he asked.

"One of our sponsors wanted to use it in a photo shoot." Sonia gave a lackadaisical shrug.

Jaxxon sighed. "Ours were also stolen from a publicity event."

Freddy should've connected that detail too. He needed to focus on his job, not let himself by distracted by Jaxxon. It was time to be sharper and make the connections he ought to make.

"We did the photo shoot on Friday after FP1 and the trophy was returned to our offices and put under the usual security."

"Which is?" Freddy asked. His frustration at his lack of ability to pull the pieces of this mystery into something useful started to outweigh his heightened lust around Jaxxon. The audacity of someone taking a trophy from a secure team truck began to sink in. How dare someone fucking steal the symbol of someone's success?

"What's the matter?" Jaxxon asked. The concern in his tone hit him in the chest, like a button that released all the energy pent up inside him. He couldn't display lust, but he could focus on the other feelings that this theft brought up and let out some tension instead.

"It makes me so angry. I know how hard it is to win one of these trophies. I came close a few times and how dare someone steal the symbol of that?" He was shaking and he squeezed his hands into fists to try and stop the flow of emotion. When he'd been a driver, he had much better control than this, and for some reason, it was worse to lose it with Jaxxon's keen eyes on him. He hadn't quite lost it yet; just like that moment of oversteer when everything was about to go sideways if he didn't accelerate through the lack of traction in the backend to stop the car spinning out.

"It can't have been easy to achieve. If your truck is

anything like ours, there is always someone here and we keep it locked down quite tight to keep the team's data secure." Jaxxon's observation helped recentre Freddy. It did no one any good to fly off the handle.

"We have already considered that the thief had help from someone on our team." Sonia's admission made Jaxxon raise his eyebrows, and he probably had a matching expression. He'd already wondered about the possibility of an inside job, especially given what he knew about how tight their security was.

"It happens." His voice combined with Jaxxon to say the same thing, and they stared at each other. Freddy's pulse leapt, loving the way their brains merged for a second.

Sonia glanced between them. "Do tell." From her astute glance, he couldn't help wonder if she knew his inner thoughts. Maybe she could see the lust painted all over his skin. It certainly felt like his cheeks were too hot, so they must be pinker than usual.

"You can have the honour, Freddy." Jaxxon waved his hand in Freddy's direction.

"How did you get involved with this, Freddy?" Sonia emphasised the 'did' and Jaxxon coughed. After a long moment of silence, Freddy's initial burst of frustration eased into a much more familiar curiosity. Why had Jaxxon coughed, and what was he hiding?

"Do you have something to say, Jaxxon?" he asked.

"No. How did you get involved?"

Freddy's immediate reaction was to blame Jaxxon for drawing him in but he forced himself to be a little more reticent. "Socrates and I have a long working relationship. You know how it is between media and Team Principals..."

Except he didn't want to fuck most of them. Only one. His mouth was too dry and swallowing didn't help much.

"And?"

He cleared his throat. "I assisted Socrates after they caught the saboteur over the break. You must remember that story, Sonia?"

"Yes. Gamble Racing has had a tumultuous few months."

He swallowed. "Anyway, I helped Socrates with the press releases around that, crafting them to help give sponsors confidence that they'd resolved their security issues." He glanced at Jaxxon whose lips were pinched together. "And I was at the Gamble Racing car reveal when their trophies were stolen, and I offered to talk to a memorabilia collector friend of mine."

"With Socrates?" Sonia's raised eyebrows asked the question that Freddy wanted the answer to as well. Interestingly, she didn't leap to the conclusion that Gamble Racing still had a security problem. Knowing her, she'd probably tucked that one away quietly in case she could use it for her own team later. He made a mental note to mention it to Jaxxon later, although judging by the twitch in his jaw, he probably already had worked that out.

"No. Socrates wasn't at the car reveal this season. He is —" Jaxxon closed his eyes for a moment. "Unwell."

"Gamble Racing has been using that story for a while now. It must be serious."

Jaxxon lifted up one hand. "It's not something I can discuss. Shall we get back to the trophies? Is there any evidence that it's the same person, or people, who took Socrates' trophies? Or just a coincidence?"

"It could be a copycat crime." Freddy was far out of his depth. What did he know about something like this? He wanted to hunt down information and try and figure out an answer, for his own satisfaction. Yeah, he needed to stop kidding himself. He wanted to prove to Jaxxon that he wasn't just some privileged asshole who talked to drivers and looked pretty on television. He wanted Jaxxon to respect him, because then he might kiss him. Fucking stop, Freddy. His crush had gone too far if he was trying to talk himself into being good enough for Jaxxon. Getting involved with someone in the paddock was a terrible idea and he had the history to prove that. Bad idea. Bad.

"What do the trophies have in common, aside from being trophies?" Jaxxon asked another pertinent question. Damn. If he had this amount of chemical attraction to anyone else, he would've acted on it already. He really didn't like this circular angst about a little bit of inconvenient lust.

"Isn't that enough? Why do we need to understand the motivation of the thief?" Sonia rubbed her temples. The simple gesture pulled him out of his bloody head and back into reality. "We want Seb's trophy returned."

"Don't forget the Montblanc rumour."

"What happened there?" Sonia asked.

He'd had a chat to Graham a few days ago. "They think their cleaner must've moved it. They noticed it missing during a dinner party but they found it later that evening in another room. I mean, it makes sense to be something random like that because why take only one trophy when both of Montblanc's trophies would've been sitting together on a shelf."

"I think we can ignore that as an unlikely coincidence," Sonia said.

Jaxxon tapped the table with his finger. "Remember when you said that trophies only come on the market occasionally, if a family needs to sell one for money?"

"Yes." He had said that.

"There is one thing both Seb's trophy, Montblanc's trophies, and Socrates' trophies have in common."

"What's that?"

"Money."

"Do you mean because none of those three drivers needed to sell their trophies for money, which means they couldn't be purchased by a collector, only grabbed by less savoury means?" he asked, and Sonia sat up straighter in her chair.

"That wasn't what I was thinking, although it's probably useful to understand." Jaxxon's eyes narrowed. "I think we should offer a financial reward for details that result in the return of all three trophies. Let's remind the thief that we have money behind us. They might be counting on the police not having the resources or jurisdiction to do much about finding the trophies, even if they can connect the two crimes. We need to act first and use the considerable resources of our respective teams." Jaxxon's implication that both team's pride was on the line; that the notion that someone could steal from them and the related security problems that would come from having someone access ...

He half-stood up. "What if it's not about the trophies at all?"

"Excuse me?" Sonia's question was mirrored on Jaxxon's face.

"Well, think about it—" He hoped Jaxxon would forgive him for pointing this out in front of his rival, and belatedly realised that he ought to hope the same for his old team too. "—doesn't the two thefts prove that each team's security is fallible?"

"Fuck." Jaxxon and Sonia swore together. "Fuck."

"A trophy is a useless treasure. It only matters to the people who won it. But if you can prove that you can get past a team's security to grab one, then—"

"You don't need to labour the point." Sonia flashed him a look, the same one she used to give him when he'd crashed as a driver. Grand disappointment in one look.

Jaxxon's jaw muscles tightened. "It's obviously a concern. We are in the process of reviewing all our security. Socrates' trophies were taken from his home, not from anywhere near any team data, but obviously combined with the fact that someone managed to infiltrate our logistics team to sabotage our cars, it's a problem."

"We are going to need to be very careful in the way we word a press release." Sonia recovered first.

"While you guys do that, I'm going to ask Cliff what he thinks about who might be interested in collecting the stolen goods." Freddy couldn't help each team with their security, but he could assist in finding the trophies by using his own connections. He hated to disappoint anyone.

"Cliff?" Sonia asked.

"He's a friend of my family who specialises in memorabilia collection."

"How does that help?"

Freddy had never felt awkward about his family or his wealth until he'd met Jaxxon. He knew it was his problem and he needed to get over himself. He swallowed. Jaxxon was a stunning example of someone who'd overcome the lack of all the opportunities Freddy had, and it reminded Freddy that his own accomplishments had been easier to achieve. "When the very rich collect things, they don't particularly care about provenance. Cliff has a good ear for when someone is using less than legal methods to acquire items."

"He's a gossip, like you." Sonia winked and he laughed, surprised that she would say that because her job as Sponsorship Manager was reliant on knowing everything about anyone with wealth or resources who could potentially help the team, aka all the gossip.

"Yeah, we are a regular pair of old assholes sitting at the bar talking about everyone else to avoid our own problems." Having an excuse to be himself and make a joke felt bloody good.

Sonia clapped her hand over her mouth. "You rascal. I shouldn't be laughing when we have a major security problem like this."

"Perhaps we should do a joint press statement in a couple of days with the reward." Jaxxon ignored the two of them to focus on work.

He could do that too and prove his worth in this discussion. "You'll need a few days to work out how to structure a reward, so you don't get overwhelmed with a million fan messages. You know what the internet is like." He paused as they both nodded. "You'll need to structure the reward notice to ensure you get concrete answers, not just bullshit."

Jaxxon looked at him as if he'd stated the bleeding

obvious and he wanted to shrink under the table. No, he would square his shoulders and prove himself.

"Good. Leave it with me," Sonia said. "Jaxxon, let's meet back in England in two days and go over the reward concept. I'll update Marcel and have a look at his schedule. He will want to be involved in that stage." Sonia stood up and stuck out her hand. They'd been dismissed. Jaxxon shook Sonia's hand with a tight smile, and Freddy waited his turn before they left the truck and walked back out into the paddock. He waved to Maddock, then pulled out his phone to check his hair and face and that he was standing in a good position with the team brand in the background, before taking the microphone from Maddock's assistant, Lilya. He pressed the button on his earpiece.

"Carol. I have the story. Are you good to go live?"

"Two minutes."

He nodded.

"Are you going to break the story before they get to do a press release?"

"Yes."

Jaxxon frowned.

"It's literally my job, Jaxxon. Do you want to be in the shot?" He would have to change the narrative into an interview if Jaxxon didn't move.

"No." Jaxxon strode away and for half a second, Freddy relaxed because Jaxxon was leaving, but no such luck. Jaxxon stood just behind Maddock, ensuring that when Freddy looked at the camera, he'd also be staring at Jaxxon. After a few long slow breaths, he forced himself to be ready. One brilliant, sexy man couldn't be allowed to distract him from being a professional.

CHAPTER 7

Jaxxon's position next to the camera person gave him an excellent view of Freddy with the truck they'd just vacated in the background. In a few days he was going to meet Marcel Levante, Team Principal of one of the leading teams. This time last year, he was a race engineer and meeting the other Team Principals had been a goal. Now it was his life. He was one of them, doing a job he'd worked hard to get, and he could be damned proud of himself. It wasn't the most ideal circumstances to begin the job, and it probably made him a dick to be a little bit glad that the missing trophies problem had expanded to become someone else's issue too.

Freddy tilted his head slightly, listening to his ear bud, then nodded. He waggled his fingers at the camera person who handed him a microphone, waited for a while, and then he introduced himself to the camera in the usual fashion.

"Here in the Series One paddock, we love our fans.

Without fans, this sport is merely a bunch of rich people spending money to see who has the fastest car, which, to be frank, could potentially be rather boring. Our fans turn Series One into an interesting spectacle and the popularity of our sport ensures more investment and that has resulted in a vast amount of innovation over the years. Innovation which ends up in the hands of our fans through road cars. It is the fans who take this pursuit of speed and innovation and engineering; and give it purpose. Fans make our sport human. We love our fans." Freddy's introduction was heart-warming, if a little pointless, but then his open expression became fierce.

"Sometimes a few fans take it too far and risk ruining everything for everyone. I stand here outside my old team's pitlane with some unfortunate news." Freddy paused and Jaxxon held his breath too. He couldn't believe he'd been drawn into this story so easily. What a skill Freddy had, and his competence made him more handsome. It took him from merely a well-constructed face with symmetric features into a real, passionate person who knew what he was doing, and who obviously cared deeply about Series One. His demonstrated ability was Jaxxon's catnip.

"The 2010 World Championship Trophy, won by Sebastian Damiamo, was in the paddock for some publicity photos. What a season that was." Freddy's half-smile was a delight. "The championship went down to the wire with three drivers all in the hunt for the championship heading into the second last race. Complex calculations were being run by all the teams to work out who had to finish where to give themselves a chance. In the end, it didn't matter as

Damaimo won the second last race decisively and only had to finish in the points in the last race to win the World Championship. Fans will remember how exciting it was." He paused, a little melodramatically. "And now those memories have been tainted. I'm terribly sorry to report that the 2010 World Championship Trophy has been lost, presumed stolen, during today's race." Freddy blinked a little, pausing as he composed himself. If he was acting, it was incredibly well done. Jaxxon believed Freddy was on the verge of tears. "You might think ... Oh it's just a trophy. Who cares?" Freddy squared his shoulders and looked at the camera, which felt like he was staring right through Jaxxon.

"I do. I care." Freddy tapped his chest. "And you should too. A trophy isn't a pretty piece of metal to be placed on a shelf and stared at. It's a symbol of the hard work that a whole team does in pursuit of victory. Almost a thousand people working all year to produce a consistent car, with great strategies for every race and every scenario, and most of all a talented competitive driver who works in unison with the team to win a World Championship. A trophy symbolises the efforts of many people, working towards a common goal, and if that isn't the entire point of humanity, I don't know what is." Freddy cleared his throat. "It would be easy, and perhaps even foolish, to blame an overly zealous fan for this ... alleged theft. For someone to achieve such an audacious theft ... alleged theft ... takes a great deal of planning to get past the incredible security that Series One teams have. This can't have been an opportunist." Freddy shook his head as if to stop himself mid-sentence. "None of that is important right now. There are a lot of people working hard to find the trophy."

Freddy glanced at him, then blinked rapidly. Jaxxon tried to send him a supportive look.

"A missing trophy might disappoint those who worked so hard to earn it. It might even demoralise a team as we finish the first race of the season and head into another Series One season of racing. We aren't going to mourn this trophy as if it were human. It is not. What this trophy represents is the achievements of many humans. We, the fans, are going to help find it. If you know anything, you can send a message to the number on the screen and your information will be passed to the authorities tasked with finding this trophy." Freddy lowered his microphone, and the camera person also tipped his camera to point at the ground.

"How was that?"

"Good, man." The camera person said.

"Thanks Maddock. A man of few words as usual."

"It's why I'm on this side of the camera."

Freddy smiled. "Jaxxon?"

"Are you fishing for compliments?" He didn't wait for Freddy's response. "You must know that it was excellent. You crafted a story, you connected with people, and you told them why they should care about this."

Freddy blushed. "Oh. I wasn't really asking for such a detailed compliment."

"I'm surprised that you didn't mention Socrates' trophies too."

"Too complicated." Freddy shook his head slightly. "For breaking news, it's best to stick to one topic and not bring in anything overly complex or the main message gets lost."

"Shit. Did that go out live?" Jaxxon needed to talk to Socrates now before he heard the news from Freddy's broadcast.

"Yes."

Jaxxon grabbed his phone and paced away to find a slightly more private spot. He ducked between two of the trucks, hiding in the shadows away from everyone. He rang the rehab centre and listened to the receptionist answer.

"This is Jaxxon Loharani-Jones. Can I please speak to Socrates Drayton?"

"No. Phone calls to patients can only happen between ten and twelve in the morning."

"I'm aware of your policy and I also know that you will connect me to a patient for an emergency call."

"What is the nature of your emergency?"

Jaxxon breathed in sharply. The rehab centre had very strict guidelines for external contacts to help their patients through their process of recovery, and he knew that a missing trophy wouldn't meet their guidelines, so he'd have to lie through his teeth to get to talk to Socrates. "It concerns his racing team and I'd rather he heard this news directly from me than from the television."

"That doesn't answer my question."

"Can I please speak to his counsellor? This is important. I understand your rules and why you have them, and I definitely don't want to set his recovery back."

Those magic words did the trick. "Transferring you now."

After a few rings, the call connected. "Dr Heather Walton."

"Hi. I'm Jaxxon Loharani-Jones. I want to talk to you

about Socrates." They'd talked a few times already, so he didn't need to do the full introduction.

"Yes?"

"I presume you know that it was the first race of the new season today for his racing team."

"Yes."

"Did Socrates watch?"

"No. I was going to call you first to discuss whether he should." She probably should have discussed this with him before the race weekend. He should've called. It was no excuse but he'd assumed that they'd let him watch and he'd been too busy doing to his job, caught up in being the Team Principal for the first race of the season. Jaxxon let out a long breath.

"Thank you. The race itself is fine. The team did well and I don't believe Socrates is so fragile that he can't watch the whole weekend live."

"And yet you are calling with an emergency."

"The broadcast just broke some news that I believe will upset Socrates and I wanted to tell him myself."

"Is everyone okay?"

Jaxxon slapped his thigh. He should've opened with that. "Yes. All the people are safe and well. It's not bad news about the team, but it is adjacent news that is of a concern."

"Tell me."

"If you recall, both of Socrates' World Championship trophies were stolen from our car reveal."

"Yes. He had a major setback after that."

Jaxxon swallowed. "Another one has been stolen. Not one that Socrates is connected to, but obviously when the news breaks, it's going to remind him of his own trophies."

"I have one question."

"Okay?" Jaxxon held his breath.

"Why do you feel that Socrates needs to be given a warning about this news, and yet you also say he's capable of watching the racing live without being adversely affected?"

Jaxxon smiled. "This news is personal. His trophies are personal. He knows Seb, he understands how Seb will be feeling about this latest theft. It's hugely different to the race. Racing is racing. Socrates lives and breathes racing. He will be going—" He stopped himself from using an ableist slur about Socrates' mental health. "He'll be more agitated by not being able to watch the whole weekend live than he would if our team had a difficult weekend. Trust me. I've worked for a long time in car racing. I understand the psyche of racing drivers better than most people."

Dr Walton hummed, a tight sound, and he knew he'd offended her.

"That wasn't a slight against the wonderful job you do, and I admit to not understanding how to help an addict. Socrates is a racing driver first and foremost. There's one thing I do understand and it's racing drivers and the way they approach risk. If we had a bad weekend, Socrates would be angry. He wouldn't be fragile."

"I will let you talk to him."

"Thank you."

"It will on speaker phone. I will supervise and I will end the call if I believe it is not in Socrates' best interest."

"Thank you. I really appreciate this."

"I will call you back in ten minutes." Dr Walton hung up.

Jaxxon leaned against the wall of the truck, hidden in the shadow between two trucks, sagging as he'd hopefully managed to sort out this situation for his boss before it hurt him. He wouldn't know until he spoke to Socrates.

"Addict?" Freddy asked. Jaxxon jumped, standing stiff and straight.

"How much did you hear?" He scanned the surrounding area, but it was just himself and Freddy.

"Not much. Where is Socrates? Why did you say he would be angry and not fragile? Who were you talking to?"

Jaxxon shook his head. "Not here. And definitely not on the record."

"Your office?"

Jaxxon shouldn't do this. He weighed up the options; he could tell Freddy the truth and swear him to secrecy, or he could say nothing and let Freddy be a journalist and keep poking until he discovered the truth. He'd have to tell him and trust him to keep it quiet, because if he let Freddy go hunting, he'd never be able to keep Socrates' secret away from the press.

"Yes." He pushed past Freddy, shoulders brushing, and ignored the way his skin sizzled with heat.

Jaxxon paced into his office with Freddy close behind him. The door closed after Freddy with a little click and Jaxxon sank in his office chair. He leaned back and placed his hands behind his head, as Freddy placed his phone, screen side up, on the desk between them, then sat down carefully.

"This is so you can see that I'm not recording."

"I trust your journalistic integrity, Freddy. What do you want to know?"

"You said on the phone that you didn't understand how to help an addict, but that you understood drivers and risk, and that Socrates would be angry, not fragile."

"And your question?"

"When Gamble Racing say that Socrates is dealing with a health issue, what issue is that?"

Jaxxon leaned forward. "I'm sure you can guess."

"I could but I might guess wrong."

"Socrates doesn't want people to know. Not because he's ashamed, but because he believes the S1 gossip mill will make it harder to recover. He wants to tell people when he's ready."

"Understood. What doesn't he want people to know?"

Jaxxon swallowed. "I'm not being deliberately obtuse or evasive. I made a promise not to tell anyone, and you are media, so this is the worst-case scenario."

Freddy's keen gaze softened. "If you think about it, I'm the best person to tell."

"How so?" Jaxxon's pulse raced, revving as if the throttle was stuck. Trust the media. Fuck, no. His instincts screamed that this was a terrible idea and he should ignore the little voice whispering a seductive chant that he'd already lost control of the situation so it wouldn't hurt to tell Freddy everything. It had nothing—everything—to do with the open expression on Freddy's face, and the empathy glowing in his hazel eyes. Jaxxon wanted to submit to the urge and tell Freddy everything.

"I understand the media and I can help."

"Fuck. I should've been more careful." He'd panicked when Freddy had said the broadcast had gone out live. A lot of his job was about putting out fires and making sure they weren't lit again. He should've thought this through and not acted without a pause.

"Don't worry about that. What exactly are we dealing with here?"

"We?"

Freddy shrugged slightly, as if to say that they were a team now, thanks to Jaxxon's lack of care. Fine.

"Off the record."

"Absolutely."

"Socrates had a minor stroke and fell down the stairs at his house. When they admitted him to emergency, they included some questions about alcohol use. Apparently it's common for long-term alcoholics to suffer strokes, and the doctors were very concerned about the amount he'd been drinking." He scratched the back of his neck. "It's why I asked about an athlete dying twice."

Freddy didn't look shocked, just intense. "He was using alcohol to cover up missing driving?"

"I don't think it's that simple and by the sounds of it, his drinking slowly increased over the years, from a few wines at dinner, to one at lunch, etc. Because he was always able to do his job well, no one noticed or thought it was a problem."

"A functioning alcoholic." Freddy summed it up. "There are plenty of those around."

"Yes. Socrates chose to admit himself to a rehab facility that is helping him with the health issues associated with his stroke as well as dealing with learning sobriety. It's complicated and will take a long time."

"I can see how it would happen." Freddy's steady

empathy helped build trust and Jaxxon started to relax. It would be an unlikely friendship given the differing needs of their respective jobs, and he couldn't let himself relax completely.

"You worry about yourself?" Jaxxon had to know more. He could lie to himself and say that it would help him understand his boss and how to help him. Or he could admit that he wanted to know more about Freddy. He didn't want to know so that he could understand a driver's psyche as a generalisation—that would be an excuse only and he did try not to lie to himself—he wanted to understand Freddy's specific way of looking at the world. Every time they talked, Jaxxon was drawn closer and closer to Freddy. Lust hummed underneath every word they exchanged.

"No and yes. No, I don't believe I have an alcohol issue. I tend not to drink most days, although the pressure to drink which socialising in the paddock can be intense.

"And yes?"

"I understand how Socrates could slowly end up where he has. Being a driver was such an intense time in my life, and presumably it's the same for others, that it's hard to adjust when it ends. Afterwards, it's like the winter break but endless. The pressure is removed immediately, which is initially a relief, like putting down a heavy weight, but then I was faced with never picking it up again. It surprised me because I'd made a deliberate decision to retire and I was lucky that I was offered a commentary job, so I had something to go into."

Jaxxon nodded. He'd seen it before with other drivers;

that sense of being lost when there wasn't a job to do anymore. "Socrates was forced into retirement after a crash. It was why Mike believed that having his own team would help him adjust."

"Do you think it was too much pressure?"

"I don't know all the details. If I had to make an assumption, I'd say that the few seasons leading into Whitehall's sacking didn't help. The team was failing, stuck at the back of the grid." He didn't tell Freddy that the decision to employ Victor...

"I understand that sacking Whitehall and employing Victor Tsui as the new Chief Engineer wasn't what Socrates wanted." Freddy already knew. Jaxxon's shoulders relaxed. It was good to talk to someone who understood without having to explain every detail. Freddy knew Socrates and he knew the team's history; probably better than Jaxxon did. No that's not true. Jaxxon had been, unofficially, Socrates right hand person for a couple of years as part of his long-term plan to learn the job of Team Principal so he could advance his career there one day. He'd advised Socrates to take Paulo, the money, and a new engineer. He'd helped pick Victor from the list of engineers who were available.

"Not initially. Obviously he's come around to the decision, what with Victor's cars being much quicker."

"And the fact that Whitehall's son sabotaged the cars to get revenge."

"Yes. It's been a tricky couple of years."

"I wish I'd noticed something. Socrates always seemed to have everything so well under control."

Jaxxon hadn't noticed either. "Don't feel bad. No one else noticed either, not even Mike, and they are married.

Socrates hid it well and I believe he didn't notice either as it was such a slow creeping change."

"I wish I could help."

"We all feel the same way." Now he had to wait for Dr Walton to call back and deal with the immediate problem.

CHAPTER 8

Freddy wished he could say he was surprised to discover that Socrates was an alcoholic. Many retired drivers had demons and dealt with the ends of their careers—not being able to race or chase that adrenalin high—in different, often self-destructive, ways. He'd been lucky that he got to stay on the circuit, spending his life in the same routine without the old pressures of racing that he'd lost the taste for. Jaxxon had opened up and told him private information, which was a huge privilege, and he felt the need to return the favour.

"Do you remember Henry Kerrigan?"

Jaxxon frowned for a moment. "The name doesn't immediately come to mind, sorry."

"He was an S2 driver. Very quick. My team decided they wanted to get the junior driver requirement out of the way early in the season, so they put Kerrigan in my car for FP2 at Spain. He hit a sausage curb and well, you know how the cars basically become airplanes once they leave the ground..."

"I remember that accident. It was horrible." Jaxxon covered his mouth and Freddy could tell that Jaxxon was replaying the accident, just as Freddy was. His car, with Kerrigan aboard, had hit the barriers and rolled onto its side. The engine caught fire, and the marshals pulled him free from the car. No one ever knew if he'd become paralysed from the crash, or when the marshals had pulled him away from the fire.

"A crash like that ... they happen, you know. It was Kerrigan's fault. He missed the apex and hit the curb. I used to be able to brush those off and stay focused on my own work. For some reason, I couldn't let that one go. Whenever I closed my eyes, I saw my own car bursting into flames with Kerrigan being dragged free by the marshals."

"That's when you decided to retire?"

"Now, when I look back, I wonder if I shouldn't have given up my seat to the next rookie standing in line—"

Jaxxon shook his head slowly. "You would never. No one would. Drivers fight so hard to get a seat and then to retain their seat. It wouldn't cross your mind to give it up, especially so early in the season."

"You are right. I didn't decide to retire until the silly season, when my agent asked where I wanted to move to. My results hadn't been great since Kerrigan's crash and my team was going break my contract and replace me." Freddy had given up as soon as he'd heard that. It was one thing to be struggling and have the team supporting him with sports psychologists and everything he needed to get back to his best, and another entirely to hear that they wanted to replace him. They'd had to pay out his contract—the only good thing that came from the mess—and it was sometime after that when Chester had started his Duke nonsense, which was absolutely the last thing he'd needed. He couldn't even remember the timing of it, time had blurred the mess of it all into endless noise and hurt.

"What's Kerrigan up to now?" Jaxxon's question helped pull him out of his memories.

"He married some actress and lives in the states. He's on the USA wheelchair basketball team."

"Once an athlete, always an athlete." Jaxxon smiled. His phone rang, and he answered it on speaker phone with a zip gesture to Freddy. He responded with the same gesture, a promise to stay quiet.

"Dr Walton."

"It's Socrates. These fuckers won't let me watch the race. What happened?"

Jaxxon winked at Freddy. "Are you asking me for the result, or do you want to watch the replay first?"

"Give me the spoilers. Can't trust these people to actually show me the whole thing. Is the car fast?"

Freddy pinched his lips together tight and stared up at the ceiling so he wouldn't catch Jaxxon's eye and burst out laughing.

"The car is fast. Ondrej finished fourth and Paulo seventh."

"Yes. Points for both cars. Brilliant. Don't tell me any other results. I'll watch the race soon."

Jaxxon grinned, an indulgent grin that Freddy probably wore too. "I've asked that they let you watch each race weekend live."

"Fucking yes. Thanks for having my back, Jaxxon."

"Of course. We all want you to heal and be back in the paddock."

Socrates coughed. "Thanks. I know I'm supposed to appreciate what they are doing for me, and I know I chose to come here, but these assholes are making me do ridiculous exercises every day and the food isn't as good as what Angie cooked. I could put up with all of that to heal, but to not be allowed to watch my own cars race. It's too much."

"I'll make sure I email Dr Walton the schedule and ensure you can watch everything. All the practice sessions, quali, and of course the race."

"And all the talking. Did you get in touch with Freddy, like I said?"

"Yes."

"Good. Now, I have one other thing to say."

Jaxxon pinched his lips together and Freddy tried to send him a supportive glance, but this was Socrates and anything was possible.

"I have to face reality, Jaxxon. I'm going to need you to stay as Team Principal permanently. This is going to be a long road, and I agree with Mike that I can't do a high-pressure job even once I'm allowed to come home. Look after my team."

"Absolutely." Jaxxon nodded slowly, and Freddy counted the slow breaths as the news sunk in. It'd been a temporary job? It made sense that Socrates wouldn't want to give up his beloved team so easily.

"Socrates, there's something else we need to discuss. Firstly, everyone is safe. However, there's some other news from the paddock."

"I know that tone. Something else bad has happened."

"Yes and I worry that the news will be confronting for you." Jaxxon breathed in deeply, his broad shoulders rising and falling.

"Tell me."

"The 2010 World Championship Trophy has been stolen."

"There's a trophy thief in the paddock?" Socrates asked.

"It seems that way."

Socrates didn't talk for a long while and Freddy hated the wait. He couldn't look at Jaxxon in case he made a noise that punctured the silence and gave away that he was here, and he clenched his jaw to stop himself talking.

"This is good news." It was a typical Socrates pronouncement.

"Excuse me?" The look on Jaxxon's face told a whole story of disbelief. Freddy squeezed every muscle in his body, trying not to laugh. Bloody Socrates; he really saw the world in an unique way.

"If it's the same person, then it means more evidence. It gives us a better chance of finding my trophies."

Jaxxon stared out over Freddy's shoulder, as if he couldn't meet Freddy's eyes. "True. Your perspective is always valuable, Socrates."

"Don't butter me up."

Jaxxon laughed, a release of tension into a soft chuckle. The sound rippled over Freddy's skin and he wanted to be the one who made Jaxxon laugh like that.

"Socrates. I'm not. You picked me for this job because you know that I would never do that. I was so fucking stressed that you'd be upset by this news, but I didn't want you to hear it from anyone else."

"Oh, I'm upset. I'm fucking pissed off about this. Some asshole is stealing trophies. But if he keeps doing it, he'll make a mistake and we'll find him."

"Skye is going to help out."

"Brilliant. They'll be able to find similarities. Their attention to detail is absolutely what this problem needs. And talk to Freddy Hiptonstall—"

Jaxxon raised one eyebrow as his gaze met Freddy's.

"Because?"

"He has a lot of contacts. He's helped me with my own collections in the past."

Jaxxon's eyebrow raised even higher. Freddy clamped his hand over his mouth and nodded because he couldn't talk but he had to 'say' something. He had sourced a few antique vehicles for Socrates when other peers had offered them for sale, quietly so that no one would know someone was selling off pieces of an estate.

"I will."

"Just watch him. He has a bit of a reputation."

"For?"

"Being great in bed but never committing to anyone." Fucking Socrates. Freddy's face burned bright hot, and he used his hands to cover his cheeks. It was the truth, and yet, he didn't need Socrates to warn Jaxxon away from him. Jaxxon swept his gaze over Freddy, one eyebrow raised, assessing him. He refused to look away. His muscles trembled as he tried to stay still and hold Jaxxon's enquiring gaze.

"I'll keep that in mind." What did that mean?

"On second thoughts, it's fucking boring in here. I've always wanted to know if the rumours were true. Maybe give Freddy a taste of his own medicine and then tell me all about it."

"Socrates." Jaxxon's warning tone had a touch of indulgence in it. "You know I don't gossip about my private life."

"Mores the pity."

"I'll talk to him. ... About the trophies, Socrates. And I'll keep you updated on our progress."

"Goodbye, Mr Loharani-Jones. That's enough excitement for Socrates today." Dr Walton's crisp tones filled the air before the call was ended.

"Bloody Socrates." Jaxxon leaned forward, resting his face on his hands with his fingers pinching the bridge of his nose.

"Yeah. He's a special type of rascal. I'm glad he hasn't lost his sense of humour in all that."

"I'm not going to fuck you." The fire in Jaxxon's stare made a lie of his words. Freddy's body went hot, then cold, as if he were alight with need, then plunged into an icy pool of longing.

"I'd do a good job."

"That's what Socrates said."

"My reputation is well earned." He was surprised that Socrates had mentioned him in that way, but it was Socrates, so not really a surprise at all. They'd joked about it before, years ago when Chester had accompanied him to dinner with Socrates and Mike. Socrates was a nosy old gay who liked to shock people, and he'd asked Chester about Freddy's capability in bed. Chester had called him a spectacular fuck, and the reputation was born. He closed his eyes, not wanting to think about how good things had been with Chester before it'd gone wrong, before Chester had proven himself to be a sneaky narcissist who'd only complimented Freddy whenever he wanted to get something from him.

"What's the matter?"

"Nothing."

"People don't frown like that over nothing."

He shrugged, trying to make it look casual. "An ex told Socrates that I was a spectacular fuck. That's where the reputation comment comes from."

"And are you?"

Damn. He needed a drink of water. The only upside to this was that Jaxxon hadn't asked about Chester. "I couldn't comment on my skills in bed."

"Oh, how obvious of you to use a humble brag."

"Excuse me?"

Jaxxon's intense stare felt like lasers beaming right into him. "It's one thing to relay information that someone else has said about you, and quite another to avoid the question when asked."

"Is there a question in that?"

The twinkle in Jaxxon's eyes made Freddy want to know everything. It was dangerous.

"I'm curious as to why you wouldn't own such a reputation. Isn't it good to be known as a—"

"Spectacular fuck? Yes." He stopped himself from admitting that the phrase was tainted by who had said it. That was a whole discussion he wasn't prepared to have today. Or ever.

"Why did I not know this?" Jaxxon drummed his fingers on the table.

"I don't sleep with people in the paddock."

"Okay." It was almost a question. Jaxxon leaned back in

his chair. The air crackled as he waited for Jaxxon to say something else. It intensified until Freddy was ready to crawl over the table and kiss Jaxxon and fuck his own rules.

"Why is that?" Jaxxon's head was tilted slightly to the left.

"Why is what?"

"Why that rule? I'll concede that not many people in S1 have sex with each other, mostly because the paddock is full of straight men. It seems like an unnecessary rule for you to hold yourself to." Jaxxon grinned and those damned eyes of his sparkled.

Freddy wanted to kiss that smile right off Jaxxon's face. He'd give him a reason to stop smiling, or maybe it was a reason to smile some more. "Most of the paddock except Gamble Racing. The gay team."

"That is what some people say about us. I doubt that we have a much higher percentage than other teams. We are merely more open about accepting people."

He smiled back at Jaxxon. "Which is why you'll have more queer people, because they know they'll be safe with you."

"Socrates has always wanted Gamble Racing to represent the world as he sees it."

"Gay with an abrupt nosy sense of a humour?"

Jaxxon threw his head back and laughed. "Fuck me. He's such a rascal and we adore him."

Freddy stood up. "It sounds like he's in the best place for him. I'd better go and have a chat to Cliff."

"You haven't answered my question."

"Which one?" He knew which one—about why he didn't sleep with anyone in the paddock. Jaxxon simply raised his eyebrows and waited. It took him a moment to find a way to avoid the question; a 'what would Socrates do' moment.

"I assume you are insistent on this one because you want to discover if I am indeed a spectacular fuck?"

Jaxxon didn't say no. He simply held Freddy's gaze, and the heat between them simmered and crackled. He was going to give in, wasn't he? The quiet buzz unsettled him.

"Do you think I should break my own rules for you? Are you so special?" He gave in.

"Do you have any other specific rules?" Jaxxon's question avoided answering his own. Were they going to play a game where they just asked questions of each other in avoidance of answering one forever? How absurd ... and also, how interesting.

"Not really. Consent matters. Safety is sexy." He was on PrEP, and he always used condoms. That was about it. He wasn't quite sure why he was answering Jaxxon's question, or in fact, why Jaxxon was asking them.

"Those are good rules." Jaxxon's voice lowered half a tone adding a little growl to his already deep voice.

"I think so." Freddy's biggest curse was that he loved talking. He knew it and he couldn't stop himself, especially when someone growled at him with such a sexy note in his voice. "I wouldn't dare boast about being good in bed, it's not something I can decide, only whoever I am with. I do know that I rate other people on their ability to stick to those simple rules. It applies to a lot of life, really, not just sex. Consent and safety. They are two basic principles that create an ethical basis for life."

"What about when things are blurred?"

"Consent is never blurry. I only want an enthusiastic yes. Coercion is revolting." He knew that from the other side of the fence and would never do that to someone else.

"Is your rule about not getting involved with anyone in the S1 paddock related to your passionate use of the word coercion?"

Freddy couldn't stop a grin stretching his cheeks. "Nice. Your very astute question is a good reminder not to get into a debate with someone so switched on."

"You can't get out of this with a compliment."

"Why do you want to know? You are pushing quite hard. Anyone might think you want to coerce me into breaking my no paddock rule."

Jaxxon frowned and blinked a couple of times. "No. I'm curious, that's all."

"Curious with a side goal of getting me to change my mind?"

"Fuck off. You aren't that sexy." Jaxxon spun in his chair and grabbed a pen from a shelf on the side of his office.

"I think you are protesting too hard." He hadn't been imagining the chemistry between them.

"Perhaps." Jaxxon turned back to stare at him.

He didn't expect that. A shot of heat blasted up his spine. "Perhaps?"

"It doesn't matter if you have an unbreakable rule. Let's park it in an irrelevant information box and move on. I have work to do."

He'd been dismissed so he stood up. "I had a bad experience once, and it followed—" Stalked. "—me for a whole season." He left quickly before Jaxxon could ask more questions. Getting involved with Jaxxon would be a terrible idea. Reckless. He knew how bad it could get, and they both had jobs to do that meant they'd have to interact with each other all year. He stood outside Jaxxon's office and leaned his head against the metal wall of the truck. Everything inside him was pumping with energy, cranked up to high revs, past the limit of what he ought to be able to endure. And damn, if he didn't want to ignore all the reasons why this was a bad idea and drown in the irrational, necessary, want for Jaxxon. It could only end up poorly. Shit.

"Freddy?" Maddock called out his name and reality came rushing back. He swallowed.

"Yeah?" It was time to get back to work, to focus on what he could have. Which absolutely wasn't Jaxxon. Yeah. He let out a wobbly breath and followed Maddock to wherever he was needed now.

CHAPTER 9

AUSTRALIA

Jaxxon hated the Australian race. Even in his jetlagged state he knew it wasn't the race that he hated. He loved racing. He hated getting here—twenty-four hours on a plane—and the way he didn't cope well with being in an opposite time zone. He stood in the hotel breakfast room staring at the barista, a smiling Asian man who was far too chirpy looking for Jaxxon.

"What would you like?"

"Coffee."

The barista stared back. "Mate. You have to pick which type."

Type. Couldn't the barista just take some of that early morning energy and guess? He should be used to dealing with people in desperate need of caffeine. Jaxxon was being a dick; too tired to behave kindly towards the retail staff. He'd worked in his parent's bakery as a teen. He knew what customers were like; being jetlagged and out of sorts was no excuse for treating staff like shit.

"We'll both have a flat white each." Freddy's breath on the back of his neck didn't help his blurry displacement. Jet lag. Lust. Both upset his usual balance and confidence. "Come on. Have a seat with me."

Jaxxon followed Freddy automatically. He'd crashed in his hotel room last night after arriving in the evening. The theory for dealing with the jet lag of being on opposite time to England was to arrive after dinner and sleep. Then he'd wake up on daylight time, or something.

"Jet lag sucks. Sit here." Freddy held out a chair as if he were a delicate princess, a notion that made him smile as he accepted the seat because it was lovely to be cared for.

"You don't have to talk. Just sit there. I arrived here a couple of days ago. My nephew Archie is at university here in Melbourne, so I came directly from Jeddah to spend a few days with him."

Jaxxon rubbed his temple. "You have a nephew old enough for university?"

"I already told you. I'm a second son. My brother, AA, is older than me and has five children."

"Your brother is called AA?"

"Archibald Athol, Marquess of Swain, heir to the Duke of Horlenmont."

"Your brother named his kid after himself?" It was the least offensive question he could ask, given the pretentiousness of being named Archibald Athol, let alone all the titles. He was far too exhausted to process any of that stuff. Using AA was probably the best option with a moniker like that.

"Family tradition."

"Sounds confusing. Why are you Freddy? If you are second, shouldn't your name start with B?"

Freddy grinned. "I might be second, but everyone in our family is named to be an alpha. My full name is Alfred Alexander, Lord Beautravers."

"I can see why you picked Freddy."

"Says the guy whose name is Jackson but spelled wrong."

Their coffees arrived at the table before Jaxxon could growl at Freddy. After a couple of sips, his brain kicked in.

"My father's name is Jack." His parents had spelled it like that because they wanted him to stand out. It was a tribute to his father—one he carried with pride—and something uniquely his. He hadn't met another one until a few years ago when a fan had asked Ondrej and himself to sign a shirt for his kid, Jaxxon.

"He named you after himself?"

"Isn't that what your brother did with his son?"

Freddy smiled, an open delightful grin. "Touché. And now your name is trendy in certain parts of America."

He sighed. "Yeah, it's a problem. People look at me and assume I'm American."

"Your accent must confuse them then." Freddy's smile widened. Just like the barista, he was far too awake and happy for this early in the morning. Jaxxon sipped his coffee and ignored Freddy's nonsense.

"Want to come bouldering with me this morning?"

"What?" He'd intended to spend today catching up on emails, since he'd spent so much time travelling here.

"What is bouldering or what am I doing inviting you?"

"Yes." Jaxxon shouldn't be tempted. Their last conversation had been bloody wild. Fucking Socrates had to go and mention that Freddy—who already tempted him too much—had a reputation for being good in bed. And then Freddy had used the phrase, spectacular fuck, and it'd spun freely in his head during every spare moment. Thankfully, during the season, he didn't have many spare moments. They'd had two great races with Ondrej finished fourth and third, and Paulo getting points in both races too. There was always room for improvement, especially now they knew the car was good enough to podium. His new mantra was that there was always more work to do.

"Bouldering is like rock climbing without the ropes."

"Sounds like a bad idea." Everything about spending time with Freddy was probably a bad idea. He just wanted to kiss the man, not think too hard about Freddy's 'no paddock' rule, or worry that he might be coercing him into changing his mind.

"It's not about height. It's more technical."

"Why are you inviting me to do a social thing with you? I thought you had a rule about that."

Freddy blushed. "You are right. For some reason, I can't resist you and I keep being tempted into doing things I shouldn't."

"We haven't done anything yet." Oops, that came out a lot more whingey than he intended. He drank more of his coffee. It must be stronger than anything he had at home in England because the fog in his head disappeared and became alive with energy.

"No. We haven't." There was something a little ... sad? ... in Freddy's tone. Freddy glanced around the room. "I shouldn't admit this."

"Then don't." It was too early in the day and Jaxxon was too jetlagged for a heart-to-heart.

"You tempt me beyond reason, Jaxxon." Freddy had leaned in closer, his voice barely able to be heard.

"Okay."

Freddy sat up straight, as if he'd been slapped.

"Sorry."

"It's fine. I knew getting involved with someone in the paddock was a bad idea. This is a bad idea. I'm sorry for flirting with you. I'll keep my distance now."

Jaxxon peered at Freddy. "What? No. It's not that. You must know that I—" He waved his hand awkwardly. "I am also tempted by this bad idea."

"But you just said okay in a tone that was very dismissive."

"I'm exhausted, jetlagged, and have a lot of work to do today."

Freddy's mouth moved in the flicker of a grin. "Are you saying it's not about me at all?"

Jaxxon looked up from his coffee. "Yeah. Give me a day."

"Awesome. Bouldering tomorrow?"

"Fine. Yes." Only because it made Freddy look so adorably happy. "Text me." He finished his coffee, and stood up, grabbing a couple of chocolate muffins on the way out of the dining room. He needed to tackle his emails and maybe have a nap. Nap first, then work.

. . .

Jaxxon was a lot less blurry eyed when he went to breakfast the next day, but he still startled when Freddy breathed on the back of his neck in the coffee line again.

"Jesus, Freddy."

"Two flat whites, please."

"Fine." He followed Freddy to a table, noting that there were more people from the paddock here today. By tomorrow, Thursday, everyone would be here, getting ready for FP1 the next day. He nodded to Marcel who was sitting with a couple of his engineers, then sat down.

"Today we are going bouldering."

"I thought we weren't going to get involved with each other."

Freddy held up his hands. "It's sport, not a date."

It felt like a date, sitting here having breakfast together with several Team Principals glancing sideways at them; a Team Principal having breakfast with the media. Rumours were going to fly around the paddock all day—not about the two of them—most likely about Socrates or engine upgrades.

"Will anyone else be joining us for this bouldering mission?"

Freddy's faint blush was likely an admission. "No. Just us."

"But not a date. We are simply two friends hanging out together doing sport? Or is this you being a member of the media trying to get a Team Principal out of his comfort zone so he'll spill all the team secrets?"

"You are so fucking cynical."

"And you are being incredibly confusing."

"How so?" Freddy leaned back in his chair in what had to be a pretence of relaxation.

"You acknowledge the chemistry between us, but you don't want to date someone who works in the S1 paddock for unspecified reasons. And yet you are inviting me on a not-date date today with some degree of enthusiasm."

"You are making this much more complicated than it needs to be."

Jaxxon chuckled. "I am? I'm not the one who is being unclear about motivations."

"Maybe I don't need a motivation. I love bouldering. I thought you might enjoy it, and if you don't, I will enjoy seeing you land flat on your ass."

The competitive streak in Jaxxon blossomed. He'd looked up bouldering on the internet yesterday and it looked quite fun; like rock climbing but on a short wall with very technical elements. "I'm not going to fall."

"That's a yes, then."

"Yes. I will go on a non-date with you to climb a few walls. Yes." His coffee arrived and he was glad to have something to do with his hands. Freddy's grin and the excitement shining in his eyes sent flashes of heat across Jaxxon's skin. Dating Freddy—for real, not this pretence—was starting to feel inevitable; they couldn't seem to resist each other.

"It will be fun, you'll see." Freddy's playfulness was such a joy. He might be a privileged son of a Lord, with a handsome face and life that had given him pretty much everything a person would want and almost none of the difficulties. His enjoyment of life still had to be a choice because Jaxxon had met too many people who had everything and weren't content with it, always chasing more and more without ever being satisfied. What a miserable way to have deal with having plenty.

"Okay."

Freddy rolled his eyes. "I can never tell what you mean when you say okay like that. Is it acceptance, or judgement, or sarcasm, or..."

"It's a basic statement. Okay. Nothing else."

Freddy's nostrils flared as he breathed in, then nodded once. "Cool. Okay, then. I've booked a place for ten, so meet me down here an hour before and I'll get the hotel to order us a car."

He had been on the S1 circuit for four years before he'd become Team Principal, spending his time with Socrates and other rich people, and he still found it hard to compute when people were so casual about things like that. He still accounted for every dollar he spent and weighed up different options; a habit of growing up among the lower middle class. They hadn't been poor, he'd always had the basics, but the wealth he was surrounded by at work now was on a level that he found a little incomprehensible. It'd been a useful trait as Team Principal because the budget caps meant they had to work harder to get value out of every dollar spent, and it was the one area where he had a massive advantage over the other Team Principals.

"You already booked it?"

"Yes."

"Isn't that rather optimistic? What if I'd said no?"

Freddy shrugged. "Then I'd go alone and the place would make a bigger profit than usual." Rich people. Jaxxon didn't know what to say to that, except another okay, which he didn't think was a great idea, so he just sat there and sipped his coffee.

"Shall I get you some breakfast? It's a good idea to have some protein before we go. Bouldering takes a lot of muscle control."

Jaxxon almost swallowed his tongue trying not to make a flirtatious comment about Freddy's muscles. If this wasn't a date, what the fuck was Freddy thinking?

"I can get my own. Thanks." He sipped some of his coffee. It was warm and delicious; the coffee in Melbourne almost made up for the jet lag. Freddy jumped up, leaving him to his coffee. He flicked through his phone, reading a few emails, and filing the ones that didn't need a response. He'd get to the others later. Once he'd finished his coffee, he stood up, slipped his phone into his pocket and wandered over to the breakfast options.

"Protein." Freddy held a plate filled with bacon and eggs, and mushrooms on toast.

"Your reminder is noted." He rushed over to get himself a plate before Freddy could make some snarky response to his own snarky response, and then they'd get into a sarcasm battle. Damn. He wished. He was so screwed. The pastries smelled great; almost as good as the croissants his mum made in the bakery. He grabbed a couple of those, some of the bacon and eggs, and a pan-fried tomato that he sprinkled with tabasco sauce. A few hashbrowns made up his breakfast choice—if he was going to go all out on a full English breakfast, he may as well get everything.

"I talked to Cliff." Freddy hardly gave him a chance to sit down again.

"Anything useful?"

"Nothing."

Jaxxon sighed and started eating his breakfast.

"It's actually notable that he knew nothing, or at least, that's what he said. This type of thing is exactly up his wheelhouse and he's heard nothing. Nada. Zilch. Zero."

"I get it, Freddy." He bit into one of the pastries he'd selected.

"Yes, but do you understand that it's useful that he knows nothing?"

Jaxxon finished his mouthful. "How?"

"It rules out all the usual suspects and means that it—"

"Could be any of the other seven billion people in the world?"

Freddy's nose wrinkled as he grinned. "I think we could narrow it down to S1 fans and rich people."

"So that's like a few million?"

"I guess that doesn't really help, does it?" Freddy looked so defeated.

"Perhaps Cliff will hear something soon. It was nearly two months between our theft and Seb's trophy."

"True." Freddy looked up. "Let's focus on bouldering for today."

Jaxxon couldn't understand the obsession with climbing up a few rocks. It really shouldn't make him so curious to find out why Freddy loved it. But he'd already given up on not being intrigued by Freddy. It was a lost cause. The only question left was what he was going to do with his curiosity.

CHAPTER 10

Jaxxon walked into the big warehouse, having spent the forty-minute drive answering emails and ignoring Freddy who'd talked to the driver the whole time. It'd been a productive drive for him, although the update from Skye that they'd discovered nothing, had been an irritation. The warehouse smelled like chalk and sweat and bleach. There were a surprising number of people climbing the walls inside—ha, he needed to make that pun later—given that it was mid-morning on a Wednesday. Didn't people work normal hours in Australia?

"Have you been here before?" He assumed yes, given that Freddy flashed his ID and they waved him right in.

"No, Georgia found it for me and booked."

"Georgia?"

"My PA. Couldn't live without her."

Jaxxon nodded. "It is good to have a strong team around you." Stepping up into the Team Principal role had been a lot easier thanks to Socrates' staff who knew all the admin ropes and sorted out all the flights and accommodation for him, as well as dealing with HR and the other myriad of details that it took to run a team of six hundred people. A leader was only as good as the team.

"What size shoe are you?" Freddy asked, pulling Jaxxon back to reality. The reality where he was expected to haul himself up a wall for fun without falling off and hurting himself. It sounded like the kind of wild thing that a retired driver would do for fun. Risky.

"Thirteen."

Freddy blinked, then grabbed some from a shelf for him. He took off his running shoes and put on the climbing shoes, doing up the Velcro, and wiggling his toes inside the soft soled shoe. They were weirdly flexible, and he was glad to be wearing his own socks because the shared shoe situation was a lot like a bowling alley. Fine if you didn't think too hard about every other person who'd put their feet into the shoes.

"Put all your stuff in our locker and then we can start."

He stuffed his phone into his laptop bag, beside his already stashed laptop, wallet, and hotel key-card, and handed it, along with his shoes, to Freddy who put them neatly alongside his own things in a locker and punched in a four-digit code.

"It's 4554." Freddy's racing number had been forty-five.

"Your racing number."

"Yes. I don't use it for my bankcard, so don't get any ideas. Just for things like this that aren't too important."

Jaxxon grinned as Freddy slapped him on the shoulder.

"Let's go. Shall we start with something easy?"

"Why don't you show me how it all works?" Jaxxon

followed Freddy into the warehouse. The big area was split into several walls covered in little fake brightly coloured rocks with big plastic mats underneath.

"Okay, so the climbs are all colour-coded for difficulty. Blue is the easiest. There's usually a code on the wall somewhere. Yeah, over there." He pointed to a sign that showed the difficulty levels. "Put some of this on your palms." Freddy held up a bottle labelled liquid chalk and squirted a coin sized drop into his own palm and rubbed it on his hands. Jaxxon held out his hand and after Freddy's squeezed some onto his hand, he did the same. It dried out into chalk. Cool.

"I'll just do an easy one and show you how to works?"

"Sure."

Freddy stripped off his t-shirt to expose a little singlet. It was bloody obscene. The singlet clung to Freddy's body with his arms completely exposed. Combined with the shorts he wore, there wasn't much left to Jaxxon's imagination. Freddy stretched, first with a lunge, then a bunch of arm stretches. It was mesmerising and his gaze lingered on every inch of Freddy's exposed skin. The man was just stretching; it wasn't a warm up for sex, or a burlesque show for one, or anything. And now he was making it weird by not being able to look away. Bloody hell. He wanted to fan himself and blame the warm Aussie weather. It was definitely hotter in this warehouse than outside.

Freddy apparently finished his series of stretches and walked over to the wall, completely focused on his interesting hobby. He pointed to the wall at one of the rock thingies. "These little arrows indicate the starting point, and then you have to plan your own pathway up to the finishing hold at the top."

"Hold?"

"The fake rocks are called holds." Freddy grabbed a fake-rock, a hold, and proceeded to climb up the wall. He made it look easy. The muscles in his back and shoulders popped out, especially as he reached the top hold and hung off it, holding on with one hand. Hell. Freddy couldn't have chosen a better 'sport' to show off his body. He dropped to the ground, landing like fucking spiderman.

Jaxxon waited until Freddy stood up again, then rolled his eyes deliberately. Anything to make light of the situation, rather than listen to the sparks in his belly.

"What?"

"You look—" Fucking sexy. "At home here."

"It's a challenge. I like it for that reason. Come on, your turn."

Jaxxon walked up to the wall. The floor was spongy, basically a big thick mat to cushion anyone's fall. It gave him confidence, although he wasn't sure he wanted to fall and look like a goose in front of Freddy, especially after his whole spiderman act.

"Place your hands here." Freddy took his hands and guided them to the hold with the small arrow stickers beside it. His breath warmed the back of Jaxxon's neck, and damned if this didn't feel like a date. Just as he almost leaned his head back and sank into Freddy's touch, it disappeared.

"Off you go. Plan your route. Keep your weight close against the wall."

He put his foot on the lower hold and hoisted himself

up, immediately dropping back to the ground. It was harder than it looked, balancing on a tiny fake-rock, pressed up against a wall. He'd much rather press against Freddy than embarrass himself hauling himself up a bloody wall.

"Stick close to the wall." Freddy reminded him why they were here. He tried again, this time twisting his knee to the side, like a bloody crab. It worked and he shifted up to the next hold. He wanted to yell out 'it worked' but he was clinging on with his fingers to a damned fake rock and so he focused on each hold, taking the first few ones slowly, until he got the hang of the balance required and eventually made it up to the top.

"Nice. You can either jump down, or you can use the pink ones as a ladder to get down again."

He wasn't going to do Freddy's whole show off spidey thing, so he used some of the holds to get halfway down before dropping to the mat on the floor.

"How was that?" The impish enthusiasm on Freddy's face was a delight.

"You really want me to enjoy this, don't you?"

"Yes. I love it. The physical challenge of it. Planning a route, making it work, it's great. I want to share that with someone."

"Anyone?"

Freddy's cheeks and ears flushed pink. "Everyone."

"Do you realise that other people can have hobbies that aren't the same as yours?"

"Of course. I don't mean to sound selfish. I can try out your hobbies too." Poor Freddy, he was so thrilled to share this, Jaxxon shouldn't imply that his enthusiasm was a problem. It really wasn't.

He cleared his throat. "Isn't that getting a little close to show me yours and I'll show you mine?"

Freddy's laugh echoed around the warehouse. "Jaxxon."

"Oh right, I forgot. This isn't a date. It's you being 'the media' and wanting to get me off balance so I'll share team secrets with you." He was glad that Freddy hadn't quizzed him further about his hobbies. He didn't really have any because he didn't have time for a hobby. Racing was his hobby. And his job. Damn, that sounded borderline obsessive. He'd wanted to be Team Principal so much that he'd given up everything else in the quest to get there. Had he really been contemplating doing that for another decade in pursuit of this job? Yes, absolutely with zero regrets.

"No. It's not that." Freddy blinked a couple of times. "Never mind. Let's try a more challenging route."

"Sure." He wasn't going to object to watching Freddy climb. His clothes—or lack of—bordered on pornographic with the way his shorts stretched over his ass, and the way his singlet didn't hide much of his pale skin or lean muscles. Damn it. It was going to be impossible to climb if he got hard from watching Freddy. For a non-date, this had all the elements of a date.

"This one looks fun." Freddy walked underneath an overhanging section of wall and used his finger to point out the different green coloured holds. It looked ... challenging, as Freddy called it.

"You go first." He'd rather observe how Freddy attacked the route, or that's what he told himself. Freddy nodded and squirted more of the liquid chalk on his palms. He glanced over his shoulder, with a serious expression, before he approached the wall. All Jaxxon could see was Freddy's back as he placed his hands on a hold, then started to climb up the overhang. His body dangled under the wall, with only his fingertips and toes touching the various holds, and all his muscles straining. The long lines in his forearms were accentuated and his shoulders bulged. Not only was he holding his entire body weight on his fingers and toes, but he was lean and agile. Fucking hot. And everything Jaxxon wasn't. He shook off that insidious thought; fucking society could fuck off with its preference for certain types of bodies. Besides, he didn't care for a comparison. He was himself, and Freddy was incredibly hot. Jaxxon should look away and think about something else. The absolute betrayal of his brain and the inability to think of anything, bar Freddy's athletic form dangling off a few rocks, should've been irritating, except he stood there, unmoving, staring at Freddy as he stretched out, reaching for the last hold. This sport was designed to make someone look fuckable. The outstretched arms, the turn of his calf as he used the tip of his toe to push off a hold, and most of all, Freddy's shorts pulled tight over the curve of his thighs and ass.

"Do you take many people bouldering for a first date?"

Freddy dropped off the wall, landing feet first. He spun around and stared at Jaxxon. "You are obsessed with the idea of this being a date."

He glanced around but they were the only two people in this section of the warehouse. "It has all the elements of it."

"Fine. It's a date."

"But you don't date anyone in the paddock?"

"I didn't say I was logical." Freddy spread his arms out wide and grinned, as if to say 'what can you do?'

Jaxxon winked. "Therefore, you are admitting that you asked me here because you know it makes you look good."

"You think I look good?"

"Freddy. Your job is to look good on television. You don't need a compliment from me."

Freddy smiled softly. "You are right. I don't need a compliment from you." He paused, his gaze intensifying. "But I would really like one."

Danger signals clanged in his head. "A compliment from me would be meaningless. We are a pair of old queers who are... Actually, I can't speak for you. Never mind." He didn't want to admit that he was going to be a middle-aged gay man who hadn't had a proper long-term relationship beyond a few months because he was always working. His career took all this focus; his need to make his parent's hard work and sacrifices for him worth something. Since his first job out of university, he'd been with a racing team and travelled the world. The constant lack of a home had been hell on any attempt to have a relationship.

"You aren't old. Not even forty yet."

"I'm thirty-eight." He wasn't that old, it was true. And he was only beginning to reach the prime of his career. If he stayed focused, he'd be able to be Team Principal for at least a decade, maybe two. Series One was the pinnacle of motorsport; he wasn't going to get bored with the challenge of thriving in this environment.

"I know. Everyone knows. You are the second youngest Team Principal in the history of Series One. Just as everyone knows that I'm forty-two because my driver stats are public knowledge."

"The answer to life, the universe, and everything."

"I wish." Freddy mustn't have read that old geeky book. "I'm just an old retired driver who spends all my time talking about my glory days." Freddy hinted at a melancholy that Jaxxon had noticed in Socrates occasionally. It must be hard to deal with an aging body—not that forty-two was very old on Jaxxon's career scale—when it'd been one of the best in the world as a younger man. Being an athlete had a very different timeline to being a manager.

"For an old man, you are very agile and fit."

Freddy laughed and slapped Jaxxon on the shoulder. "Why did that sound like a backhanded compliment?" Freddy stepped closer and brushed Jaxxon's shoulder where he'd slapped him. "Sorry."

"For?"

"I left a chalky palm print on your arm."

"It's fine." His skin reacted to Freddy's gentle touch with gooseflesh, chasing the sensation of his hands moving against his shoulder in a way that was both careful and careless at the same time. Freddy dropped his hands.

"I think I made it worse."

"Don't worry about it. Should I give this one a try?"

Freddy bent down to grab the liquid chalk. "Yes. You look like you have the strength for it."

Jaxxon smiled softly. This man and his incessant flirting would be the end of him. He held out his hands and Freddy squirted a small amount of chalk into his palms. Freddy stood too close, the light sheen of sweat on his skin tempting. Jaxxon swallowed and stepped around Freddy to walk towards the beginning of the climb.

"Here?"

"Yes. The trick is to use your legs for strength, keep your weight on your toes, and use your arms for balance."

"While upside down?"

"Try it. You'll soon figure out what I mean once you feel it for yourself."

Surely Freddy hadn't meant that to sound like a euphemism. Jaxxon focused on the wall. The main thing here was to give it a go and not fall on his ass and hurt himself. He shook out his hands, grateful that the chalk absorbed some of the sweat on his palms. With a deep breath in, he reached out for the holds, and stepped onto the lowest hold with his feet.

"That's it. Now reach up to the next one and push with your thighs. Step out to that small one on your right." Freddy started to talk him through it; it was less like coaching and more enthusiastic encouragement. "Keep your body close to the wall in this stage. Yes, that's it. Now reach over your head. The trick now is to keep your arms long."

"Long?"

"Elbows straight. Um, it's less work for your biceps."

Jaxxon tried it and it helped. He moved his legs, listening to Freddy's instructions, but when he reached out for the final hold, he missed and dropped to the ground, landing on ass.

"Are you alright?" Freddy rushed over and hovered beside him.

"Yeah." He eased himself up. "I just missed the last hold." He brushed his hands down his thighs, leaving streaks of chalk on his clothes.

"I noticed."

"It's fine. I bounced." Jaxxon grabbed the liquid chalk, spread some on his palms, and had another crack at it. Freddy talked him through each hold again. The man just loved talking, and slowly Jaxxon inched his way to the final hold.

"Yes." Freddy's excitement echoed in the warehouse and Jaxxon dropped to the ground, this time landing on his feet.

"Thanks."

"I told you it was fun." Freddy kissed him on the cheek, then jogged off to another wall and began climbing, leaving Jaxxon to touch a couple of fingers to where Freddy's lips had brushed his skin.

CHAPTER 11

Freddy was glad that bouldering took concentration because he still couldn't believe that he'd spontaneously kissed Jaxxon on the cheek. And now he wanted to ask Jaxxon to have lunch with him. Jaxxon spent the ride back to the hotel working on his laptop. It felt like Jaxxon was ignoring him, even though he'd reassured him that he had a few things to do, and he wanted to take advantage of the car ride to catch up. A few things. Jaxxon had been tapping away on the laptop for nearly forty minutes. He breathed out slowly; recognising the anxiety spiral. He wasn't being ignored on purpose. It was just that Freddy should've controlled himself better. It was one thing to flirt with Jaxxon, and another to kiss his cheek because he'd been so relieved that he was fine after falling.

The speed of Jaxxon's tapping had been interspersed with the occasional moments of staring out the window. Freddy was fascinated by watching Jaxxon work; his focus and intensity screamed of competence. Obviously, he had to be good at what he did, or he wouldn't be a Team Principal before his fortieth birthday. Fuck, the pressure of running a whole team with all the financial side of things was more stress than Freddy wanted to take on. He was quite content being in the media. Close to the action, getting to spend all his time thinking and talking about Series One. He'd thrived on the pressure when he'd been a driver. Pressure as a driver was different to being Team Principal because he only had to focus on one job; get around the track as fast as possible for the whole race distance. Outside the car, he spent most of his time training and it'd been all about one singular task, being faster and more consistent. Team Principals had to juggle several threads of information and people all the time.

Their ride-share pulled up outside the hotel.

"Wasn't that fun?" Fuck. He sounded like a needy teenager, not a forty-two-year-old man. People accused him of playing his way through life and he really wasn't helping himself. Something about sitting next to Jaxxon as he did proper, serious, work made him feel like his own work was inadequate. Logically, it wasn't. Every job in the paddock was useful; he sold Series One to the public with his enthusiasm and he often had feedback from fans who loved his insights into why a car or driver reacted in certain ways.

"Sure. Thanks for inviting me." Jaxxon packed his laptop back in his bag and stepped out of the car. "Thanks, driver."

Freddy scrambled to follow. It was a glorious Melbourne day, with bright blue sky and properly warm air. He enjoyed working here as press more than he'd enjoyed driving here. The jetlag was always an issue, and the cockpit of his car was hot enough without adding Australia's summer weather to it. Singapore was worse though because of the humidity. He followed Jaxxon into the hotel, checking for people they knew, but no one was around in the foyer, so he stepped into the elevator with him.

"What are your plans for the rest of the day?"

Jaxxon glanced up from his phone. "I'm going to have a shower, then head down to the track to see how the logistics team are going with the set up. The cars arrived this morning and should have cleared the airport by now."

"Can I—"

"No. You can't come with me. Freddy, we need to have some boundaries."

He cleared his throat. "Fine. I'm sure there will be someone around to interview or annoy."

"Stop fishing for compliments. You aren't annoying."

He was, though. He always had been an annoying presence in the world. His father treated him like the second son whose presence was inconvenient—existing just in case anything happened to AA—and he'd spent his childhood trying to get the attention of his father and brother, to no avail. The Duke had been pleased when Freddy's racing had taken him away from the family. "Kept him busy," was a euphemism for the Duke not needing to expend any time on Freddy, and there was no surprise that winning races had been incredibly validating when his family weren't. He'd become addicted to winning until the day he couldn't shut out the risks anymore.

"Wait a second."

Jaxxon pushed the button for the elevator. "Yes?"

"Why do you think we need to have boundaries?" He

shouldn't get his hopes up with a question like that. Jaxxon probably just meant a work boundary with the media restricted from seeing team data in case something became public knowledge when it shouldn't. Freddy hoped, rather hopelessly, that Jaxxon referred to a possible relationship between them. Freddy already knew he wasn't going to be satisfied with a hook up with Jaxxon. It was all or nothing, really. This pull towards Jaxxon should scare him since it made him want to ignore all his own good sense.

"Like work ones, or?" Freddy was the one who needed boundaries; to stop another Chester situation; and yet, he couldn't resist Jaxxon. He still couldn't believe that Jaxxon had gone bouldering with him. He'd asked for permission, then taken a few photos of Jaxxon as he climbed and he knew he'd probably stare at them tonight when he was alone. Jaxxon's broad shoulders and strong legs had looked fucking amazing as he'd climbed. After a few climbs, Jaxxon's light blue t-shirt had clung to his body. Freddy loved how the colour of the shirt was so aesthetically pleasing against Jaxxon's dark skin, and while he wasn't as fit as Freddy, Freddy had found Jaxxon's rounded middle much sexier than he expected. Much sexier. He wanted to hold him and be held by him, pressed up against him like a ... well, he couldn't think of anything better than Jaxxon himself.

"Freddy." Jaxxon stepped out of the lift and walked along the hallway.

"Yeah?"

"Come in." Jaxxon swiped into his room, and kicked off his shoes, leaving them just inside the door. Freddy took off his shoes, making sure they were neat and tidy, trying not to get his hopes up about what Jaxxon might say. Who was he kidding? His little crush on this glorious man was growing every day into something big and dangerous and irresistible.

"I'm here."

"What are we going to do, Freddy?" Jaxxon placed his laptop bag on the desk in his room, pulling out his laptop and plugging it in.

"About?"

Jaxxon turned to face Freddy and waved his hands in the air, a stiff awkward movement. "Us. This. Whatever this is, or might be, and how we navigate it."

"Are you saying you want to date me?"

"Before we even make that decision, we need to discuss this, right? There's a chemistry between us that isn't going to go away if we ignore it. We have to make a conscious decision, either way."

Freddy swallowed. "What do you mean, either way?"

"The sensible choice—" Jaxxon paced across the room. "I've only been Team Principal for two races. I ... The sensible choice is to focus on work and not let myself be distracted by you."

"I'm a distraction?" He had assumed the chemistry was all one way; from him. That he was the only one who felt this, like he came alive whenever he was near Jaxxon. Fuck. Jaxxon had said that there was chemistry between them. He must feel it too. Freddy was doomed and he was ready to embrace every sensational moment of his own downfall.

"If we decide not to be distracted by this, then we need a plan."

"And if we decide to see where it goes?"

Jaxxon raised his eyebrows. "We still need a plan."

"You like plans?"

Jaxxon spread his hands wide, palms up, still covered in chalk. "I've always wanted to be a Team Principal and from the first day of my engineering degree, it was apparent that I'd need to work a lot harder than anyone else, and have plans, to get here."

"Because you aren't rich?" Freddy knew it was more likely about race but he wasn't sure how to raise the issue without making a mess of it.

"I'm Black. And yes, also because I don't have any wealthy connections."

"Yes." He'd spent the plane ride to Australia reading about the impact of race in western society. It was only a start and likely no amount of reading would ever be enough. He'd never have the lived experience, but he could listen and learn, and try not to fuck up. Fuck, he really didn't want to fuck up, but from all that he'd read, he knew he would, probably more than once, and he'd have to practice how to apologise without making it about him or his reactionary feelings.

He could begin with the one thing that seemed to matter to Jaxxon. "If you think we need a plan, then let's have a plan."

Jaxxon's frown disappeared. His face relaxed into a slow smile and the unveiling of it made Freddy's chest feel like it was bursting open. He'd fit in with any of Jaxxon's plans to see that smile again and again.

"Good. Plans have helped me get to where I want to be. There's a structure in having a plan that supports a goal.

Even when plans have to change or adjust to new information, they are still useful, still what I need."

"If you need it, let's have it." Freddy didn't have an opinion on plans. They'd been useful when he was a driver and away from the track, he'd rather just go with the flow and see where life landed. Most of the time that had been enough, except for the only time he'd needed a plan—to get rid of Chester—and even then, he'd employed Georgia to sort that out for him. When he'd been a driver, his job was to execute plans and he'd been good at it. He could do the same now—not because he was particularly obedient—he just knew his strengths.

"What will it be?" Jaxxon asked.

"The plan?" He deflated a bit; not sure what Jaxxon was asking.

"Will we decide to focus on work and do nothing about ... us?" Jaxxon's use of us was a shot of heat into his heart, at odds with what Jaxxon was actually saying.

"No. I don't think that's a good idea." If left alone, or purposely ignored, the chemistry between them would erupt like a dormant volcano, spilling mess over everyone. "It makes more sense to deal with this head on." Maybe if they kissed, they would get it out of their systems. Maybe it was driven by curiosity and once they both knew, then it would be boring, and they could move on. Or... He held his breath as Jaxxon walked closer to him, a deep frown between his eyebrows.

"What about your no one from the paddock rule?"

He coughed as his breath caught in the back of his throat. "I don't know." It was a good rule, removing the possibility of another Chester and making sure he didn't have to be awkward around a one-night-stand gone wrong, or whatever.

"We are sensible adults. We don't have to be weird around each other." He didn't need to say—later when it all ended.

"Hence why we need a plan."

Freddy shook his head. "Who uses hence in a sentence?"

"Someone who isn't going to let you avoid talking about this." Jaxxon sent him such an indulgent look that Freddy knew there was only one option.

"I'll give up my not in the paddock rule for you." His mouth went dry. He was basically inviting drama into his life, but the way Jaxxon looked at him made him want to try again. "I can't seem to resist you. It's only been a few months since—" Since he interviewed Jaxxon about his promotion. Before that, he'd been aware of Jaxxon as part of the Gamble Racing team but hadn't really interacted with him.

"I can't stop thinking about you either. I keep telling myself that it's a terrible idea. What kind of cruel joke from the universe is this? I should be maintaining a proper distance from the media, and I really, really shouldn't spend every evening wondering about you."

Jesus. The longing in his voice would be Freddy's undoing. Jaxxon really would be the death of him. He shoved his hands into his pockets to stop himself drumming them on his thighs. One day Jaxxon would discover that Freddy was a disaster who tried too hard to impress the wrong people.

"Maybe you should stop wondering. You'll find out

soon enough that I'm…" He didn't get to finish because Jaxxon interrupted him.

"You are worth it."

"You can't know that."

Jaxxon peered at him with an odd expression on his face. "Actually, you are correct. I can't know that. We've only just met and barely know each other. … But you've given me no reason to doubt your worth as a person." Jaxxon tilted his head. "Of course, that could simply be lust talking. This is mostly lust—" Jaxxon's admission that he was unable to be logical thanks to the chemistry flickering and igniting between them had Freddy so hard and wanting, he wanted to end the agony and kiss Jaxxon right now.

"It's impossible to know where this might go or if it is worth the risk." Jaxxon's reminder was a shot to the heart.

"And there are risks." He knew better than most. Being forced to think about his stalker ex was the greatest cure to a mighty erection ever. Tension built in his shoulders and his spine went rigid.

"Yes. It's also important to note that whatever happens next, we still need to talk on television at the next twenty-one races. I intend to be Team Principal for many years, and I imagine you aren't willing to give up your job, so we need to find a way to continue in our work whatever goes down between us." Jaxxon's understanding being punctuated with sexual innuendo increased the warring feelings inside him; as if his stomach and chest were rioting against each other. Their jobs, which involved talking professionally to each other in front of an audience of millions, was only one part of the potential mess they were about to embrace. Freddy couldn't decide if his worries were just fears that he should overcome, or if it would all play out into the ugly catastrophe that he'd experienced before. He didn't think Jaxxon would stalk him, but there were countless ways this could go terribly wrong. There was only one thing for it.

"I want to kiss you." This might be the best or the worst choice he'd ever made. "I can't spend all year playing this game, wondering what it will be like. I have to know."

Jaxxon strode across the room and placed one slightly chalky palm on his cheek. "I need to know too." Jaxxon leaned in and Freddy almost closed his eyes, except he wanted to be completely present for this; their first kiss. He placed his hands on Jaxxon's elbows, and waited, holding his breath. Jaxxon's breath—coffee and mint and a little salt, a reminder of the way they'd sweated at bouldering— whispered over Freddy's lips.

"Please." He stretched up and kissed Jaxxon—his extra few inches of height were fucking perfect—unable to wait anymore. From the moment that their lips touched, the kiss was everything that had been promised in their banter. Jaxxon kissed him as if he'd been planning it since they'd met. It was deliberate and precious, hot and sexy, and some- how, impossibly, imbibed with Jaxxon's sarcasm. He could almost hear Jaxxon's sardonic tone saying some seemingly throw away comment that got right to the core of the matter. This kiss began as an introduction and grew into a wild, uncompromising demand for more. Jaxxon shifted his hand, gripping onto Freddy's skull, pulling him closer. The pressure of Jaxxon's fingers threaded through his hair created a source of heat at each connection point, prickling in the best way. There was so much heat and need in the kiss that Freddy didn't move, couldn't move, rendered speechless and motionless by a kiss with only his mouth capable of any response. He flicked his tongue along Jaxxon's bottom lip, asking the question, and Jaxxon lashed his tongue into Freddy's mouth. Their kiss became demanding; a deep tangle of mouths and tongues until all Freddy could taste was Jaxxon. A lick of sweat from their earlier efforts at the bouldering place, and oddly, a hint of buttery croissant. Trust Jaxxon to taste decadent and rich, the buttery perfection of a meal cooked at a starred restaurant. Jaxxon's gaze stayed focused on him, and he gave Freddy the impression that he never wanted this to end, but also that he'd stop immediately if Freddy asked. God. He never wanted to stop. He wanted to strip off Jaxxon's clothes and kiss him everywhere. He wanted to suck Jaxxon's cock, to taste the saltiness of his cum. He wanted to find the places, unique to Jaxxon, that made him moan and beg for more. He wanted it all. Everything. He wrenched his mouth away, gasping for air.

"Shower." He didn't want their first kiss tainted by old sweat and chalk from bouldering. He wanted to be reckless and lick Jaxxon all over.

"Okay." Jaxxon dragged his hand through Freddy's hair, across his cheek, and over his bottom lip. He tried to lick Jaxxon's finger.

"Mmm, chalky."

Jaxxon spluttered. "Let's have that shower, then."

"Where does this fit into your plan?" He needed to know. He wasn't going to tease Jaxxon into jumping into the shower with him; it needed to be something he enthusiastically wanted. And Jaxxon had already said he loved having a plan.

CHAPTER 12

A booming laugh caught in Jaxxon's throat. "A plan. I plan to get you naked and lather you in soap all over." A daft joke about planning made him want Freddy with an extra urgency. More than the jest, it was the notion that Freddy had been listening and he knew plans were important to Jaxxon. Being listened to truly was the fucking hottest thing ever.

"I like that plan." Freddy slid his hands down Jaxxon's forearms and held his hands. It was strangely intimate. Nice. One of those moments in time that ought to be preserved, savoured, except Jaxxon's cock was hard and he didn't want to waste time. Having Freddy touch him consumed him. He let Freddy guide him into the ensuite of his hotel room. The team had booked him a suite—the benefit of being the boss was getting a room with a separate bedroom so he could use the lounge space as an office if needed during the race weekend—and the bathroom had plenty of room for two men to stand on the tiled floor, holding hands, and breathing rapidly in time with each other. A shudder ran up Jaxxon's arms from where Freddy held his hand, all the way into his chest, and down to his aching cock. He flicked a glance up and down Freddy's body, over the tiny outfit he'd worn to bouldering.

"I can't believe you go out in public in these clothes."

"What's wrong with them?" Freddy tilted his head up with a dazed expression.

Jaxxon leaned in close, brushing his lips over the curve of Freddy's neck. "They are obscene. Barely covering your body at all. What a show off, you are."

"You like them?" Freddy swallowed, his throat moving up and down, and Jaxxon traced his finger all the way up Freddy's arm, over his bicep, and pressed it lightly under his Adam's apple. Freddy's breath sped up, ragged and quick. The air grazed Jaxxon's skin, an electric caress, bringing him alive, and aware of every inch of Freddy's body.

"You know that I do. I particularly enjoyed the way your shorts stretched over your ass as you climbed." He reached around Freddy's body, pulling his close, and traced his hand over the curved muscle that he hadn't been able to look away from. Freddy's body seared against his, their aroused dicks grinding together. Hell. This was more than he'd imagined, and he had an excellent imagination.

Freddy blinked. "I wanted to tempt you."

"I'm tempted." More than tempted, he had to act and touch Freddy. He spread his hands on Freddy's spine, pushing up the cotton shirt he wore over the tiny singlet and finally, after a bit of a fumble of fabric, he was able to touch the lean muscles of Freddy's back and shoulders. Having his skin under his palms sent erratic spikes of heat surging through him, and he kissed Freddy again. The absolute tangle of limbs and lips and fabric as they raced to undress each other only made it better because it wasn't perfect. He nearly punched himself in the temple as he dragged his shirt up, unwilling to stop kissing Freddy, and yet needing to so he could remove his clothes. Jaxxon didn't want to stop touching Freddy, even for something as useful as getting undressed, but he needed to get his skin against Freddy's. Now that they'd made this decision to see where this chemistry would take them, he was going to enjoy every moment of it to the fullest. Freddy spread his hands over Jaxxon's waist. Oh. The intimate touch on his paunch jerked him back to reality; a reality where he was a little self-conscious about his size. Freddy was an athlete, still incredibly fit and physically beautiful with hard lean muscles rippling under his skin, even years after he'd retired, while Jaxxon was... well, himself. Ordinary. He didn't usually think about his body like that; it functioned, and it kept his brain alive.

"I'm sorry." He mumbled, unable to stop his apology, even knowing that he shouldn't compare. God knows, the world was fat-phobic enough without him doing it to himself.

"For?" Freddy frowned and Jaxxon wanted to take it back but he had to know what Freddy thought before they took this any further. Freddy had invited him bouldering, for fuck's sake. Fucking worrying about living up to societies standards was a curse, and terribly distracting from what he wanted to do, which was kiss Freddy and ... damn it. He'd started this now. He had to follow through. Lust mingled with foolishness and churned in his stomach, but if he pressed his hand to it now, it would give completely the wrong impression.

He gulped. "For not being as fit as I could be. I'm not an athlete."

Freddy squinted at him. "If I wanted to fuck someone as fit as me, I would do that. I happen to find you sexy. All of you." As if to prove it, Freddy placed his hands on Jaxxon's stomach. He didn't have abs, he was fat, especially around the middle, because his job meant he spent most of the day sitting down. Before he was Team Principal, he'd been a race engineer, spending his workday staring at data on computer screens and trying to find the keys to the race strategy among numbers. They had a gym at the Gamble Racing headquarters and the drivers and mechanics used it as part of their fitness regime. He'd never prioritised his time to include going there because it didn't matter that much to him, and now he'd made it an issue when it mostly wasn't one. He didn't want one tiny moment of insecurity to become a whole thing. Shit. He should've shut his mouth and used it to kiss Freddy again.

"Jaxxon—" Freddy slid his hands down to Jaxxon's hip, resting them gently. "I've broken my own rules to be here." Freddy shifted his hips, grinding his cock against Jaxxon, and he forgot everything. "You are sexy as you are. You shouldn't do something just because someone else thinks you ought to do it. Please don't change to impress me. Trust me, I'm already impressed."

"Okay." Going to the gym hadn't mattered to him until now, as he stood half-naked in a hotel bathroom with someone older than him and a lot fitter. Freddy was right, though, and he could let himself believe Freddy.

"Seriously though. You are gorgeous." Freddy touched his stomach, lightly at first, tracing circles on his flesh. Freddy's fingertips were calloused from bouldering, roughness adding awareness that went woosh over his skin, sending dancing shivers of sensation. He swallowed back a moan.

"Freddy."

"Yes." He glanced up.

"Keep doing that, please."

"We need to shower. I'm leaving chalky smears on you." Freddy moved and for an awesome second, Jaxxon thought he was going to drop to his knees in front of him, but he reached into the shower and turned on the water instead. His outstretched arm and hairy forearm reminded Jaxxon of the way Freddy reached and stretched on the bouldering wall; a foreplay to now. Freddy held out his hand under the flow, then adjusted the temperature.

"Come on. Hop in with me." Freddy's voice lowered as he dropped his shorts and undies to the floor. He stepped into the shower and held out his hand for Jaxxon. "You can always say no at any time."

"I know I can. I don't want to say no." He adored that Freddy happily accepted his non-athletic body that had been raised on too many pastries in his parent's bakery and now only existed to keep his brain alive. He shimmied out of his shorts, then placed his hand into Freddy's outstretched palm and joined him in the shower. The water was hot, steam surrounding them, and when Freddy stretched up to kiss him, he couldn't tell if the steam increased because they'd stepped into the shower adding body temperature to the water or because the kiss created a heat of its own. He wanted to squirm against Freddy, and with Freddy's words hovering around him about how he was sexy as he was and he shouldn't change for anyone, he did as he wanted. He wrapped his arms around Freddy's waist, pulling them closer together and it was exactly what he'd imagined. Heat sizzled. Water flowed between their bodies. Sandwiched together, with their dicks clamped between them, Jaxxon was in erotic heaven. The steam of the hot shower added to the glaring heat of Freddy's gaze, and he kissed Freddy, lashing his mouth with his tongue, literally begging for more with every swipe until Freddy groaned and squirmed, bucking his hips and grinding against Jaxxon's body. All doubts fled. The promised chemistry became a magnesium fire, brilliantly hot and so bright it ought to blind anyone who stared directly at the light being emitted. Fireworks were dull compared to this explosion of touch and hisses of breath as they kissed.

"Fuck, you are so delicious." Freddy half-turned, twisting in Jaxxon's arms, to grab the little bottles of hotel soaps and the water streamed over his short brown hair, sending rivulets down the arch of his neck and spine. Before Jaxxon could lean in and kiss him there, Freddy had turned back to face him. Using Jaxxon's hold to balance, Freddy leaned back and squirted some body wash into his palms. He dropped the bottle onto the shower floor. Jaxxon barely heard it hit the ground because Freddy spread his hands between them and placed his soapy palms on Jaxxon's chest. He lathered the soap, using his hands on Jaxxon's chest, creating a mess of bubbles in his tight black chest hair.

"Look at you. I love your chest hair."

"Yours is also..." He glanced down. "Um, a lot."

Freddy had a lot of chest hair to match the thick hair on

his legs and forearms, and if he looked closely, he could see where it'd been sculpted.

"Do you?"

"Yes. Yes, I get it sculpted." Freddy's face flushed as he interrupted Jaxxon's half-question. "I know it's very vain, but if I don't, it spreads out everywhere. All up my neck and across my shoulders, and there's a certain image that I need to project."

"Project?" He low key adored the way they talked and teased each other, as if being naked in a shower and feeling alive from touching each other still wasn't enough. They connected through words too, and it made their chemistry irresistible. It combined into searing flashes of glory, simultaneously easing the tension so he didn't come right there, and building it into more and more, a deeper connection than merely two bodies enjoying each other.

"My job is on television. Very hairy men were fashionable in the seventies, but smooth is in now."

Jaxxon grinned. "Then you are lucky that I don't care for fashion. It suits you to have an excess of hair."

Freddy grinned back at him. "Are you saying that I'm excessive?"

"Yes."

"Let me show you excessive."

Jaxxon shivered. "Please." He needed Freddy's touch. Holding him was only the beginning. Jaxxon needed more … of everything. The hotel soap smelled of flowers and pine nuts, and he bent his head to nuzzle at Freddy's neck. There was still a remnant of sweat from the morning's efforts, salty on his tongue. He kissed all the way towards Freddy's earlobe, lapping at the water flowing over his skin. For a while, Freddy's touch flowed over his chest and shoulders, a sweet and light sensation, exploratory, and then ... he pinched Jaxxon's nipple. The sharp pain turned into a wild wrestle where the two of them grabbed and caressed and touched each other everywhere, as if trying to compete for who could cover the most amount of skin with the soap. It was slippery and raging and so bloody perfect. Jaxxon rubbed his hard cock against Freddy's body and the groan he made was erotic.

"Jaxxon." Freddy grabbed Jaxxon's cock, stroking hard. If it wasn't for the soap and the water, it would've been too much, too rough, but it was just fucking perfectly slippery. He spread one hand on the back of Freddy's neck, pulling him in for the kiss, and with the other, he joined their cocks together, helping Freddy.

"More soap." Freddy dropped to his knees. Water streamed over his head and down his shoulders. If he decided to lick Jaxxon now, he'd come. He squeezed his eyes shut. The drop of cool liquid soap onto the end of his cock made him jump and his eyes flashed open.

"Are you alright?" Freddy stood up again, a lithe easy movement, nimble, just like he'd be in bed.

"Yes." He ground out the word between clenched teeth. Freddy reached up and massaged the tension in his jaw with one finger.

"Are you sure?"

"I'm trying not to come." His face burned with heat at the admission, but Freddy's responding smile made it worth it.

"I think you should." Freddy slid his hand over Jaxxon's cock again, spreading the soap everywhere, then he took

Jaxxon's hand and wrapped them all together. Jaxxon's insides turned to boiling soup, bubbling furiously, just a fiery ball of heat pulsing in his veins and everywhere, with all the heat sourced from Freddy's hand as he stroked them together, slowly. Too gently. Jaxxon needed more.

"More. Faster."

"Like a racing driver. Push mode."

It was a bit absurd and it should jerk him out of his head, except it didn't. It did the opposite. Jaxxon growled. If he was a driver, he'd put his foot down, and accelerate to a glorious end.

"Let's go." He moved his hand faster, trying to show Freddy what he wanted, and when Freddy pumped them quickly, it was almost enough. Bright flashes of lights flickered and desire lashed his body until his muscles trembled and he moaned. Nerve endings deep in his torso fired with life, and every fibre of every muscle contracted, tighter and tighter, wound towards the impending release that they were chasing.

"Freddy." He cried out and Freddy wrapped his other hand around the back of Jaxxon's neck, pulling his face closer until he kissed him with a ferocity that matched the galloping thud of his heartbeat. They kissed and they stroked until they groaned into each other's mouth. Jaxxon clutched Freddy, clinging on tight, as Freddy kept up the endless, perfect, pumping around their cocks. And when Freddy bit him on the bottom lip, he came with a roar. A roar that echoed and multiplied in the small space of the shower.

"Freddy. Fuck." He opened his eyes to see that Freddy had flung his head back under the water of the shower, coming together. He trembled, knees weak, and slumped against Freddy. He rested, his breathing slowly becoming steadier, with the constant fall of the shower water and the soothing caress of Freddy's hands over his stomach and hips and spine.

"Thank you."

Freddy didn't answer for far too long, long endless seconds.

"This must be what it feels like to have a five second stop and go penalty."

"What?"

"Say something."

Freddy lifted his face and slowly shook his head. "I think we are completely fucked." He closed his eyes and nestled his head against Jaxxon's shoulder. A million awful scenarios raced through Jaxxon's head, so fast that he could barely catch any of them to put into words. He sucked in a trembling breath.

"Why?"

Freddy didn't answer. He curved his hand around Jaxxon's bicep, a possessive hold, then Freddy slid his fingers over Jaxxon's elbow, cupping it gently, slowly tracing the lines of his forearm, until he held Jaxxon's hand and lifted it up to his mouth. Freddy kissed each finger, sucking the end of each digit, one at a time. Freddy worshiped his hand, and fucking hell, he never wanted to leave this shower. Maybe that's what Freddy meant. Now that he'd tasted Freddy and experienced this quick urgency of their cocks grinding together, he wanted more and more. Despite the warmth of the shower, gooseflesh broke out over Jaxxon's skin. He grabbed the shower head and used it to rinse all the remaining soap suds off Freddy, then quickly did the same to himself, and shut off the water. Freddy, unusually, still hadn't spoken. Jaxxon grabbed a couple of towels, wrapping one around Freddy's shoulders and another around his waist. Freddy didn't move.

"Freddy. Please talk to me. I'm worried about you."

Freddy shook his head. "I'm good." He didn't sound convinced.

"Really?"

Freddy looked up, his eyes shimmering. "We are so fucked."

"Come here." Jaxxon guided Freddy out of the shower, towelled him off, and sat him down in the chair in the main part of his hotel room. He grabbed a bottle of water from the fridge and handed it to Freddy who drank it like a thirsty man.

"Now tell me. Why are we fucked?"

"Jaxxon. How can you not know? You must feel this."

He held his breath. He had had a wonderful time, but Freddy looked devastated and it made Jaxxon's chest tighten and compress. If Freddy was wrecked by this—and not in a good way—then he couldn't enjoy this either. Maybe that's what Freddy meant.

CHAPTER 13

Freddy was fucked. He wanted to hold Jaxxon and never let him go. He stood there in the shower, wanting more than he could ever ask for, and with every breath, his squirely brain started to think that he was just like Chester. Obsessively wanting to keep Jaxxon at all costs. And then Jaxxon had to be kind. Drying him off, caring for him, giving him water, hovering with a worried expression. Hell.

"Please tell me what you feel." Jaxxon knelt on the floor in front of Freddy with his hands placed gently on Freddy's knees. It didn't help, it only made him want more than he could ask for.

"I thought..." He drank more water. It didn't soothe his throat as much as he wanted it to. "I'm a fool. I thought kissing you would make this go away. Things are never as good as I imagine them. Why were you so good?"

Jaxxon's fingers tightened on his knees. "Freddy?"

"Yes?"

"Are you having a crisis because you want to kiss me again? Because you enjoyed this?"

He leaned back in the chair, wanting to do something dramatic like place his hand on his forehead. "Yes. Don't you feel that?"

"Feel what?"

"The need to hold you and possess you and never let you go." He was deranged.

Jaxxon blew out a long breath, and it whistled in the air. "I'm flattered. I had a great time too. From the bouldering, which pushed me into trying something new and challenging, to being with you intimately."

"I'm being dramatic."

"Yes, Freddy. You are."

His heart stopped pounding, easing into an elevated but not frantic rhythm. "Hey." He sat up straighter and attempted to glare at Jaxxon, who only shrugged one shoulder.

"Well. You asked."

"What now?" He didn't know how to handle this. Before Chester—and definitely afterwards—he'd always been one to fuck and leave without caring about anything beyond the immediate enjoyment. Being with Jaxxon had meant more and it scared the shit out of him. He hadn't felt this since the early days with Chester. Right. That's why he was freaking out. He was completely freaking... The. Fuck. Out.

"Now we make a plan, and we work out what to do next."

He swallowed, unable to stop a delayed shudder. Sex was supposed to be fun, not this incredible fantasy come to life that surged inside him, throwing him around like the handling of an S1 car in the wet, slippery and impossible to keep on the racetrack. He was supposed to be able to leave afterwards without caring too much, not aquaplane into a concrete barrier.

Jaxxon stood up and kissed him lightly on the mouth. "Relax. I'm not asking for a plan immediately. First, I need to go to pitlane and check out the cars. Why don't you stay here and take some time to figure out what you want? We can have dinner and talk about it."

"A plan." It made sense. And being alone for a while was good. He could call Georgia for advice, or maybe Ricky Dee. They'd been mates when they drove against each other —the bromance of the paddock as the media used to say— and while their lives had taken very different turns since retirement, they texted all the time and still caught up for a beer and a chat a few times a year when their schedules coincided.

"All things can be managed with a good plan. Overwhelming problems can be broken down into separate pieces and each piece dealt with." Jaxxon's good sense helped, but the reality was that Freddy was going to have to be brave and tell Jaxxon the whole bloody story about Chester. He'd run away from relationships since then with purpose and now he was being pushed into the ground by the weight of these new feelings. Fucking emotions.

"I can do that." He waved his hand, trying to look more relaxed than he felt. "Go. Work. Make those cars fast."

Jaxxon smiled. "They are already fast. Victor did that and our mechanics keep them fast. It's a team effort."

"Saying that makes you a good leader. I can see why

Socrates picked you to take over from him." Freddy started to feel normal again, until Jaxxon kissed him on the damned forehead and the warm buttery scent of him wafted over his skin. Just like a real lover might do. Fucking fuck. The wash of emotions threatened to overwhelm him again. He didn't want any of this; except that he did. No, what he wanted was to have fun with Jaxxon without all these pesky feelings. If only he could go back to before, when it was just flirting and potential, before he knew how fucking spectacular Jaxxon was, and before he had the taste of his skin and his kiss on his tongue.

Hours later, Freddy walked into one of the hotel bars and found a quiet spot where no one would bother him. Because time zones sucked and he was on the wrong side of the world, he'd woken up Georgia and she'd groggily told him not to be a fool, both for waking her and being worried about that and for stressing about all of this. She'd reminded him—warned him—that if Jaxxon mattered, then Freddy had better be honest with him regardless of how hard that conversation might be. Okay, so she'd been surly about being woken at some ungodly hour, and her advice had been tersely given. He'd needed to hear it and he'd decided—perhaps doubling down on the foolishness— that he should have this conversation over dinner in public, but far away from anyone in the paddock. He nearly asked the waiter for a glass of Shiraz and then he didn't want to be the retired driver drinking alone in a hotel bar cliché; mainly because the revelation about Socrates being in rehab with a drinking problem that no one—not even Socrates—

had noticed had been quite confronting. Since then, he'd been out of sorts, although how much of this unsettled churn in his stomach was due to the progression of his relationship with Jaxxon? Most of it.

"I'll have a fresh juice."

"I'll get you a menu." The waiter walked off and Freddy pulled out his phone. Time to do this.

Freddy
Are you still good for dinner?

The waiter arrived back with a menu filled with exciting options, like The Cleanser which sounded like something no one would want, but comprised of blended apple, beetroot, carrot, ginger, kale, and lemon; and the much better named Green Goddess which as far as he could tell was basically the same as the other one but with cucumber and spinach instead of beetroot and carrot.

"I'll have a Sunshine." Maybe it would help him return to his usual sunshine state. It was filled with grapefruit, mango, orange, and pineapple.

Jaxxon
Yes.

Jaxxon
I'm on my way back to the hotel now.
Give me an hour to get ready.

Freddy sent him a thumbs up. When the waiter arrived back with his unassuming looking juice in a plain glass, he booked a car for an hour's time. Now he needed to find somewhere to go. It had to be somewhere that Jaxxon would be comfortable, so not one of those degustation places that served seventeen successive meals on huge plates. He didn't want to remind Jaxxon of his wealthy background—he wasn't ashamed of it—he simply didn't want to put Jaxxon in a potentially uncomfortable situation. The whole discussion was going to unflattering and awkward, and he wasn't sure he could do it without sounding like a wanker.

And it had to be somewhere that no one in the paddock would go, therefore it needed to be somewhere far away from the track and this hotel, and off the radar. Nothing that could be easily found on the internet—nothing Instagrammable—and he didn't particularly want to head into a suburb then wander aimlessly, like he might have done if it was just himself exploring a new place. He needed purpose and he had an hour to find something. He waved at the waiter, a young South Asian man.

"I have a question."

"Yes sir?"

"I was hoping for a recommendation for somewhere to eat tonight."

The waiter nodded. "We have several restaurants here. I can get you a menu."

"I'm looking to get away from everyone tonight."

"Everyone?"

"Series One." He forgot that people didn't automatically recognise him from television if they weren't fans.

"That's the car racing thing? The boss said that most of our guests this week are part of that."

"Yes. The car racing thing." He grinned. "You are obviously a local and I was hoping to get a recommendation for somewhere that isn't here."

The waiter frowned. "You want my advice on a local place to go that isn't near here? I am supposed to encourage you to eat here."

Freddy should've known. It made sense that the staff were taught to keep the money in house. "If it makes you feel better, I'll be here for a week and most of the time I'll be eating here. This is a one-off thing, away from work."

"Understood, sir. What is it that you are looking for?"

"I want to experience something with a good vibe and excellent food, and I want to do it away from my colleagues. Something in Melbourne but not local to this hotel, if that makes sense."

"Melbourne is known for its cuisine and quirky restaurants. What type of food are you interested in?"

"I'm taking someone who has a soft spot for pastry —" He'd noticed that Jaxxon always picked the pastries at breakfast in every hotel they stayed in, and he'd mentioned that his parents ran a bakery, so it made sense. "Um, I don't really have a preference. I'm looking for an experience rather than a specific cuisine from any culture."

The waiter nodded. "What type of vibe are you looking for?"

"Great question. Fun, flirty, private." How many ways could he say date without mentioning the word?

"Give me a second." The waiter walked off and attended to a couple of newcomers, Carol, his boss, and his colleague John McMurray. He waved at them, then bent to stare at his phone, hoping they'd stay over at the bar. He sipped his juice, but of course, both Carol and John slid into the seats at his little table.

"How's things, Freddy? Haven't seen you all day." John was about fifteen years older than him and was the legendary voice in S1 broadcasting. His 'lights out and away we go' had even been remixed into a song. Hashtag goals?

Freddy tried not to smirk. "Just did some exercise, then had a rest. It's the jet lag, you know."

"Isn't it the worst?" John sipped his white wine, and Carol ignored them both staring at her phone with a deep frown. "You have plans for dinner? Come and eat with us."

"Thanks, but I'm meeting a friend in—" He checked his phone. "—forty-five minutes." With every minute, he distracted himself with chatter. They talked about their plans for the weekend, and all the latest gossip, and who were 'must interview' subjects in the paddock. It was early in the season, so the news was quite boring, just differences in cars from last year to this and how the rookies were settling in. None of it was news, just rehashing the schedule, and he didn't really need to pay attention to be part of the conversation. He sipped his juice incredibly slowly, until it was time to walk to the foyer.

"See you all tomorrow." He shook their hands, and as he was walking out the door, the waiter handed him a piece of paper.

"Here are a few options. I asked the chef and he's recommended some funky places that might work. There's also my cousin's restaurant if you want to try Pakistani cuisine."

"Wow. That's awesome. I really appreciate this. Is there some way that I can tip you as part of my gratitude?"

The waiter shrugged. "We don't really do tipping in Australia."

"Could I donate to a cause that you care about?"

The smile on the young man's face was endearing and lovely. "Thank you. There's a charity who takes used cricket gear from clubs and ships it to kids in need in other countries. They always need help with the shipping cost."

"I love that idea. Write the name down for me." He handed the piece of paper back to the waiter who grabbed a pen from the bar and scribbled something. Freddy tucked the paper into his pocket and shook the waiter's hand. "Thank you for everything."

"Anytime, sir."

"And I promise to eat here for the rest of the week, so you won't get in trouble with your boss."

"Thank you, sir."

With a deep breath out, he walked out of the bar towards the foyer. It was almost time to confront his demons and tell Jaxxon why he was so scared about wanting Jaxxon this much. All his fears disappeared as he walked into the foyer and saw Jaxxon standing there. He wore a crisp dark grey suit and was talking on the phone to someone. The suit was tailored perfectly to Jaxxon's body, hanging off his broad shoulders. He looked every inch the powerful executive, and Freddy's insides buzzed. Jaxxon had an intense expression, his eyebrows furrowed together, as he listened to whatever was being said by the other person. Usually if Freddy saw a Team Principal with this expression, he'd wait until they'd finished and quiz them to find out what was going on, but he was overwhelmed by how incredible Jaxxon looked; powerful, competent, and so fucking sexy. Jaxxon's fingers were wrapped around his phone as he held it to one ear. With his other hand, he fiddled with the collar of his suit and as soon as he saw Freddy, he shook his head, so Freddy nodded once and walked outside to wait for their car. He started to look up each recommendation on his phone. Their car pulled up and Freddy slid into the back.

"I'm waiting on someone. I'll tip for your time." He sent Jaxxon a quick text with the make and model of the car and the licence plate, then went back to checking out the list of recommendations. He even had enough time to send a donation to the charity the waiter had written down for him. Eventually, the door opened and Jaxxon got in.

"Sorry about that."

"It's fine. It's your job. Now, spicy or not spicy?"

Jaxxon smiled. "Not too spicy, although I do love a good curry."

"Excellent. I was thinking we'd go to a Pakistani restaurant." He gave the address to the driver who set off.

"Why Pakistani?" Jaxxon sent him a 'that's random' quizzical glance.

"It's run by the cousin of the waiter in the hotel bar. He gave me a bunch of other recommendations too, so we don't have to go there if you'd rather try something else."

"Let's do it. It'll be nice to support a local family business."

Freddy grinned. "That's what I thought too. And he mentioned a cricket charity that I've just donated to." He cringed, worried that he sounded like a pretentious ass, self-promoting his donations.

"Cricket? Did you play at school?" Jaxxon's easy question was like a warm hug, relaxing.

"Opening batter for the thirds!" Freddy had only wanted to drive cars, but his school had insisted that he play cricket for them too. "And you?"

"Everyone plays cricket and football. I was a keeper and batted okay."

"And football?"

"Goalie. I grew early, and the coach thought that my height and size would help in goal."

Freddy reached out and held Jaxxon's hand. He wasn't sure what to say, except that school had been a shitty place for him and it sounded like Jaxxon had a terrible time too. "School sucked."

"Not for me. I enjoyed school. I was good at it, just not the sport parts of it."

"You didn't get teased for being gay?" Other students had known before he had. Being bisexual had been incredibly confusing when he was young, because he understood all the teenage lust over hot women, but he also didn't really fit in and he'd been teased for being gay when he hadn't really known what that meant.

Jaxxon made an odd noise. "Not really. My size tended to keep people from opening their mouths too much." He laughed. "I'm not even that big, only six foot, but I grew early. The teachers all loved me because I actually did the homework."

"What?" He would've been on detention for months if he'd tried to opt out of homework.

"I went to a government school in a poor suburb. A lot of kids didn't get fed and had boatloads of intergenerational trauma. It was tough. I used to bring yesterday's bread from the bakery to give to people so they'd get a decent meal for the day."

Freddy's heart grew a size. "You are incredible."

"No. Just practical. If the other kids in my class could get food from me, they'd leave me alone so I could study. I always knew I had to do well, to get out of the cycle of poverty, and the thing is, we weren't even that poor on the scale of things. My parents had a steady job and we had a place to live. I had a solid base to grow from."

The differences in their upbringings couldn't have been starker and Freddy was glad he hadn't complained about being called dreadful names for tying his school tie wrong, or having slurs graffitied on his locker.

"School is such a microcosm of society." He deserved the look of disdain Jaxxon shot in his direction. "I mean it's obvious that we had very different experiences at school. I was teased—" Taunted. "—A lot for being queer but even then, I was still the son of a Duke with a title of my own, so I held some status above the untitled nouveau riche." What a wanker that made him sound like.

CHAPTER 14

Jaxxon didn't know whether to laugh or throttle Freddy or hug him and empathise with being called slurs. "You do realise that makes you sound like a right wanker."

"Yes. I'm a privileged fucker. I know."

Empathy won. "It can't have been easy having to listen to people disparage your identity."

"No." It was amazing how one little word could carry so much weight.

"It would be easy to tease you about your upbringing, but I also have a strong sense of smugness about my own. It's a blurry line between I'm better than these people and the idea that I understand why others aren't able to achieve big things." His parents had been good at helping him understand this difference, that if he was too superior in his attitude, people would actively bring him down and more importantly, his own arrogance would prevent him from seeing the whole picture. He was forever seeking that balance between confidence in his abilities and the egotistical lack of awareness caused by arrogance.

"Oh. I never thought of it that way. I was always just pleased that when I was able to get away from school to go racing. Between the karting circuit when I was teen, and then getting into S3 when I was sixteen, I missed a lot of school."

"But you graduated?"

"Yeah, I guess. I got my GCSEs and officially left school."

"Sixteen is the leaving age, isn't it?"

"Yes. My team insisted I get my GCSEs as part of my contract, and I loved racing so much that I did it for that reason only."

"It's just a piece of paper." Jaxxon didn't really believe that; for him, his degrees had opened doors that would've been firmly locked to him otherwise.

Freddy scoffed. "Says the guy with double degrees from England's most prestigious university. It's not just a piece of paper and saying that insults both of us." Trust Freddy to get to the heart of the matter succinctly.

He swallowed. "Yes." He probably should take some time to understand why he wanted to dismiss his own achievements to make Freddy feel better about his lack of education, especially when Freddy specifically said he was content with what he'd done.

"It's valid to take different paths. You don't have to disparage or dismiss your path to make me feel better." Freddy reinforced it and Jaxxon wanted to protest that he wasn't doing that, when it was exactly what he was doing.

"Yeah."

"You've just said that you loved school. I was the opposite. I couldn't wait to leave school and I thought I was so mature when I got my seat in Series Three."

"Hold up. If your S3 team insisted you get your GCSEs, then you must've been only sixteen? You were the minimum age when you got your seat?" He'd read that somewhere but to hear it directly from Freddy highlighted what a great achievement it was.

"Yes. My connections helped and of course I was a silly teenager with far too much ego when my fellow drivers were—"

"Aren't most S3 drivers also teenagers?" He didn't know too much about the rules for the feeder racing levels in Series racing, since he'd spent most of his career in rally, before leaping directly into Series One.

"Not really. Each year, there are only a couple who are under eighteen. Most S3 drivers are between eighteen and twenty-two." Freddy managed to make his achievement even more impressive.

"Come on. You are all about different pathways and that I shouldn't dismiss my degrees, while you dismiss the fact that you made a series team at the minimum age."

Freddy chuckled. "Yeah. True. Fuck, I thought I was so grown up, getting to leave school to be a race car driver. And to be honest, I was happy to be escaping the toxic culture at the school I went to. I mean, car racing is full of rich people, but there's generally less entitlement than in the very exclusive school I went to."

"You mean to say that people who are going to inherit titles think they are better than everyone else?" Jaxxon winked at Freddy.

"I know you think you are joking, but it's not that funny."

"Because?" He didn't have to wait long.

"It's taken me a long time to sort out the impact of growing up in a hierarchy. Um, I was unlikely to ever inherit the Dukedom, and even less likely now that AA has five sons. I knew I would never be at the top of the pile but I was still raised to be smugly superior to everyone else. I have a title of my own—"

"You do?" Jaxxon wanted a little bit of time to think about this concept of smug superiority, and especially how it related to their discussion on different pathways. He grappled with the same concept, just from a different starting position, as the first person in his family to go to university. It wasn't a puzzle that he was going to resolve now, however. Not when Freddy laughed and pushed him on the shoulder.

"Haven't you looked me up online? It's not a secret."

"Okay." He wasn't overly interested in any of that stuff, although anyone growing up in England couldn't avoid knowing how the aristocratic system operated. Titles didn't say anything about someone's character, just as his degrees didn't make him superior to people who didn't have his good fortune to have supportive parents who encouraged him to do his best, or people who made different choices based on their different talents. But people often elevated him, especially with a racial flavour, as one of the good ones and he didn't want to buy into that nonsense.

"I mean, whatever, right. My last boyfriend cared too much." Freddy turned to look out the window of the car, just as it pulled into a parking spot near the curb. "Oh, look we are here." He tapped on his phone, then leaped out of the car, leaving Jaxxon wondering if that meant Freddy considered him his boyfriend. Relax, Jaxxon, they'd been on one 'not really a date' date, hooked up this afternoon, and now were going to dinner. It was hardly a relationship. Yet.

"Thanks driver." Jaxxon followed Freddy. The restaurant was tucked into a Victorian red-brick building, similar to his parent's bakery, with what looked like the owner's accommodation above the shop. Aside from the weather, Australia had a very familiar homely feel, and this suburb could've been any run-down suburb in Liverpool with the mix of different languages written on faded shop signs. Freddy held the door open for him with a little grin on his face. Dressed in casual jeans and an unbranded polo shirt, Freddy looked good, with an effortless elegance that came from having gorgeous looks and from growing up wealthy. Freddy charmed the person at the front of the restaurant and soon they were seated at a private table near the rear of the restaurant. The waitress brought them some water and ran them through the menu.

"I think we will have a selection of your traditional meals." Freddy was so at home in places like this, the consummate traveller who glided through life, and Jaxxon was grateful that he could simply follow along. Before his first job in rally, he'd never travelled, never left England, and now he'd been all over the world working, he tended to stick close to work and the team. Freddy's ease could only have come with practice at adventuring around unfamiliar places. Once the waitress had taken Freddy's order, Freddy poured two glasses of water.

"Now, I suppose we need to talk about what

happened earlier." Freddy had been so lightly chatty and comfortable this evening that the reminder about Freddy's shutdown after their shower earlier today was a jerk back into reality.

"Only if you are comfortable. I was worried about you." It all came rushing back. The way Freddy blankly stared at him repeating that they were fucked, and the sinking in his stomach that he'd done something wrong.

"Thank you. I need to tell you a story."

"Okay."

Freddy wiped his hands on his napkin and sipped his water again. "There's a reason for my no paddock rule."

He'd assumed so. He nodded, and kept his gaze on Freddy, waiting. Freddy wrung the napkin around in his fist until it tore. Jaxxon reached out and held his hand softly.

"Um, thanks." Freddy sighed deeply and his shoulders slumped.

"You don't have to tell me. You don't owe me this story or your pain. We are—" Well, he didn't actually know. Were they friends, or lovers, or had it been a one-time thing and they were just a couple of blokes who'd had a hook up? Boyfriends? Freddy had hinted at that in the car just now, hadn't he?

"Actually, I don't know what we are."

"Isn't that why we need your plan?" Freddy's eyes twinkled for a second then the shine faded. "Fuck. I was stalked by an ex who I met in the paddock, that's why I have that rule." The words came out fast and scrambled, muffled into Freddy's napkin.

Cold air blew sharply over his neck. "Excuse me. Did you say stalked?" He couldn't have heard that correctly.

Freddy's nostrils flared and his face was blotchy with colour. "Yes."

"That sounds bloody intense. Fuck."

"It was, rather." Freddy closed his eyes.

"You don't have to talk about it if it's too hard. It's okay."

Freddy opened his eyes, the hazel darkening to mostly brown in the faded light of the restaurant. "I do because this morning, after..." He paused and pinched his nose.

"Take your time." Jaxxon didn't want to push Freddy to tell a story that so obviously was hurtful to him.

"It's not too hard to tell the story of my stalker. It's just facts, something that happened to past me."

"Okay. You still don't owe me anything."

Freddy raised both eyebrows. "Are you kidding me? I freaked out today and scared you. How can you say that I don't owe you an explanation?"

"I—" Jaxxon paused to sip his water and sort out exactly how to respond. "I think the reason behind your no paddock rule is explanation enough." To say that Freddy had had a stalker told him enough and he didn't need to drag Freddy through the whole drama again for the sake of his own satisfaction. What a dick that would make him. 'Hey, re-live your pain for me.'

"Chester Ormsby—"

"Hold up." Jaxxon held up one hand. "The guy who is married to Terry Josund, the fertiliser billionaire?" Socrates had approached him for sponsorship before they'd taken on Paulo and Sanchez Shipping, and the meeting had been memorable for the way Josund's husband had fawned over him. Just because someone was queer didn't mean it was a good fit for their team, and Socrates had agreed that the whole thing had been too awkward to continue to try and build a business relationship with Josund.

"I don't know, but Chester marrying someone who made his fortune in shit is a nice touch." Freddy's mouth twitched, an unsteady attempt at a smile. Jaxxon squeezed Freddy hand, tracing his thumb over Freddy's wrist.

"Could be a coincidence. Sorry for interrupting."

Freddy's pulse raced under Jaxxon's thumb and he kept up the gentle caress. "Don't stress about it. Chester worked for Sonia, doing graphics for the team. I didn't really know him, but he was in the paddock on the day of Kerrigan's accident and comforted me afterwards."

"Seeing Kerrigan crash your car and not walk away must've been a huge shock." They'd talked about how the crash which paralysed Kerrigan had been a big factor in Freddy retiring as a driver. Accidents happened in motor-racing. He'd lost a driver in the New Zealand rally early in his career as a mechanical engineer and it'd been a stark reminder of the dangers of the sport they chose to work in.

"It was. And Chester provided comfort. It wasn't until later that I suspected he'd sought me out that day and used my emotional shock to weasel his way into my life. Back then, I'd assumed it was genuine."

"As would anyone."

Freddy didn't answer for a long time, and it wasn't until the waitress arrived with their first course that he managed to speak, if only a quick thanks to the waitress.

"Here is the Mutton Aloo Gosht." She placed two plates on the table, one with the gorgeous smelling curry and another piled up with chapati.

"Want some?" Jaxxon spooned some into one of the small bowls and handed it to Freddy.

"Thanks."

"This one is the Charcoal Fish Lahori." The waitress placed a plate covered in deep fried strips of fish with a tamarind chutney dip.

"I love this style of eating with share plates in the middle." Freddy smiled, hesitantly. "I like trying a bunch of different things and this way I can order a few options and know that I don't have to choose only one option."

Jaxxon was content to let Freddy chatter away about food. He'd tell the story of his stalker when he was ready. He wasn't going to push. The mutton curry was filled with soft meat and potatoes and he couldn't help thinking that this was the Englishman's ultimate meat and three veg meal with proper spices. It melted on his tongue as he used the chapati to eat it.

"Try the fish. It's incredible." Freddy handed him a small bowl filled with several strips of fish. The crisp outer coating was covered in masala spices providing a perfect contrast to the soft fish inside. He dipped some in the chutney to add a little sweetness to the experience. Hell, he could eat far too many of these.

"That's amazing. How did you find this place?"

"It's owned by the cousin of the waiter in the hotel bar."

"And you just took his recommendation?" Jaxxon tended to do more research before he spent any money. "What if it was no good?"

"Then we'd have an experience and something to talk about. Life is an adventure."

Jaxxon grinned. "You've obviously never saved up your money for something and worried about whether it would be worth it."

"No. But surely you have enough money now not to worry about that?"

"Old habits die hard. I have plans for my money."

"Plans." Freddy's eyes sparkled. "I would counter that with life is for living … but—"

"You don't want to exchange positive affirmations with me?" Jaxxon ripped off a piece of chapati and ate some more of the gosht so he didn't grin like a Cheshire Cat.

"I can exchange things with you all night, Jaxxon."

He nearly choked.

"Do you need some water? Is it a bit spicy?" Freddy's concern was lovely, although his expression hinted at his lack of seriousness.

"The only spicy thing here is you."

Freddy's cheeks flushed and he waved his arm in the air. The waitress appeared. "Can we please try the chicken karahi?"

"That's our spiciest option on the menu. Are you sure?"

"Yes. Bring it on." Tomorrow, his stomach might regret letting Freddy taunt him into this adventure but given way Freddy looked at him with a twinkle in his eye, only added to the buzz between them. He wanted to impress Freddy, a dangerous idea that sent an involuntary shiver up his arms.

CHAPTER 15

Their ride-share car pulled up outside the hotel and Freddy wanted to invite Jaxxon into his room because … basically, he wanted to kiss him again. It was the natural conclusion to an amazing dinner; except he was caught between freaking out that he'd broken his no one from the paddock rule and the yearning for Jaxxon. Jaxxon's response to his very brief mention of Chester had been perfectly reasonable. Freddy knew it wasn't his fault. It'd been Chester's bad choices; it was merely that Freddy had had to deal with the consequences of it, and his weaselly brain got in a little jab at that because he'd fobbed a lot of those consequences onto Georgia, paying her to deal with them instead. He sat up straighter in the ride-share. He refused to let Chester continue to have any power of him and he was going to stop being worried that the situation would repeat. Seriously, he'd have to be incredibly unlucky to have two stalkers... Except the real problem was that he stressed he was going to be the Chester in this new relationship, that his own intensity had somehow caused the problem and he couldn't help but become his own worst nightmare. *Fucking shut up, Freddy.* He might be a privileged son of a Duke, but he could try and recognise his own self-centred bullshit and make it stop.

"Do you want to come to my room to discuss the plan?" He wanted Jaxxon. It should be simple.

"The plan?"

"Yes." It was absolutely a euphemism for sex and besides they could sleep in tomorrow. "FP1 is at two."

"I am aware of the timings of the practice sessions, Freddy."

"What time do you need to be at the track?"

"On Friday, or tomorrow?"

Freddy swore under his breath. He was so caught up in his own head—selfishly—that he'd forgotten it was only Wednesday night. "Are you going to the track tomorrow?"

"Yes. It's my job."

The car stopped. Jaxxon thanked the driver and hopped out of the car, leaving Freddy to scramble after him. Maybe it was a sign from the universe that he needed to take the space that Jaxxon offered and take his time. He didn't want to become obsessive like Chester had been; he'd been on the other side of that mess and he wouldn't want to inflict that on anyone. Life was simpler when he went to gay bars for hook-ups, or to his club to have sex with other people who also went there for the purpose of fun sex with no strings or feelings attached. Now he was a bundle of emotion, churning in his chest, and he didn't like it.

His phone dinged and he blinked. He was standing in the foyer of the hotel, all alone.

Jaxxon
Are you still interesting in talking about
the plan?

Trust Jaxxon to write in complete sentences. Freddy—whose job it was to talk—could barely articulate any of the mess in his head.

Freddy
Yeah. 732

Jaxxon
What is that number?

Freddy
My room

Jaxxon
I will meet you there in an hour. I need to
have a chat to someone in the bar first.

Freddy
Someone I know?

Jaxxon
Are you jealous?

Freddy
No

This was ridiculous. He shouldn't be grinning at his phone as he texted Jaxxon.

> **Jaxxon**
> One of our sponsors wants to have a
> beer and talk about a few things.

Freddy sent a thumbs up, and then a gif of someone rolling in cash.

> **Jaxxon**
> Freddy

How did he manage to make a text sound like a warning? He walked towards the bank of elevators and pushed the button.

> **Freddy**
> Jaxxon

> **Jaxxon**
> Maybe I'll be longer than an hour.

> **Freddy**
> Is that a threat or a promise?

> **Jaxxon**
> I'm not sure what you mean.

> **Freddy**
> Do you want me to be waiting with
> impatient anticipation?

> **Jaxxon**
> Freddy.

Freddy
I could sit on the 'edge' of the bed while I wait.

Jaxxon
Freddy!

Freddy
If I keep making euphemisms, will you call me Lord Beautravers?

He wasn't sure he wanted that, but he really wanted Jaxxon to say—type—his name in that tone again.

Jaxxon
That's your title?

Freddy
For my sins

Jaxxon
I am not comfortable calling you that. I don't think the aristocracy is a good concept.

Freddy laughed as he stepped out on his floor. He could tell Jaxxon the truth—that he agreed despite the benefits to himself—or he could make another joke. Or combine the two...

Freddy
Are you saying that hundreds of years of inbreeding and wealth collection hasn't been good for the world?

> **Jaxxon**
> Did you just

> **Jaxxon**
> Sorry. My finger slipped.

> **Freddy**
> Are you going to finish that sentence?

> **Jaxxon**
> No. I have to go. My meeting is here.

> **Freddy**
> I'll be waiting for you.

> **Jaxxon**
> Freddy

> **Freddy**
> Plans are afoot. Or abreast. Or…

He couldn't think of any other words with body parts in to continue the theme.

> **Jaxxon**
> Please stop now.

He typed, 'are you saying you can't resist replying to me?' but he deleted it before he sent it. This was the restraint that he ought to be practicing. He stood outside his hotel room door and stared at it for a while. It was silly to hang out alone in his room when he could be getting all the gossip from the paddock. He spun on his heel and went back down to the hotel bar.

Jaxxon didn't reply, and he wasn't in the main bar either. It took John's teasing for him to stop checking his phone.

Talking to people in the bar had taken a lot longer than he'd anticipated. The extra time was completely worth it, it'd paid dividends and now he had news. He rushed along the hallway to Jaxxon's room, needing to tell him now, and he knocked enthusiastically on Jaxxon's door.

"Let me in. I have news."

"Go away."

"I have news."

"It's midnight. Tell me tomorrow, Freddy."

It was? He pulled out his phone. He had a text from Jaxxon two hours ago, saying he was outside his room, then another ten minutes later saying he was going to bed. Damn. Freddy had been so caught up in talking to people about this news—so excited to be chasing information down the rabbit hole—that he hadn't heard his phone beep. He'd lost track of time, and he'd forgotten his appointment with Jaxxon for sex, or to discuss their plan, which was basically the same thing. Regret surged in his stomach, and he swallowed down the bitter taste of bile.

"Shit. I'm sorry." He was a disaster and it was yet another sign that this whole thing with Jaxxon was a bad idea.

"I'm sleeping now."

Bad ideas, be damned. This news couldn't wait. "No, let me in. You'll want to know this news right now."

A minute later, the door opened. Jaxxon wore only a pair of blue boxer shorts. Freddy forgot why he was there, jolted in the chest at the sight of Jaxxon's bare torso and arms. The little frown between his black eyebrows and the glare emitting from his dark eyes sucked all the air from Freddy's lungs. Jaxxon growled, and heat sizzled over his skin, reverberating like a well-struck gong.

"This better be good."

"It is." He brushed past Jaxxon and tried—and failed—to ignore the zing of heat at the small contact with Jaxxon's bare skin. The hotel door shut behind him with a little snick. "It really is. But first, are you okay? I lost track of time and I've only just seen your texts now."

Jaxxon sat down, elbows on the table beside his laptop. "Yes. You didn't answer so I came here and slept. You woke me up." The annoyance in his voice hardly registered. All of Freddy's attention was drawn to Jaxxon's bare skin. The poor man was exhausted, he was resting his body on his arms, propped up by the table, and Freddy was ogling him.

"Sorry. This is worth it, I promise."

"What?" Jaxxon's voice was rough, and it sent a shiver along Freddy's spine. Lust immediately turned into care. He needed to tell Jaxxon this news quickly so he could tuck Jaxxon back into bed. The urge to rub his back and listen to him drift off to sleep was shockingly like being in an actual relationship. His neck went cold then hot, and he breathed in deeply. First things first. The news.

"John overheard someone talking about the Gamble Racing car reveal night and he went over to chat. It was one of the sound check guys, Mark."

"And?"

"Mark had been asked by Carol to turn off the cameras after they were set up."

"Turn them off? We were told by the production team that there was no footage of the stage until you and Blasi walked on." Jaxxon leaned heavier onto his arms.

Freddy frowned. "That can't be right. We usually do extensive light tests before we begin. There should've been at least an hour of footage of the stage."

"You just told me that Carol told someone to turn them off."

"Yes. Right. So that was unusual, and John thought so too. He asked Carol about it, and she said that she hadn't said that. It must be a mistake."

Jaxxon leaned forwards. "Convenient mistake to make. Do you think Carol is in on it?"

"No. Why?"

"What do you mean, why?"

"Carol wouldn't steal a trophy. For starters, she's not really a fan of S1."

"But she works on the circuit."

"As she says, women can't turn down an opportunity to produce a major sporting program. She makes no secret that this is a steppingstone for her in her career. Don't get me wrong, she's really fucking good at her job, but she's not an avid fan."

"It'd be quite strange to steal such a specific item then."

"Yes. Completely out of character. She's a stickler for the rules; pisses me off sometimes with her pedantic need to do everything by the book."

A grin flickered on Jaxxon's face, almost a smile, before it disappeared again. "That statement doesn't surprise me."

"Are you saying that I'm a loose unit?"

"Is that what it's called?" Jaxxon smiled, his eyes sparkling.

"I'm good at my job."

"And you are a retired driver with friends everywhere."

"That's why I got the job. It's not why I keep it." He wanted to growl at Jaxxon's assumption that he only had his job because of his past. Not every retired driver made a good tv presenter. He was fucking good at his job. Right. He was probably tired after a long evening of unreleased lust. Seeing Jaxxon leaning with exhaustion removed all remnants of desire and he wanted to get this conversation done quickly so he could help Jaxxon sleep. He breathed in slowly. "Shall we get back to the point?"

"Which is?"

"Someone told one of the crew to turn off the cameras. And Carol claims it wasn't her."

Jaxxon nodded. "You've given some strong reasons why it wouldn't be her. Who else might it be?"

Fuck. That was a great question. "I can ask Maddock."

"Maddock?"

"My cameraman. You met him in Bahrain when Seb's trophy got stolen."

"Maybe tomorrow."

Freddy checked his phone. "It is tomorrow."

"I need to be in pitlane early, so I'm going back to bed." Jaxxon stood up and walked towards the bedroom in his suite, leaving Freddy awkwardly alone. So much for helping Jaxxon and demonstrating care. Obviously Jaxxon didn't want his assistance. He could leave. He probably should leave … Unless there was something implied by the fact that Jaxxon had simply gone to bed without turning off any lights in the lounge of his suite. Jaxxon didn't strike him as the kind of person who would waste electricity simply because the hotel would pay. This could be a terrible idea, or he could take a chance and get into bed with Jaxxon. He liked risk and making decisions quickly. It was why he'd been a good driver. Freddy walked around the room, turning off lights and making sure Jaxxon's laptop was plugged in and charging, before he put all his things in a neat pile on a side table. It wasn't much, just his wallet, phone, and hotel swipe card.

He quickly went through the boring motions of getting ready for bed, putting all his clothes neatly on a chair, then opened the door to Jaxxon's bedroom. Everything was dim, although the light from the street coming through the window was enough to see that Jaxxon was already asleep, sprawled under the covers with his arm wrapped around the pillow. Freddy realised he was tip-toeing around the bed, even though the carpet was soft enough to muffle his footsteps. He pulled the curtains shut, removing the last of the light, and slid into bed. The bed dipped a little with his weight and he held his breath, but Jaxxon didn't move. He didn't dare cuddle him, so he lay there, stiff on his back for ages, staring into the dark room, listening to Jaxxon breathe. For once his brain didn't whir incessantly, somehow calmed by Jaxxon's steady breathing.

CHAPTER 16

Was there a fucking puppy in his bed? Jaxxon had slept deeply and he woke up to the soft sound of muffled snoring. He must be dreaming. He rolled over and his foot connected with something hard.

"Ow, fuck."

"Freddy?" He'd kicked Freddy in the shin?

"Did you just wake up and chose violence?"

"I don't think that's supposed to be used literally." Jaxxon rubbed his eyes. "What are you doing in my bed, and why do you sound like a puppy?"

"Are you saying I'm cute?"

"Sure. Take that part of what I said and roll with it." Jaxxon closed his eyes for a moment. "Why are you in my bed?" He knew they hadn't done anything, so it was a bit of a mystery. Mystery ... wasn't there something Freddy had said about that? Fuck, he needed caffeine before he tried to put all this nonsense into something coherent.

"I came to tell you news and then you just went to bed."

"And you thought the best plan of action was to join me?" Jaxxon would've sat up and glared at Freddy, except he was rubbing his foot against Jaxxon's leg, and it was rather nice.

"I hoped you wouldn't mind. I mean, we've already—"

"—fucked in a shower? Yes. I suppose that might give you ideas about what is appropriate."

"I'm not being appropriate?"

"We were supposed to make a plan first."

"We can do that now." Freddy sounded far too hopeful, like an enthusiastic puppy wanting to be taken for a walk. Jaxxon had probably stretched that metaphor too far, but he hadn't had any coffee yet and his brain was fixated on Freddy being in his bed.

"What's the time?" Jaxxon needed to go to work. The cars had arrived and had been assembled yesterday. He had a fresh team for this event. To prevent burnout among the mechanics across the 23-race schedule, they rotated their staff at different races as well as between S1 and their other teams, which also helped upskill the younger mechanics into the pressures of S1. Today would be finalising all the checks before FP1 tomorrow and doing pitlane practises to ensure the team was ready to work together for the race.

"Let me check." Freddy leaped out of bed, actually leaped, far too enthusiastic for this time of day. Jaxxon was not a morning person. At all. But when Freddy stood by the window—butt naked—and drew back the curtains, Jaxxon began to appreciate that there might be some benefits to being awake just now. The taut muscles stretching from his shoulders down his spine to his rounded strong ass. Freddy turned around, his arms spread out wide. Daylight framed his body, putting him into shadow, which made him appear like an artistic pornographic dream. Holy Jesus. Jaxxon groaned, his gaze glued to Freddy's perfect cock, erect, jutting out of his neatly sculptured hair. Jaxxon's own cock tented the bedsheets and he rolled onto his stomach to hide his reaction.

"Shall I follow you?" Yes, anywhere.

Jaxxon buried his head in the pillow, a useless attempt to hide from the heat surging inside him.

"Jaxxon?"

"Um, sure." He grabbed his phone to check the time, except there were a million notifications from Aurora and Victor and Mike and Skye, and he started scrolling through them until he'd done enough work for his erection to fade. Skye was back in England, so it'd be evening there.

> **Skye**
> Looks like a staff member let in one of the camera crew. I've got some fussy imagery of someone bundling out Sebastian Damiamo's trophy, but I can't tell who. Vid in email.

He sat bolt upright, and opened his email to read Skye's comment about why they'd assumed it was a camera person or staff member at the other team. Too much knowledge of the security systems and the angles of the cameras they had. He watched the video and all of Skye's comments made sense.

"Everything okay?" Freddy leaned against Jaxxon's shoulder, a comforting presence. Jaxxon had been so focused on his email that he hadn't noticed Freddy climb back into the bed. A quick glance over found sheets covering Freddy's spectacular body and a confusing twist of gratitude that he'd covered up and being gutted at the missed opportunity made him shiver.

"Yeah, just an email from Skye about Seb's trophy."

"Oh. Good news?"

"Not really. Why don't you watch it and see what you think?" He held out his phone for Freddy and hit play again. The security footage was a little grainy, and the person who took the trophy off the shelf kept their head ducked away from the cameras.

"Is that Mark?" Freddy asked.

"Who?"

"One of the sound engineers." Freddy gasped.

"Fuck." They swore together.

"John said in the bar that it was one of the sound engineers, Mark, who mentioned turning off the cameras at the Gamble Racing launch." Freddy wrapped his arm around Jaxxon's waist, still leaning against him. It shouldn't feel so comforting. If anything made sense in this world, it was that Jaxxon was commander of people, he didn't need comfort while he organised his thoughts. But it was nice to have Freddy's naked body pressed against him.

"Then we need to find this Mark person and talk to them." He kept his focus on the problem at hand, not the way Freddy's hands rested lightly on his waist.

"Shower first and breakfast."

"And coffee. I'm not doing anything without coffee." Jaxxon flicked through the rest of his messages, but it was nothing that couldn't wait. He quickly replied to Mike, pleased that the rehab centre would let Mike visit to watch the race with Socrates, and let him know that Skye might have found something about Seb's trophy but not to get his —or Socrates—hopes up. He didn't mention the connection with the sound guy on purpose. He needed more information first.

"Come on. Let's get ready for the day." Freddy's upbeat enthusiasm as he pushed away from Jaxxon and grinned motivated Jaxxon to get moving. He wanted to see Freddy's hazel eyes flicker and darken, like the ever-changing colours in the forest, with browns and greens and a little bit of gold like the sunshine attempting to shine through the growth to reach the forest floor. Jesus, now he was being all poetic about someone he'd hooked up with once.

"You just want to get me naked and in the shower. It's like you have a thing for showers..." Jaxxon's teasing sounded off to himself, but Freddy grinned as if he knew what Jaxxon had meant and adored his attempt.

"Is this going to upset your plans?" Freddy was still smiling but the glow faded a little.

He put his phone down. "We haven't made a plan yet."

"We should."

"Why?"

"It's important to you. You said that."

"It is. And yet, you've managed to just be in my life without it needing to matter yet."

Freddy swallowed and half-turned away, before looking back over his shoulder; his naked shoulder. He liked how comfortable they were with each other, how easy it was to talk to Freddy... A chill wind breezed over his spine and he put his phone down. Freddy's job was to make people want to talk to him. Had he simply fallen under the same charming trap?

"That's not a great reason to not plan, Jaxxon." Freddy disappeared into the ensuite before Jaxxon could agree with him. He paced up and down the bedroom a few times. This was silly. He was a grown man. He enjoyed being with Freddy. He should just embrace this while it lasted. And yes, they would need a plan to deal with the fall out if it didn't work out. Freddy's mention of a stalker in his past at dinner meant Freddy would likely need some reassurance that Jaxxon wasn't going to do any too intense; although how he would achieve that seemed impossible. He could hardly just state that he wasn't going to stalk Freddy. Aside from being weird and intrusive, it wasn't exactly something anyone could promise. He wasn't going to stalk him. But simply stating that wasn't ever going to be enough. Actions meant more than words when dealing with an awful moment in the past.

"Freddy." He walked into the ensuite ready to have the discussion, but the sight of Freddy in the shower covered in soap suds stole all his words. "Gah."

"Is that a good gah or a bad one?" Freddy caressed him with his gaze, sending trails of heat all over Jaxxon's skin. "Never mind. I see the evidence that it was a good gah. It's nice to see that I can reduce you to vague sounds." Freddy's gaze locked onto Jaxxon's cock.

He licked his lips, suddenly very dry, and had to dig deep to say something remotely more intelligent than another gah. "We need to do a SWOT analysis." He would've cringed at how dorky he sounded, except Freddy's eyes widened and his cheeks flushed as he dragged his gaze over Jaxxon possessively.

"Yes."

"You have no idea what a SWOT analysis is, do you?"

"Nope, but it sounds sexy when you show off your business acumen. Analyse me." Freddy dragged his hand over his chest, trailing it down his stomach, across each of his abs, and down to his hips. He moved his hips, thrusting out his cock, and Jaxxon nearly choked. Freddy's hand emphasised his lean athletic body, and as he stared at Jaxxon, it felt like he was daring Jaxxon to do something about his blatant erection.

"Yeah, no." His breath rushed over his lips, a reminder of the hot desert wind in Kenya, when he'd been on the rally circuit there.

"I could make it sexy." Freddy lifted his hands over his head and stood so the water flowed over his athletic form, and before Jaxxon knew it, he was in the shower too, hands on Freddy's chest. Freddy leaned forward and kissed him, a quick brush of lips, then he nuzzled against Jaxxon's neck. The sudden intimacy had his cock ramrod hard, and he pressed his body against Freddy's lithe form. His heart thumped, yes, yes, yes, wild and needy, with the water from the shower prickling hot patterns on his skin. Freddy's hair was wet, strands against his forehead with the sandalwood scent of his shampoo filling Jaxxon's nostrils. Freddy had managed to grow a decent amount of stubble overnight, and it was rough against Jaxxon's skin, opposing the texture of his lips and the water. The onslaught of sensation made Jaxxon dizzy and he clung to Freddy, fingers digging into his flesh.

"Jaxxon Loharani-Jones." Freddy's use of his media voice beckoned him. "Tell me about this SWOT business."

Jaxxon spluttered, as if he'd choked on a mouthful of shower water. "Basically—" He couldn't talk while Freddy was torturing his neck with his soft lips and rough stubble. He rested his face against Freddy, buried against his wet hair and let the water try to distract him from the surging sensations in his cock and belly. It didn't work. His legs trembled and his vision went hazy with desire.

"Nothing about you is basic, Jaxxon."

"What?"

"When you say, basically, you know I'm waiting for some complex concept that probably sounds simple to you..." Freddy undersold himself—the man could talk for hours about racing data—and Jaxxon pushed Freddy away, taking one step backwards in the shower. He needed space to be able to respond to Freddy's words. How on earth could the man talk while touching him? It was beyond comprehension. It was enough to stay upright while electricity surged in his veins, centred in his impossibly hard cock. He ached.

"What?"

"Explain SWOT to me." Freddy's nostrils flared.

Jaxxon blinked. "SWOT is simple." He closed his eyes for a second, removing all temptation, except now he could smell Freddy's masculine sandalwood shampoo. "It stands for strengths, weaknesses, opportunities, and threats. You just go through—"

"Just?"

"Yes." He cleared his throat. "You go through each of the four items and write down whatever comes to mind, then it forms the basis of your plan because you use those notes as the basis of understanding for the situation."

"Only you could make basis of understanding sound hot." Freddy placed his hands on Jaxxon's ass and pulled them back together, close again, with their cocks touching. Heat surged, like a fever dream, but for the very best reasons. Desire ruled and he responded with needy grasping hands. He had to touch Freddy everywhere. This man and his enjoyment of Jaxxon's ambition was everything. A low growl rumbled against his chest, and he realised it'd been him, the noise vibrating from deep inside himself.

"Kiss me."

Freddy licked his collarbone instead, the heat from his tongue dragged down until he circled Jaxxon's nipple with his mouth and sucked. He didn't care what they'd been talking about. It could wait. He wanted all of Freddy's mouth. Now. Everywhere. He plucked Freddy's right hand off his ass and pushed it between them, wrapping both their hands around their cocks. Just like last time. Freddy shook his head and pushed Jaxxon's hand upwards until both their hands were splayed across Jaxxon's stomach instead, away from their cocks. The more innocent touch, a light caress as Freddy held his hand, slammed desire into his groin and he moaned.

"Concentrate on the plan. What was the first one?" Freddy whispered. The first what? All his attention was on the way Freddy's fingers entangled with his hand, firm enough to prevent him from touching their cocks again, but light enough that Jaxxon could move if he really wanted to. It took him a moment to process what Freddy had asked.

"Strengths." Jaxxon swallowed; an early morning without coffee and the overwhelming lust of being here in the shower with Freddy made it impossible to think of anything beyond Freddy. "Not physical strength, although I do appreciate your wiry athleticism."

"Do you?" Freddy let go of Jaxxon's body and posed to show off his biceps, so Jaxxon planted a kiss on them, first the right one, then the left, but when he went to hug Freddy again, Freddy put his hands on Jaxxon's chest and kept them apart.

"Freddy." He whined a little in the back of his throat, uncaring how needy he sounded. "You know I do, and you know it's a strength of yours too, since you took me bouldering to show yourself off."

Freddy lifted his head. "It worked."

"Obviously." He showed Freddy just how much he enjoyed Freddy's physique, taking his time to explore every lean muscle with his hands.

"Before you get too carried away..." Freddy's voice trailed off.

"What?"

"I mean—"

"Would you like me to stop?" Jaxxon dropped his hands to his sides. Consent mattered more than any other consideration and overwrote the surging need which made his pulse accelerate like a car coming out of a hairpin.

"No, but you have to. You wanted a plan and we still don't have one."

Jaxxon closed his eyes for a second. "We've already decided to give this a go."

"Have we, though?"

"Maybe not in words, but our actions have. We can't seem to keep our hands off each other, so I'd say we have." He slid his hands over Freddy's ribcage and down his sides to his hips. He used his hands to frame Freddy's cock, loving the erotism in the contrasting tones of their skin, with the shower water running in rivulets over Freddy's body. He wanted to lick the pathways of the water, as it flowed over and around each muscle.

"Okay. Is that the plan?" Freddy shook his head and water sprayed in odd directions. "I don't need a plan. This is your thing, and I want you to be certain."

"Maybe we should keep it simple. Let's agree not to be assholes to each other. We have to be professional out there in the paddock." He hadn't been in this situation before and honestly, all he wanted was Freddy's cock in his mouth. It would be the easiest thing in the world to drop to his knees, with his hands keeping hold of Freddy's hips and sink his mouth over Freddy's cock. Nothing else mattered; except the tiny voice in his head reminding him that Freddy was right to remind him. Plans always made things better.

"I am older than you and therefore more experienced. If you want a plan. Let's have a plan."

Jaxxon laughed, trying to ignore the flash of hurt that flickered on Freddy's face for the briefest split-second. "Yes, old man." It was easier to tease him that wonder what that look was about.

"Why are we still talking anyway?" Freddy dropped to his knees and slid his mouth over Jaxxon's cock. He instantly went from firm to achingly hard as Freddy's hot mouth sucked him. Fucking hell. Freddy doing the one thing Jaxxon had wanted to do, had planned to do, was a lot. His heartbeat sped up to triple time, a wild frenzy.

"I like this plan." His brain was fuzzy; from Freddy's mouth and the overwhelming sensation of his attentions and from not enough caffeine, although that had to be an excuse. This was the best way to start a day. He threaded his hands through Freddy's wet hair, tugging in the rhythm he wanted. It didn't take long. He'd already been taken to the edge by Freddy's insistence on trying to work out a plan for … whatever this was going to be. Hopefully more than blowjobs in the shower. Fuck, he wanted so much more and logically the very last person who should have his mouth around his cock was someone in the press. This could go very wrong, and yet, it felt so incredibly perfect that he didn't care. He clung to Freddy's hair, closed his eyes and just let himself feel everything. The hot slide of Freddy's mouth, the way he worked his tongue, the tightness of his throat.

"Fucking fuck. You are perfect. Freddy." He cried out as lights flashed behind his eyes and he came hard and fast. "Freddy." He grabbed the shower wall, unsteady on his feet, as Freddy licked all the way up his stomach and chest, all the way to his mouth, where they kissed. An erratic meeting of their mouths, desperate. Freddy tasted like cum, salty and fucking perfect.

"Hold me." Freddy grabbed Jaxxon's hand and wrapped his fingers around his cock. He stroked him hard. "Rougher. More." Freddy's voice was rough, well fucked, and it made his heart do weird flipping things. He stroked Freddy quickly, until Freddy's mouth hung open. Jaxxon leaned in and sucked Freddy's bottom lip, loving the way

Freddy's eyes glistened and glowed, darker than usual, and his gaze never left him.

"Yes." Freddy cried out, spurting all over Jaxxon's stomach and hand. "I like this plan." And then he leaned his head on Jaxxon's chest, eyes closed, with the shower water still drumming onto the light skin of his shoulders. Jaxxon wanted ...

"We should do this in a bed sometime."

"Everywhere. I want you everywhere." Freddy's soft sleepy murmur made Jaxxon's chest clench a little. He washed them both quickly, going through the practical motions, so they could fall back onto the bed, and cuddle for a while. They could finalise the plan later, when Jaxxon's eyes weren't quite so heavy, and his limbs were capable of holding himself up again.

CHAPTER 17

Freddy hadn't spoken to Jaxxon for almost two weeks. He missed him. Not just his kisses, or the quiet groan in the back of his throat when he came, or the clever sparkle in his dark brown eyes. It was chatting to him that he missed most of all. Fucking hell. He was turning into a sap. He rolled his eyes. Only yesterday over a beer with Georgia, she'd told him just to ring Jaxxon and stop all this agonising. The implication that if he carried on moping about, he'd become pathetic, was apparent in her tone.

Freddy
Am I pathetic?

He didn't press send. He shouldn't even let these old thoughts seep into his conscious. He deleted the text, fanning away the annoyed heat in his cheeks, and paced over to the windows, to lean on the glass. The glass was cool against his forehead. Because he wanted to remind himself how far he'd come, he scrolled through some of the notes his old therapist had sent him from back when Chester had been stalking him. One question jumped out; why did you wait for him to initiate all conversations? At the time, he'd been furious, and even now the same red mist rushed up his spine. It wasn't his fault. And they'd discussed that. Yes, Chester's choice to stalk him was completely Chester's issue. But—the therapist wanted to know—had his passiveness been a reason that Chester had found him attractive in the first place. When he told Georgia about the conversation, she'd immediately sacked the therapist and found him his current one, who'd explained about victim blaming in abusive relationships. Chester would've made his choices regardless of what Freddy did or didn't do.

All this introspection wasn't good for him, so he called John to chat about the trophy issue.

"It's not even silly season yet, and people are already discussing contracts." John's chatter helped ease the worry in Freddy's head. He half-listened to John carry on about one of the mid-field teams and rumours that they were planning to dump their rookie after he'd spun out in all three races so far.

"It's a bit soon to be making that call." Freddy should take his own advice. Yes, he hadn't heard from Jaxxon since the Thursday before the Australian race, but it was too soon to think dramatically about what that might mean. Jaxxon had been busy doing his job. During the race weekend, it made sense to stay clear of him and let him work. Freddy had his own work to do. Since then, after travelling home to his empty apartment in London, Freddy had been trying to squirrel out information about the sound tech, just for something to occupy himself.

"Yeah. Are you calling about Mark?"

"I'm guessing there's nothing new." The hollow ache in his chest had nothing to do with not being able to solve the puzzle of the missing trophies—which frankly made it sound like a 1950s comic, his favourite type of reading material—and everything to do with missing Jaxxon.

"No, sorry. Mark has been transferred to another department by the higher-ups. Carol said she had nothing to do with the move. She sounded pretty annoyed that she'd lost a good sound tech, and told me not to get involved. The police were dealing with it and we should leave them to it."

"Damned lot of good that's going to do."

"Unfortunately yes. When are you heading over to Imola?"

"Probably Wednesday or Thursday, and you?"

"Tomorrow. I've doing one of those filler pieces and I'm going to the factory where they make the crash barriers and then to Imola to film them installing them for the race."

"Enjoy."

John laughed. "Don't be jealous. You'll get the next one, I'm sure."

"Yeah. I'm not jealous of the filler piece, but you get to spend extra time in Italy eating all the good food."

"Ha, good point." They signed off with a bit more banter, and Freddy stared at his phone. Jaxxon hadn't sent him a text since they'd woken up together in his hotel room before Australia. Freddy didn't want to think too hard about what the silence meant; maybe Freddy needed the space anyway. This lack of communication was one way to continue to achieve space from Jaxxon. Lord knew that when they were in the same room, Freddy damned near vibrated with sexual tension. He missed him and even though a little part of him wanted to contact Jaxxon just to prove that he wasn't passive, he wasn't going to make the first move just because of something his sacked therapist had said. He pushed off the glass and stretched out his shoulders. Keep it simple, Freddy. He could send Jaxxon a message because he wanted to; he didn't need another reason. He missed him.

Freddy
We never did get to that plan

One little text shouldn't matter and now it was sent, he realised how much all this introspection was annoying bull-shit. He'd always been like this; except when he was driving. The world went away when he was in the car, and he only had to think about the car and the race. When that clarity disappeared, and fluff had crept in while he was driving, he'd known it was time to retire.

Jaxxon
Can you send me a draft?

Freddy
Because you are so busy and you
believe that I'm not, so I have the time to
do this?

He finished with a smiling face emoji so Jaxxon would

know he was joking.

> **Jaxxon**
> Yes to the former and I can't comment
> on the latter since I am unaware of those
> details of your job.

In other words, yes, but Jaxxon was too polite to say outright that he knew. Well, Jaxxon knew jack-shit about the work that went in behind the scenes of the live presentations of each race. Freddy resisted the urge to outline what he'd done; he'd had enough therapy to realise that the need to explain came from growing up trying to be enough to get noticed by his father. Usually whenever he became all irritating like this, he would go to his club and find someone to fuck. He shuddered. The thought of being with anyone who wasn't Jaxxon was repellent.

> **Freddy**
> How about we both do a quick draft then
> meet in Milan Tues before Imola

There was no response. Whatever, he'd book something and if Jaxxon didn't come, he'd have a nice day or two in Milan. He needed a couple of new suits, so it wouldn't be wasted time. He flicked an email to Georgia so she could organise it for him ... or berate him because he'd forgotten some other appointment. Whatever. He opened his fridge and decided it all looked boring. Perhaps he could go out for dinner, maybe to one of his clubs, just not the sex one. If only the Gamble Racing headquarters weren't so far away. It would too much of a gesture to get a helicopter flight there just to see Jaxxon, especially since they were barely dating or whatever, and Jaxxon would be uncomfortable if Freddy spent too much money on a random thing. His phone dinged, saving him from his endless introspection. God, he was even annoying himself. Ergh.

Jaxxon
How about tonight? I'm in London for meetings, so we could meet for dinner.

Freddy grinned. If he'd been into manifestation, he'd believe that simply thinking about having dinner with Jaxxon had made it a reality. Maybe he wasn't the only one who missed the other. He replied with a thumbs up.

Jaxxon
Where? When?

Freddy assumed Jaxxon would want somewhere private without cameras. Any of the ancient gentleman's clubs, like White's, would suffice, but Freddy would be glad to avoid any possibility of seeing his father. But ... He clicked his tongue a couple of times. He really did want to impress Jaxxon, so it would have to be somewhere special. Special, private, and not too flashy. He liked the challenge of that.

Freddy
Where in London are you?

Jaxxon
Knightsbridge.

Not too far from his apartment. The idea that Jaxxon had been close by for most of the day made his head spin a little, but also it meant he could take Jaxxon to his favourite little restaurant. He rang them up, using his name and fame to get a last-minute booking for two, then sent Jaxxon a text with the name and address.

Two hours later, Freddy sat alone in the private booth at the back of the restaurant.

> **Freddy**
> Ready when you are

> **Jaxxon**
> My meeting took more time than I anticipated but I am in a cab now. ETA 15 minutes

Freddy grinned at his phone. The way Jaxxon always wrote his texts out in whole sentences was so adorable. He pulled the bell-pull—because of course this place had a bell-pull in their private booth—and let the waiter know that Jaxxon was running late. He declined a drink, content with sparkling water until Jaxxon arrived, and clicked open the comic he was reading on his phone.

"Sorry about that." Jaxxon slid into his seat and Freddy blinked. He'd obviously come straight from a meeting. His dark blue tie was loose and askew, and he had his jacket slung over one shoulder. The pinstriped navy suit pants clung to Jaxxon's thighs. Freddy's breath trembled as he released it from his tight lungs, and he closed his fists tight, because he wanted to peel those pants off Jaxxon and lick him. Fuck. This attraction, the chemistry and desire, grew every time he saw Jaxxon, and he wasn't quite ready to embrace what that might mean.

"It's fine." His voice sounded like it'd been dragged over a gravel road, and he cleared his throat. "I had a book to read."

"You read?"

"No. I only mentioned a book to impress you." Freddy refused to be embarrassed by his love of comics. Letting himself enjoy them and not the serious books his father said he ought to read—to impress others—had been a hard-fought win.

"Ha. What are you reading?"

"The puzzle of the island treasure. It's a comic." He didn't see any pity on Jaxxon's face—not even a flicker of a reaction to his admission—so he barrelled on. "I had a laugh the other day because the trophy problem sounds like a comic title; you know, The Puzzle of the Missing Trophies, bracket, and how Freddy found them. End bracket."

The corners of Jaxxon's eyes crinkled as he smiled. "Did you just speak punctuation at me?"

"As part of a fictional comic title. Yes."

"I—" Jaxxon paused, then sipped some water. "Your book sounds fun."

The validation from Jaxxon's approval of his reading matter warmed him all the way through, like a big hug, and he smiled.

Jaxxon hung his jacket over the back of the chair and sat down. "How did you get a booking here? I heard this place is fully booked for months in advance."

"Yes, but they also keep this booth available every night

in case a celebrity decides to attend at the last minute."

"And you name-dropped yourself?"

Freddy shrugged. "What on earth is the point of being the son of a Duke who used to drive S1 cars and now is on telly all the time if I can't use it to get a booking at one of London's most exclusive restaurants. And we're lucky tonight as the head chef is actually here, so we will get the authentic meal."

"What do you mean?"

"Most of these famous chef big name restaurants don't have the actual chef doing the day-to-day cooking. They have a team who cooks to their specifications."

Jaxxon nodded. "That's so logical that I feel like it's something I should've known."

"Do you often worry that you should've known stuff?" Freddy wanted to know, and he hoped the burning longing in his chest was merely to do with his desire to completely understand everything about Jaxxon, and not the fucking spectacular way Jaxxon looked tonight, like someone who'd done a hard day's work and needed to come home to Freddy's welcoming arms.

"Yes. My job requires me to talk to a lot of incredibly wealthy people and I didn't grow up among them. I've worked very hard to fit in with them because it's necessary for my career. I don't like reminders of what I don't know because—" Jaxxon squirmed a little.

"Why are you uncomfortable?"

"I've never told anyone this, but I'm a bloody hypocrite."

"Why?" He wanted to rub his forehead, as if that would diminish his confusion. Freddy admired how Jaxxon navigated the S1 world as a Black man in a predominantly white sport, and he was authentic in his desire to continue Socrates' goal in diversifying Gamble Racing, not just with queer people, but across all type of marginalised people.

Jaxxon sighed, his broad chest rising and falling. "I use my humble upbringing whenever it brings me an advantage—"

"Yes, you mentioned it in our first interview. That doesn't make you a hypocrite, just a human chasing a dream and using anything to help get you to a goal. I've just used my background to get me dinner here tonight."

"Will you let me finish?"

Freddy gulped, then nodded.

"I don't want people to discover my humble beginnings simply because I've used the wrong fork at dinner or ordered the wrong type of wine with a meal, or any of the myriad of other rules rich people subtly adhere to as examples of how people ought to treat them better because they have money."

Freddy waited, biting his tongue so he didn't smile at the way Jaxxon phrased it—subtly adhere to—forcing him to stay quiet until he was certain Jaxxon had finished. "You want to control the story?"

"Yes, which makes me a hypocrite."

"No. It makes you human. You have goals and you are strategic to achieve them. We all do it."

"Thank you for finding the upside." Jaxxon sent him a strange look, then waved his hand. "I don't seek out the rules for fitting into a rich crowd because I want to be like them. I don't comply to get other people's approval, but I really don't want to stand out for the wrong reasons."

"That makes complete sense. It's a bit like being queer."

Jaxxon nodded. "Yes, I suppose it is rather like coming out. I hadn't thought of it that way before. I'm happy talking about my humble upbringing among some rich people, but sometimes I just want to fit in."

"And using the wrong fork can accidentally out yourself, so to speak."

Jaxxon laughed. "Don't make it sound ridiculous. It's not really about the forks."

"Or the forking."

Jaxxon rolled his eyes, still grinning. "Freddy." Yes, there it was. His name in that tone. Fuck, he'd adored that, probably a bit too much. It was addictive.

"Would you like a drink? I didn't get the matching drinks because it's always too much alcohol." This restaurant only had a degustation menu, which meant they wouldn't have to order.

"I'll have what you are having."

Freddy's chest swelled slightly. "Clever."

"What?" Jaxxon paused. "Okay, fine. Yes, I do often say that when I'm unsure. It's a good technique because then I know I'll fit in, but occasionally backfires."

"Don't tell me you said that to Mr Dadeireyes?" The elderly man was on the board of S1.

Jaxxon's shoulders shook as he shook his head. "Yes. No one warned me that he has very, um, interesting tastes."

"You mean that he likes a Bloody Mary but with brandy, not vodka."

"It was fucking terrible. I thought the juice was rotten."

"He also likes to dip pickles in his ice cream, and sprinkles sugar on salt and vinegar crisps."

Jaxxon clamped his hand over his mouth and cackled. "I used to dip the McDonalds pickles into their thick shakes when I was a kid, but Mr Dadeireyes is nearly ninety."

"Are you calling a Board Member childish?" Freddy could hardly contain his laughter and the absolute joy glowing in Jaxxon's eyes was worth it.

"I would never—" Jaxxon coughed. "—dare do something so disrespectful to someone in his position."

Freddy lost it at Jaxxon's dry sarcasm. The waiter walked into their booth, and he wiped his eyes before he ordered a bottle of pinot noir to share.

"Perhaps you would prefer something lighter to compliment the first few courses, my Lord?" The waiter said. He couldn't look at Jaxxon as the waiter used his title.

"How about we have a glass of bubbles each to start? That should get us through the lighter courses." Knowing this restaurant, they'd bring the whole bottle, but he didn't have to drink it.

"Very good, my Lord." The waiter left again, and Freddy breathed out slowly. He glanced at Jaxxon who wasn't smiling.

"What is the matter?"

"Nothing." Jaxxon fiddled with his napkin.

"Fuck. You aren't comfortable with all the Lord business, are you?"

Jaxxon just shook his head once.

"I'd tell you to ignore it, but maybe you should put it in your plan under ..." He waved his hand because he'd forgotten all the details of the acronym that reminded him of a fly swat but if he said that it'd be wrong.

"Would it be a weakness or a threat?" Jaxxon asked.

CHAPTER 18

Jaxxon knew it was silly to be overwhelmed by a waiter in a fancy restaurant calling Freddy, my Lord. Freddy never behaved as a man of rank. He was just Freddy; bold and funny and with a tendency to overthink. Freddy talked through his problems, seemingly able to find a solution with the illogical method.

"I'm not threatened by your title, Freddy."

"It'd be weird if you were. I'm hardly going to, I don't know, print my name on a piece of paper and force feed it to you."

"Freddy!" He couldn't believe he'd say something like that. He was saved from a longer response when a pair of waiters arrived, one carrying an ice bucket on a stand with a bottle of champagne and two glasses, while the other carried two white plates, each had four oysters neatly arranged on a bed of salt, with tiny pink and white cubes scattered over the oysters.

"Your rock oysters with gooseberry, cucumber, and

almond." Once the waiter left, Freddy leaned closer with his elbows on the table.

"Talk me through the process of creating this plan." Freddy wore a crisp white shirt with shiny cuff links that caught the light as he leaned forward.

"Essentially, I thought we could start with a SWOT analysis and use the answers to build the plan." He didn't want to admit that it would help him prepare for their inevitable break up—he'd already assumed they would sooner or later because he'd never had a relationship longer than a few months—and he needed to understand how he was going to deal with it. This one was going to hurt, and not just because they'd see each other at work all the time.

"SWOT." Relief swept over Freddy's features.

"Did you forget what it was called?" He was probably smirking, so he picked up one of the oysters and ate it. The little cubes of fruit were crunchy compared to the meatiness of the oyster, with a wonderous combination of sweet and salt on his tongue. He had another one because it was so good. The excellent food was one benefit of working in this world of wealthy people.

"To be fair, you are quite distracting." Freddy's gaze swept over him, hovering on his mouth

"Try one of these." He ate his third one and while it was amazing, he also regretted it because now he had only one left.

Freddy shook his head. "I don't like oysters. It's the texture."

"Makes sense." He'd heard others say that too. "Let's do this SWOT through word association."

"Okay." For someone who spent his life discussing racing data and complicated team strategies, Freddy looked quite lost. "You can have my oysters if you want."

"Thanks." Jaxxon reached out and touched Freddy's hand. "And relax. SWOT isn't that complicated. If we are trying to build a plan that helps us manage this situation, then we run through each section and just say what you first think."

Freddy swallowed. "Let's go."

"What do you think are the strengths of what we are doing here?"

"Chemistry." Freddy pulled his hands away and picked up an oyster. He held it out and Jaxxon couldn't resist opening his mouth hopefully. Freddy tipped the shell and the oyster with the little fruity flavours slid onto his tongue. He savoured the little morsel.

"I could feed you all night. The moan you just made was obscene." The oyster shell rattled as Freddy put it back on the plate.

"I've never had something so amazing. I could eat these all night."

"One day I'll take you to New Zealand and feed you fresh oysters."

"Promises." Jaxxon licked his bottom lip, loving the way Freddy's gaze hovered on his tongue, so he dragged it along his lip again. Freddy closed his eyes on a long blink, then grabbed the bottle of champagne and poured some for both of them.

"One day."

"Not in the summer break. There's too much to do."

Freddy lifted his glass. "Always so practical, Jaxxon.

Let's go at the end of the season, then. I've never been, but apparently they have the best oysters in the whole world."

Jaxxon tried to ignore the rush in his torso as Freddy assumed they'd still be doing this—whatever it was—at the end of the season. "How do you know they are the best? You just said you don't even like oysters."

"My brother's wife likes them. They go once a year." Freddy's tone changed, hinting at admiration.

"You like them." Jaxxon wasn't sure, but the few times Freddy had mentioned his family, it'd been with loosely disguised hurt.

Freddy cleared his throat and picked up another oyster. "Yes. It's only my father I have disdain for. Never mind that, eat this."

Jaxxon let Freddy feed him another oyster, and he understood Freddy's comment about chemistry completely. He let the flavours linger on his tongue, like swimming in the sea with Freddy's mouth against his and their hands all over each other. So good. "It's more than chemistry. I enjoy talking to you, Freddy."

"Oh, you say the sweetest things."

His cheeks warmed; he let out an unsteady breath. "What about weaknesses?" He had to focus on getting this plan sorted before he got too involved. Before he got hurt.

"Obviously I don't have any? You?"

"Freddy." He loved the way Freddy's eyes lit up whenever he used that tone, and he'd started to seek out moments when he could use it. "The plan is about us. What are the weaknesses of this plan to—" He wasn't sure how they wanted to define this.

"Fuck each other because we can't resist each other?"

He choked on a laugh. "Jesus, Freddy. Yeah ... That about sums it up."

"Obviously, the main weakness is that I'm breaking my no paddock rule for you."

"Does that bother you?"

Freddy pulled an odd face. "Bother? No. It's fucking scary. I'm basically trusting you not to make it fucking awful..."

"I'm not going to stalk you."

"I realise that isn't likely."

His frantic heartbeat slowed and he reached out to hold Freddy's hand. "But that doesn't stop you being worried about it. I get it. There's a difference between qualitative risk and quantified risk, like a driver saying the rears are losing grip, and seeing the data on the screen indicating tyre wear and traction."

"I understand the difference. Why do Team Principals always treat drivers like we don't understand data?" Freddy's eyes narrowed and Jaxxon relaxed, gratified that the conversation might prove useful to Freddy.

"Probably because Team Principals tend to be engineers or mechanics, and drivers have a more intuitive understanding of the car. It's quantitative vs qualitative risk in action. Both are required for the best outcome."

"And are we the best outcome?" Freddy picked up another oyster and Jaxxon let Freddy feed him. He closed his eyes to savour the flavour combinations, opening his eyes again when Freddy traced his thumb along Jaxxon's bottom lip. The rough callus on Freddy's thumb, from bouldering, made his balls heavy, sparks rushing down his torso, and he had to blink to stay centred in the moment, when all he wanted to do was clamber over the table and kiss Freddy.

"I've never been with someone who wanted to plan a relationship." Freddy dragged him back to earth, or to his chair anyway, and he almost protested that he was planning the end of this fling, but he didn't dare articulate that. Besides, it wasn't all about him anyway.

"I want you to feel like your worries matter to me. You've had a bad experience with someone in the paddock —" Jaxxon didn't know many details apart from Freddy mentioning that he'd been stalked by an ex, but it was enough to realise that Freddy would want plenty of agency and choice if they were going to do this.

"I don't want to be defined by one asshole who made bad choices."

"I didn't suggest that. Only that it's good to be on the same page about what we want."

"Okay. What's next in your SWOT test?"

Jaxxon glanced down. There were only two oysters left, so he sipped some of his champagne instead. The dry bubbles added to the heady swirl inside.

"It's not a test. It's a planning tool."

"And?"

"The O stands for opportunities. What opportunities arise from us being together?" He gasped and held up one finger. "And if you say that you'll get all the Gamble Racing gossip first... No. That's more of a threat than an opportunity."

Freddy placed his hand on his chest and winked. "You wound me."

"Do I though?"

"No. I've definitely thought about the advantages for my job, but don't stress, I will try—try—not to be too keen when it comes to S1 gossip."

"Thanks."

"Of course, you might want to know all the gossip from other teams before it becomes widely known..." Freddy waggled his eyebrows.

Jaxxon was tempted. "You really know how to tempt someone, but no. From a long-term point of view, it wouldn't be a strategic advantage to have other teams assume a flow of information between us. It would be bad for both of us; other Team Principals would stop talking to you and I'm conscious that I'm quite young for this job and will need to earn my place among the other Team Principals."

"That's fair. It's obvious why Socrates employed you."

"Why?"

"Listen to the way you've thought about this and realised the potential problems."

"Let's park this one under a potential threat to our jobs."

Freddy nodded. "Okay. Is this helping?"

"I think so. At the very least, it's proving that we can discuss difficult things without being rude to each other."

"Pretty low bar." Freddy leaned back in his chair, further from Jaxxon.

He was saved from answering when the waiter walked in with two bowls. "This is our Polish gazpacho with cucumber, curds, and lovage." The dark grey bowls were filled with a green liquid that was probably soup. As soon as the waiter left, Jaxxon pulled out his phone and looked it up.

"Gazpacho is a cold soup." Freddy said.

"What makes it Polish?"

"No idea. What does the internet say?"

The tightness in his chest eased when he wasn't the only ignorant one in the room. "It says that it's a cold soup made from salted cucumber and potato."

"Let's try it. I've no idea what lovage is either."

He typed that in too. "It's an herb that tastes like celery." He put his phone on the table screen side down and tried some of the soup. Sour bitterness was contrasted with the creamy texture. "I prefer the oysters."

"There is still a couple left. Have them."

Jaxxon didn't need any encouragement, so he ate the last two oysters, loving the way they tasted like the ocean, with the crunch of the sweet fruit. "So good."

"Your good food face looks a lot like your sex face."

"Freddy!" His tone came out naturally, and it made Freddy's eyes sparkle and his cheeks flushed with colour. Warm spread through Jaxxon, centring in his cock. This whole dinner was one long piece of foreplay, and that realisation only added to the anticipation pulsing in his veins.

"It's true." Freddy's unashamed enjoyment of Jaxxon's company was so special, and he knew he was already falling deeply for Freddy.

"Are you looking forward to Imola?" With a cough, Jaxxon changed the subject. He was already hard. He hardly needed the reminder that he wanted Freddy's wicked mouth to do more than talk.

"My favourite track." Freddy winked. "But you can't distract me with talk of work."

"It usually works because you are passionate about racing."

"I'm also passionate about sex." Freddy ate some of his soup, apparently unconcerned that he'd just made Jaxxon's heart gallop wildly.

"Don't you find it difficult when you are travelling all the time?" Jaxxon's few relationships over the years had always ended because he was never home and his ex's hadn't enjoyed always coming second to his career ambitions and his job. The rally circuit involved as much travel as S1 and from a job point of view, it'd been good preparation for a life lived on the road. It was hell on relationships though.

Freddy stared at him, holding his gaze until Jaxxon was tempted to look away. "You do realise that there are people in all the countries that we visit, and all you need for sex is other people."

"Like one-night stands?" It wasn't really his kind of thing, although he'd had a few here and there.

"Yes, Jaxxon, just like that. After Chester, I couldn't stomach the idea of letting someone get close to me, and I'm afraid I was a bit of a slut for a few years. I'm on PreP, and I get tested regularly." Freddy had mentioned that when they'd first hooked up in his hotel room shower.

"Is it going to be a problem?"

"What?"

"We work in the same sport, Freddy. We'll spend most of the year travelling together."

Freddy's eyes widened and he looked horrified at the

prospect of spending so much time with Jaxxon. "Jaxxon. If I'm with you, I will only be with you, unless we consent to something else. I plan to focus my high libido on you."

Oh, Freddy had been insulted, not horrified, at the idea Jaxxon might assume he wouldn't be monogamous with him. God, he wanted this man, and only this man, right now. A volcanic heat exploded across Jaxxon's skin. He stood up, paced around the table, and hauled Freddy to his feet. He kissed Freddy with all the ferocity that had built up during the evening, with teeth, tongue, and lips, all moving with desperate urgency. He wanted Freddy more than anything. Freddy tasted like champagne with a remnant of the sour soup. Freddy curled his fists into Jaxxon's shirt, clinging on as their breath mingled into rapid pants and groans. His heart banged out an impatient tempo.

"Take me home and fuck me, Freddy."

"We haven't had the main course yet."

"Make me the main course." His voice had deepened into a hoarse whisper. Freddy pressed his body against Jaxxon's, hard cocks rubbing together.

"Patience." Freddy sank to his knees, dragging his hands down Jaxxon's torso, lower and lower until his face nuzzled against Jaxxon's aching cock. "This is just a promise." He gripped Jaxxon's ass, fingers digging in, and he mouthed at Jaxxon's cock through his clothes. It shouldn't be this hot, there were too many layers of fabric in the way, and Freddy's mouth was only tracing his shape, not surrounding him. He threaded his hands into Freddy's hair and groaned.

"Please."

"No." Freddy stood up and kissed him hard on the

mouth, before reaching up and untangling Jaxxon's hands. Noise filled the air—his own whine—as Freddy stepped away and sat down in his chair. "We are going to enjoy this very expensive, exclusive dinner, and then ... And only then, will we go back to my place where I will take you apart inch by inch."

Somehow, on trembling legs, he managed to collapse back in his chair. His hand shook as he tried to eat the soup. It wasn't until after the soup had been cleared away and replaced with a tiny morsel of food artistically centred on a huge white plate that he was able to form a single thought beyond, 'now, now.'

"Try it. It's excellent." Freddy used the side of his fork to slice the small piece of fish in half, scattering the micro-herbs and edible flowers around his plate. A stack of slices of fresh tomatoes and thin slices of salty haloumi lay under the succulent fish. Jaxxon tried—and failed—to ignore the way the veins in his cock pulsed. Instead, he attempted to eat the food. It was delicious and absolutely no reflection on the chef's ability that he barely tasted it. He wanted to shovel it in, rush through the rest of dinner, so he could go home with Freddy.

"We have all night."

"Promises." The croak in his voice echoed around the room. Dinner passed in a blur of red wine, tension, point-less chatter about S1, and incredible food. He was thankful that Freddy did most of the talking, and keeping it about work, stopped him from simmering into a full-blown boiling need to strip Freddy right there. There was guinea fowl cooked to perfection with a side of green beans, and two desserts. One with baked apples, blue cheese, and honeycomb, and the other was a honey cake with plums and ice cream. The cake was succulent, soaked in honey, with similar flavours to the baklava that his mum made in the bakery, and he left the restaurant with sweetness lingering on his tongue.

CHAPTER 19

Conceptually knowing about Freddy's wealth hadn't prepared Jaxxon for the reality of it. They'd walked from the restaurant, a few blocks to Freddy's building, and the cool London evening spring air had done nothing to slow the heated tempo in Jaxxon's veins. The marble foyer made Jaxxon gasp, the place looked like a bank with the pretensions of displayed wealth, and he focused his gaze on Freddy's spine as he followed him to the elevators. Freddy swiped a card and the elevator rushed to the top floor, opening up to a small room with two doors.

"Reiko Inoue lives there, and this one is me." Inoue, as in the media mogul? The desire buzzing in his veins rapidly cooled sending chills over his skin as he followed Freddy inside. A wall of glass did the impossible and sucked all the remnant sexual tension out of his body. This apartment must be worth mega-millions. He couldn't move, just stared out over London through massive glass windows. It wasn't that high up; not in this suburb; but the view over the city was staggeringly beautiful.

"Jaxxon. Are you alright?"

"Ah, yeah." He might be having an out-of-body experience, although that seemed dramatic. The jarring change from wanting to rip Freddy's clothes off to standing in his lounge staring at one of the world's most expensive views made him dizzy.

"I'm going out of a limb here and am going to guess that you aren't alright." Freddy guided Jaxxon over to a beautiful leather couch and sat him down with a ... well, it would've been thud except the couch was soft and welcoming, like falling onto candy floss.

"I think I'm going—"

Freddy leaped up and grabbed a vase. "Be sick into this."

"You want me to vomit into a vase?" He squinted at Freddy, who appeared to think that Jaxxon had food poisoning. Probably more logical than freaking out at Freddy's expensive apartment. "I was just going to leave and go back to my hotel, not vomit."

"Hold on. Why are you leaving?"

He wasn't sure either, just that he wanted to escape this place. He didn't belong here. "I grew up in a two-bedroom flat above the bakery where my parents worked. Their rent was included in their pay cheque."

"And look how far you've come."

"Our whole flat could fit inside this room, and I bet your place is much bigger than this."

Freddy knelt in front of him. "Are you panicking because I have a nice apartment?"

"Yes. This can't work. How can this work?" He could assimilate into S1, surrounded by rich people, and do his job. He wasn't sure he could live like one of them. Certainly, he couldn't be in a relationship with someone who took that wealth for granted and lived like a fucking king on top of London.

"Jaxxon. We have a plan. It's going to be fine. We made a plan for you, because you needed one."

He needed a drink of water to soothe his desiccated throat. "Technically, we don't have a plan yet. We are in the midst of creating one."

Freddy sat on the floor, picked up Jaxxon's right foot and began to massage it. "Relax. Close your eyes. You could be anywhere."

"But I'm in an apartment that I'll never be able to afford, even if I'm Team Principal for the next three decades."

Freddy pressed his fingers against Jaxxon's foot, right in the pressure point that released lactic acid and made all the tension ease away. His fingers worked the little muscles in Jaxxon's foot, a thoroughly amazing massage, and the only sound was their breathing and the slip of Freddy's fingers on Jaxxon's bamboo and cotton socks.

"Are you worried that we aren't equals?"

"Yes."

"I'd say that you are more than my equal on every criteria that matters, except money, except I don't think that'll help right now."

He made an uncommitted noise. Rank and status shouldn't matter this much, and yet, he'd spent his life working towards having a highly ranked job in one of the most competitive sports in the world. How many times have he heard that S1 was the pinnacle of motor-racing? Freddy continued to massage his feet, releasing tension in his tendons and in places where he didn't realise he had any. The mess in his head felt disconnected from Freddy's attentions.

"Should we add a financial clause to your plan? Would that help?"

Jaxxon leaned back and stared at the plain white ceiling. He wasn't sure how that would work. "I have plenty of my own money." He was doing well on his own career path; and remembering that helped settle the churn in his stomach.

"Gamble Racing ought to be paying you well as Team Principal."

"They are."

"But you are still worried about my money?"

"It's not the money, per say, it's more the trappings of it." He gulped as Freddy encircled his ankle with his hand, pressing his thumbs gently into his flesh.

"Per say... I love the way you talk."

"You do?"

"Yes. It's like you couldn't hide your education if you tried."

"Am I flaunting it?"

Freddy smiled, his hazel eyes glowing, perhaps admiration on his face. "No. That's the beauty of it; you are just you and it comes out so naturally. I can tell when someone is trying too hard to impress."

He groaned as Freddy pressed his fingers into a tight spot on his ankle. "Aren't my feet a bit gross?"

"What do you mean?"

"I've been in meetings all day wearing shoes." It was an immediate thing to worry about because everything else was too overwhelming and he didn't know where to start unpacking it all. He'd probably overreacted to Freddy's apartment. Shit, had he hurt Freddy by stressing about this?

"It's fine. But I'm not going to wash them Jesus style."

Jaxxon slid off the couch and wrapped his arms around Freddy, burying his face against his shoulder as he laughed. "Good. That would be fucking weird."

How perfect of Freddy to say exactly what he needed to centre himself and the two of them. He was here because they'd had dinner together. The old buzz of their earlier foreplay started to grow as they hugged, squashed awkwardly together on the floor, until Jaxxon's legs started to cramp and he tried to straighten them out.

"You okay?"

"Yeah, just too old for sitting on the floor."

"Old. You aren't even forty yet." They both stood up, and Jaxxon stomped his foot a few times to bring sensation back into it. The pins and needles were at odds with the electric way Freddy's loose hold on his arms felt.

"It's incongruous, really. I'm the second youngest Team Principle in the history of S1 and I'm always so aware of that, especially at the meetings with the S1 board and stewards before each race, and yet I don't want age to be a thing in my life. I don't want to become one of those men who chases youth constantly."

"Ew, there's something wrong with men who only date much younger men."

Jaxxon nodded. "And straight men who only date young women are even grosser."

Freddy shuddered. "Oh, definitely. There's too much weird power in that one. Creepy."

"Yeah. I'm glad we are around the same age."

"You just like my experience." Freddy winked.

He shook his head. "It's not that, although I'm sure that will have its benefits. I like that you know who you are, and you are living your passion. You aren't trying to relive your athletic youth."

"No, definitely not, although I understand the temptation. I was so young, and lauded as young, when I started out in S3, that it would've been easy to cling to that sense of early achievement, but luckily for me I spent a few years in S3 and S2 before I got my S1 seat. By then, there were drivers younger than me, being championed by the media. It was humbling in exactly the way I needed to realise the benefits of experience. And now I'm over forty, it's starting to feel like the best is yet to come. I have the perfect job for me, I get to travel and see every S1 race live, and I've just met someone who I want to share it with." The sappy admission warmed Jaxxon all the way through. Doubt disappeared. The trappings of Freddy's upbringing and money didn't matter when he was so certain about the two of them.

"Come with me." He held out his hand and Freddy took it. They walked together to the huge glass windows and Jaxxon turned around so his back faced the view. He leaned against one of the steel struts between the glass and cupped Freddy's face. "The plan is this..."

"Yes." Freddy was breathless.

"I want more than a hook up with you. I want to try and have a relationship; one where we travel for work together, where we are honest with each other, and where we understand the boundaries of our jobs. I can't share all the Gamble Racing data with you, and I don't want to know the other team's gossip before it becomes public knowledge. I refuse to use this as a reason to get ahead."

"You can do that on your own, Jaxxon. You don't need me."

"Thank you. And I know it's probably too early to have this conversation, but I need it, and I think you do too."

Freddy swallowed, his throat moving against Jaxxon's wrist. "I do. I've never entered a relationship with an extended negotiation before we really start."

"Is it weird?"

"No. It's fucking hot. I love that you've thought about this, about how to cope with the different pressures of our careers and how being together might impact our jobs and our lives. I've only had one relationship with someone in the paddock and it was a complete disaster. I made assumptions about Chester, and he took advantage of that. Talking about this with you makes me feel cared for."

His breath caught in the back of his throat at Freddy's raw honesty, and there was only one thing for it. He kissed Freddy. He poured all these new feelings that he couldn't put into words into this kiss; the desperate swirl of chemistry in his gut, the aching need in his balls, the shared passion for motor-racing, the way they complemented each other, but most of all, the zing of electricity as their tongues lashed each other.

"If we both have money, how about we just keep our

own money and spoil each other at a level we are okay with. If I overstep, please tell me." Freddy placed his hands on Jaxxon's heaving chest.

"I can do that. Most of the time, I'll be okay, it's just sometimes, like walking in here, it's a stark reminder of the differences in our upbringing."

Freddy brushed his lips across Jaxxon's cheek, then whispered in his ear. "Your worry isn't about us now, it's about where we came from?"

"Yes. I know I've earned my place here and I shouldn't be insecure about my upbringing..."

"It doesn't sound like insecurity to me. Whenever you talk about your parents or your childhood, it sounds idyllic."

"Idyllic?"

"Yes. Your parents love you, they obviously want the best for you, and you've succeeded thanks to their commitment to your well-being."

His heart swelled. "That is true. I have the best parents." He wanted them to meet Freddy, all of the sudden, and his heart skipped a beat imagining them sitting at the chipped Formica table in the kitchen above the bakery. He could imagine Freddy there, comfortable in the small kitchen, and without a hint of disdain at their lack of wealth.

"Money doesn't give you love or support. Whenever you get overwhelmed by the grand capitalist glory of my life, remember that. I would give this all away to have parents who gave a shit about me."

Jaxxon pulled Freddy into a tight hug, utterly humbled by Freddy's admission. "I'm so sorry. I was so focused on my goals and what I didn't have that I forgot what I do have." The perspective was one Freddy had mentioned before, but somehow, standing here in one of London's most expensive apartments with Freddy tugging on his ear lobe with his teeth, made it finally sink in. Wealth didn't matter without love, and his heart broke for the child that Freddy had been, and he realised he adored the man Freddy had grown into despite the lack of it. Jaxxon's drive to chase career success and money had been created by his childhood and wanting to have a better life for him and his parents, and he'd forgotten that part.

"I've lost my way a little. When I first went to uni, it was because I wanted to be Team Principal of a racing team. Not for the status. Racing gripped me and I wanted it to be my whole life, and I knew if I worked hard enough, then I'd get to the top. Now that I'm here, I keep looking around for what I'm lacking, but I'm here already. I lack nothing."

"Your ambition got you here and now you can't stop chasing more."

He gulped. "More will never be enough. I need to pause and enjoy being here." And if he did, then taking Gamble Racing to the World Championship would happen without him needing to stress about whether he belonged. He belonged because he was here. His next goal was a World Championship, a constructor's title for Gamble Racing. That ought to keep him busy for a long time.

"You did it. You've made the space for yourself." Freddy pulled Jaxxon's tie off, tossing it aside, and undid the button on his collar. His warm fingers against Jaxxon's throat anchored him to this moment. The only thing missing in his life was a partner to share his success with;

and maybe, hopefully, Freddy would be that man. The power in the possibility roared in his veins. He pushed his thigh between Freddy's legs and walked them towards the couch, until Freddy sat down, and he straddled his legs, purposely surrounding him.

CHAPTER 20

Freddy couldn't think of anything better than Jaxxon's weight on him. The glorious way he was being pressed into the couch was exacerbated by the slow way Jaxxon's gaze raked over him, as if he were cataloguing every sinew and muscle. They were still clothed, yet Jaxxon's gaze stripped him bare and his cock, already rigid, ached deep down in his balls. Hips bucking upwards, he needed to rub himself all over Jaxxon. Jaxxon's hands were at his throat, undoing his shirt, button by button. He was being undone, unravelled, by Jaxxon's touch. With a tilt of his chin, he lifted his face to kiss Jaxxon, and what a kiss. It tasted of the honey cake from dinner and the rich tannins of the pinot noir, all mingled with Jaxxon himself. Their tongues danced, grappled, somewhere between a waltz and a wrestle, and Freddy was lost to the moment. Breathy noises, moans, groans, and a rumble of triumph as Jaxxon's fingers tangled in his chest hair, all intertwined. Who made which noise? It didn't matter. Lust was the antidote to overthinking. His brain was blissfully blank as sensation ruled. Exquisite.

"I have lube and condoms in the ..." Where? He willed some blood to his brain to find the answer. "Um, top drawer in my bedroom."

Jaxxon stood. His shirt was awry and his erection tented his suit pants. "Show me." He held out his hand, and Freddy allowed himself to be pulled to his feet. His knees were soft and loose, but not enough that he couldn't march to his bedroom, tugging Jaxxon's hands.

"Close your eyes."

"Why?"

"Please." His bedroom was a lot; custom designed by D&Y Designs, one of London's freshest names in interior design, and to his specifications. It'd been his indulgence when getting this place fitted out, with a massive bed that dominated the room. He never intended to have someone else in here; preferring to keep sex separate from his comforting place, although he had selected a bed with anchor points in the bedhead and legs. Just in case. For one day. He sent a quick thanks to his past self for planning for this moment. Today's bedspread was mostly black with dark red roses and a subtle gold stitch around the edge with matching pillowcases and a fluffy throw blanket tossed over the end. His housekeeper made the bed every day.

"Okay." Jaxxon allowed himself to be led to the end of the bed. Fuck, he looked so incredible standing there with his eyes shut and mouth slightly parted. Freddy pressed a few buttons on the wall, shutting out the view with automated blinds, as well as changing the lighting into something moodier.

"Jaxxon. Let me undress you." He walked back to the other man, standing behind him, and began to unbutton his shirt. He stripped it off, pressing kisses along his spine, then undid his belt and pants. As he pushed them down Jaxxon's legs, he licked the round exposed muscles of Jaxxon's ass, and used his hands to massage Jaxxon's thick thighs.

"Freddy."

"Wait. Please." He stood up, sidling up against Jaxxon's spine, loving the way gooseflesh broke along his skin, and his muscles twitched. He held Jaxxon's waist and pressed a hard kiss between his shoulder blades.

"Freddy." The pleading tone and the choppy timbre of his breath all flooded Freddy's cock with an ache that would only be appeased by Jaxxon's touch.

"One moment." He licked all the way down Jaxxon's spine, then tapped him on the ass, before stripping off his clothes in a rush, nearly tripping over his pants as he flung them aside. He grabbed the lube and a handful of condoms from the drawer, shutting it with a bang that echoed in the room, before shoving the throw blanket aside, and rolling naked on the bed. From this angle, Jaxxon looked like a fucking God. All naked flesh with his huge, hard, dick demanding attention. It was fucking glorious. He'd had it in his mouth in the shower, but he'd never seen it on display like this and he shivered. The promise of that cock had him writhing and he swallowed quickly because Jaxxon was being so perfectly patient.

"Okay. I'm ready. You can open your eyes now."

Jaxxon's eyes fluttered open slowly, his nostrils flaring, as he gasped. "Oh fuck, Freddy."

"Yes please." He bent his knees, opening himself up, and placed the lube and condoms on his stomach.

"I can't promise I'll be gentle."

Heat surrounded him. "Take me. Take what you need." His lungs were fit for bursting as Jaxxon gazed at him, taking his damned time, until Freddy wanted to scream for his touch. His gaze traversing his skin wasn't enough. Eventually—finally—Jaxxon held Freddy's ankles, and slowly leaned forward, caressing those big hands of his all the way up Freddy's legs. He brought his elbows up, half-sitting, so he could see better.

"Your abs are something extra." Jaxxon reached out and fluttered his fingers over Freddy's stomach. Every hour in the gym, every mile run on the treadmill, and every bloody sit-up was worth it. Holy fuck. He crunched a bit more, wanting to show off and encourage Jaxxon to touch him more. The bottle of lube rolled off and he caught it with his hand.

"And those legendary reflexes..." Jaxxon spread one hand over Freddy's stomach, and with the other, he gently took the bottle of lube from Freddy's fist. The brush of his thumb over Freddy's racing pulse had him moaning for more. Soon he'd be begging. And then, Jaxxon licked his bottom lip, eyes considering.

"Fuck me." The headiness of being wanted by this man made his dizzy with power. He lay back on the bed, spreading his arms wide, and was rewarded with a low, guttural groan from Jaxxon. Jaxxon moved suddenly, grabbing a condom and rolling it onto his dick, before squirting lube onto his palm. Freddy grabbed the bedcover, holding the soft fabric in his fists, as he waited. He didn't have to wait long, as Jaxxon bent his legs higher and slapped his lube-covered palm over Freddy's hole. The switch from gentle to this desperate touch sent shockwaves through his body and he released the air from his lungs on a long obscene moan. Jaxxon's gaze focused, his nostrils flaring and that little muscle in his jaw twitching. With one hand, Jaxxon dragged Freddy's body to the edge of the bed, while he used the other to open up Freddy. The hot jolt of pleasure of Jaxxon's thick fingers inside him sent sparks up his spine, igniting every nerve ending from his belly to his groin, and when Jaxxon pressed the blunt end of his cock against his hole, he made a noise from deep inside his chest, something like a mewl and a needy growl. He wrapped his legs around Jaxxon's waist, never taking his gaze off Jaxxon, who held his hips and guided himself in slowly. So slowly that Freddy wasn't going to die if he didn't hurry up.

"Jaxxon. Please." The pressure of thick cock against his prostate was a flash of fire and he dug his heels into Jaxxon's back, wanting to impale himself on Jaxxon.

"Soon." Jaxxon's voice was strangled.

"Now. Please." He needed to be fucked hard and he wasn't above pleading for it. His hands flailed everywhere, trying to grab Jaxxon and pull him closer, but Jaxxon simply pushed him on the chest. The weight of him was everything. The pressure of Jaxxon's hand on his chest, and the fullness of his cock inside him. There was only one thing for it. He grabbed his own cock and stroked it.

"Freddy. Fuck, you are so handsome."

Pleasure roared inside him, loving the compliment, and the huskiness of Jaxxon's voice. And just as he thought he'd spent too long hovering on the edge, Jaxxon roared, a rumbling deep sound that was only the beginning. Jaxxon's grip on Freddy's hip tightened, and his other hand threaded into Freddy's chest hairs creating little prickles of heat across his flesh. And then Jaxxon moved. Freddy's eyes rolled back in his head, as Jaxxon pounded into him. The slaps of their flesh and the agony of their ragged breaths were the centre of the world. The building could crumble around them, and Freddy wouldn't care, wouldn't notice, because the only thing that mattered was the way Jaxxon fucked him. His expression was all concentration, a little furrow between his brows, and his teeth dug into his plump bottom lip. Jaxxon stared at him as if he were the most precious thing in the world, and holy fuck, it was the best thing ever. He released his own cock, and placed his hands over the top of Jaxxon's, and that was all it took. Jaxxon slammed into him, all power and beauty, and called out his name over and over until Freddy's ears rang with it. He came, spurting all over himself and Jaxxon's arm, utterly spent with his head spinning. If he hadn't already been lying down, he would've collapsed, wrung out. Jaxxon's hand slipped off his chest, and he lay on him—perfectly heavy—claiming his lips in a lazy kiss.

"Freddy. You've ruined me for anyone else." Jaxxon's whisper broke through the haze of release and he frowned.

"What?"

"I want more than I should ask for."

Warmth spread over his languid limbs. "Ask anyway." He'd give Jaxxon the world if he could.

"I want to be your last lover. Your forever." Jaxxon blew out a sharp breath that was hot against Freddy's cheek. Oh my God. Freddy wanted that too. His heart thudded. He couldn't form words; his mouth was drier than the Australian outback.

"Shit. I … it's just sex. I shouldn't have said that." The panic in Jaxxon's voice jerked him back. He needed to say something, anything, before this beautiful man misinterpreted his inability to form a coherent thought as something negative.

"It's fine." Freddy wrapped his arms around Jaxxon, soothing him with long strokes of his hands up and down Jaxxon's spine. "We have a plan, remember, and I hope that includes a lot more sex like this."

"You liked it?"

Why the sudden doubt? "Jaxxon. Look at me."

Jaxxon lifted his head and stared at him, that damned frown still there.

"Jaxxon. I've had a lot of sex with a lot of people—"

Judging by the wide-eyed startled expression, he'd fucked this up.

"And this was just another bout for you?"

He purposefully raised one eyebrow. "Will you let me finish?"

"Not if it's bad news."

He ran his hands down Jaxxon's spine and squeezed his ass muscles. "It's good news. Hell, Jaxxon, that was the best sex. You are glorious." He knew he needed to prove it. "The way the tendons in your neck stand out as you come, the noises you make, holy wow, and best of all, the way you make me wait and wait until I'm desperate for you, and only when I'm going to pass out from waiting, did you slam into me."

"That was okay?"

"No, Jaxxon, it wasn't okay. I came hard enough to splash my own face with cum. It was fucking spectacular, and I beg you. I beg of you. Please. Do it again and again."

Jaxxon nodded slowly.

"I can't promise you forever. I can do right now, and right now, you are the only person I want. Trust me when I say that once isn't going to be enough. I want you in every way that it's possible to have sex with someone. I want to be surrounded by you, to be filled by you, to have you. Over and over."

Jaxxon kissed him hard, as if he could eat Freddy's words and store them inside him, or that's the way it felt. Almost too much, but still not enough. Freddy had been worried that he was so fucked by the amount he'd wanted Jaxxon after their first time together. Now that stress disappeared because they were in this together, and while he wasn't sure about forever, he adored the way Jaxxon hoped for it. He cupped Jaxxon's face as they kissed, and slowly the kiss became a dreamy slow sleepy kiss. Jaxxon rolled them together, awkwardly as their legs hung off the end of the bed.

"I'd better clean up." Jaxxon eased himself out, dealing with the condom, and stood up.

"Have a shower with me. I'm not done with you yet." For this man, Freddy would welcome him into his most private of spaces. He'd never had someone here in his home. Only Jaxxon. Jaxxon who wanted forever; and Freddy—God rest his soul—wanted that too. In Freddy's experience, it was completely unrealistic, but that didn't stop the fucking longing for it. History had taught him that people only wanted him for what he could give them, and they persisted even after he said no. It was up to him to create a boundary, and if he could keep reminding Jaxxon of the contents of his 'plan', perhaps everything would be alright. Perhaps they could simply fuck all this chemistry away until they both walked away content. The real problem was that Freddy was afraid to hope for the impossible, so he focused on now instead, because at least that was tangible. Either he would become obsessed, or Jaxxon would, and Freddy knew how that ended.

CHAPTER 21

MIAMI

"Congratulations." Freddy stuck his microphone in Jaxxon's face. Sweat beaded on Jaxxon's temples in the sticky humid conditions, and Freddy wanted to lick it off. Later. Miami was always like this in the early summer with warm, humid, days. He wore a short-sleeved shirt, cotton for breathability, and tried not to look at the way Jaxxon's Gamble Racing polo shirt clung to his body. A body he was incredibly familiar with now. A familiarity that only made him want Jaxxon more and it really should bother him more than it did.

"Thank you. It's a thrill to see one of our cars back on the podium." Jaxxon's driver Ondrej had finished in third, some consolation for Paulo ending up in twelfth after a tussle on lap twenty-two had resulted in him needing a new front wing.

"It was a good drive from Sanchez too."

"Yes. He was unfortunate not to get points after that effort."

"The car seems to be working well."

Jaxxon must've been working on his media face, as he kept a neutral expression. "Yes, we are pleased at being able to convert the quali pace into race pace, and a podium. There's a lot of room for improvement. We aren't content to hang out in the mid-field and today's drive by D'Grieg shows that the car is capable of being on the podium. Now we need to do it more often."

"The mid-field battle does look quite intense this year."

Jaxxon sent him a quick look of disdain. "Yes." It was deserved, a boring answer to a dull question. He ought to know better.

"And the crowds?"

"The fans here are amazing. We've had so much support here in America, you know it's a huge growth market for S1. It's been excellent. Without the fans, none of us would be here. There's a whole ecosystem supported by the fans; we provide the entertainment, and they allow us to pay our mechanics, engineers, find sponsors. Our fans have come to know the drivers and the Team Principals and that personal connection continues to bring new fans to motorsport, which ultimately is a wonderful thing and allows us to keep racing."

"And you have it folks. Gamble Racing loves the American fans!" Freddy moved on with his camera crew to the next interview, but not before he pulled his phone out of his pocket and quickly sent a text.

Freddy
You look hot. Cold shower with me later?

Jaxxon didn't answer immediately. A couple of hours later, Freddy had wrapped up the day's work, at least for their live feed, and was about to sit down in the crew's truck for a quick end of day meeting when the response came.

Jaxxon
No. We have an auction to attend.

Freddy
Meet you there?

Jaxxon
As planned, yes.

Freddy fidgeted through the meeting wanting to rush off and get cleaned up for Jaxxon. They'd settled into a routine; travelling together and finding time for each other in the moments between their jobs. They weren't brave enough to book a room together yet, but still spent most nights on the road in the same room. There hadn't been time between races and travel to be together back in England; Jaxxon was busy after Imola, preparing for Miami, and now the schedule would move to Spain in a fortnight. The snatched moments together on the road were special to Freddy.

———

Two hours later, he walked into the auction room. The 1959 Ferrari S1 car sat at the front of the room with two security guards beside it.

"She's a beauty."

"The first S1 car to have disc brakes." Jaxxon bumped his shoulder. "Can you imagine driving it?"

Freddy grinned. "I don't need to imagine it."

"What?"

"There's probably footage online somewhere. I drove this exact car at Imola eleven years ago as a demonstration. I can't believe that Giacomo is selling it."

Jaxxon frowned. "I don't believe you."

"What?" Freddy hadn't been boasting. "Why not?"

"The name of the vendor in the catalogue is Flavio Ricci."

"Hold up. What?" Freddy traced his hand along the frame of the car, ready to look inside the cockpit, but someone hauled him backwards.

"Sir. You can't touch the car." The security guard squeezed his shoulder in a decidedly unfriendly way.

"I think you'll find that Alfred Hiptonstall, former S1 driver, is one of the few people who can touch this car." Jaxxon's defence was so fucking hot, he was going to expire on the spot. Just self-combust in a little pile of ashes.

"Let's sit down. I want to watch the bidding." Freddy walked away from the beauty. If he had anywhere to drive a car like this, he'd probably buy it. Ten million would probably get it. Pocket change for his investment fund. They sat together while the auction, mostly of Italian art, went along at a snail's pace, until they got to the car. Freddy's leg jiggled but finally it was time for the car to go under the hammer.

"Originally owned by Giacomo Esposito, whose father drove it to victory in the 1959 S1 season, this vehicle changed hands six years ago, and now the current owner Flavio Ricci has entrusted us with finding a new owner." The auctioneer confirmed Freddy's gut feel that it had been the one he'd driven, and he elbowed Jaxxon.

"Told you so."

"Yes. I've seen the footage online."

"Sneaky. When?"

"During all the dull art auctions, of course. Don't tell me you were paying attention to that?"

Freddy had been. There were a few pieces that might look nice in his apartment, but he knew better than to spontaneously purchase art without a second opinion. "Never mind that. Now we need to see who buys the car, to see if it gives us a clue."

"Potentially."

"The thief has been stealing trophies. It's personal. This old car is different, besides, Socrates wants it." Jaxxon held up a bidding paddle, and soon it was him against someone on the phone. Freddy sent a quick text to Cliff to see if he knew who was bidding against them. The response was unsatisfying with Cliff not even aware the car was for sale.

Cliff
Upside is that it's not the same market as memorabilia

Freddy
Or trophies?

Cliff
Cars sell to car lovers. Memorabilia sells to collectors. Different market

Jaxxon had guessed as much, and shortly afterwards, Jaxxon won the bidding war, signing over $8.2million of Socrates' money for the car. Freddy was a little sad that it didn't go for as much as he had expected, but that was quickly overwritten by the realisation that if Socrates owned it, he might get to drive it again. The old familiar buzz of adrenalin shot through his veins and he closed his eyes, visualising the Imola track and how it had felt in this ancient V6 with manual transmission. After all the paper-work had been done, they sat together quietly at the back.

"How did that feel?"

"Nerve-wracking. Mike wants it to be Socrates' present when he leaves rehab. When the bidding started and the other person kept hitting back at me, I thought it was going to burn past my limit, but then it just stopped."

"I meant spending such a big amount of money."

Jaxxon shrugged. "I manage a much bigger budget with the team. After a while, it's just data on a page, not real money. I try not to think about it in real terms."

He was so fascinated by this idea, and it made some twisted sense. Jaxxon dealt with huge sums of money every day as the Team Principal, and yet when it became personal, Freddy had seen how Jaxxon still struggled to comprehend his place in the world.

"Perhaps Socrates will let you drive it." Jaxxon's reitera-tion of his own hope sent a flourish of joyful heat buzzing in his torso.

"Perhaps. He'll want to do it first." Freddy hadn't driven on Socrates' test track. He'd only seen it from the air when arriving at the estate in a helicopter.

"Have you driven the test track?"

"Me? No. I'm a mechanical engineer, not a driver."

"I should take you for a spin sometime."

Jaxxon smiled. "One day. Now, can you put on your journalist hat and find out who the underbidder was? It might be useful to know."

Freddy absolutely could do that. He pulled out a card from his wallet and waited until the final item had been auctioned, before approaching the auctioneer. The underbidder was an agent, known to the auctioneer, who gave him the contact details. A good starting place and he could head back to Europe in a few days with more information under his belt.

———

SPAIN

Ten days later, Freddy stood in a crisp suit with his colleagues before FP1 in Spain when his phone buzzed in his pocket. He pulled it out.

Cliff
I've been looking through old auction catalogues for S1 memorabilia and I've created a little database for you. It's in your emails.

Freddy
Awesome. Thanks

He opened his email, and sure enough, there was an email from Cliff with an attachment, so he forwarded it to Jaxxon and Sonia with a note. Once that was done, he flicked Georgia a text.

Freddy
Can you set up a meeting with Jaxxon at Gamble Racing and Sonia from my old team?

Georgia
I know who Jaxxon is

Freddy
This is work

Georgia
Today in Spain?

Freddy
Yes

Georgia
Ok

"Freddy, focus please, the cars are about to come out on track." Carol's reminder in his ear was more severe than he'd expected.

"Are you alright, Carol? You sound very stressed."

"My presenter is acting like a teenager, texting on his phone instead of doing his job." Harsh, but true. He clicked his phone onto silent and slid it into his pocket, before clearing his throat and nodding at Maddock.

"We have a sell-out crowd here at Circuit de Barcelona, with Series Two driver Harry Goldingstone sitting in for JP Lavinge for FP1. The teams have brought many upgrades to the race this weekend, most notably with Gamble Racing bringing changes to their floor as they hope to make their car less susceptible to understeer. This season is looking like a strong battle with the top three teams having their six drivers all within thirty points of each other, while the midfield is in a state of flux."

"It is too early to be making any calls for the Championship." Alicia Blasi was his companion reporter for this practice session, while John and Shavi were on pitlane duties.

"Yes, I agree. I'm sure our fans are enjoying how tight the battle is at the top as much as we are."

"The change to the downforce regulations a few seasons ago are certainly doing their job and making the field a lot tighter."

"Yes, I'm enjoying seeing much tighter racing and I think our fan love seeing more overtakes."

Alicia smiled at the camera. "And with that, the pitlane lights are off and the first cars are on the track for this free practice session."

They waited until they had the signal that the live feed had gone to cover the actual cars, and Freddy tried to avoid the temptation to look at his phone again.

"Hey, what's the deal with you spending so much time with Jaxxon Loharani-Jones?" Alicia asked.

"Excuse me?"

"People are talking, and I thought I'd just ask."

Freddy tried not to look startled. "Um, we are?" Shit, he meant to ask if people were talking, not that they were together.

"Spending time together? Yes. It's been noted by several of the Team Principals and they want to know what's going on."

He tried to stay outwardly calm while his stomach flipped over. He hadn't discussed this possibility with Jaxxon; their plans had been about them, not the rest of the paddock. Jaxxon had mentioned it when they'd talked about potential problems, but they'd been too busy fucking to discuss it more. Freddy's phone vibrated in his pocket and he realised he had the perfect reason to calm everyone down. "Ahh, you remember how both of Socrates' trophies were stolen at the Gamble Racing launch?"

"Yes. I was there. Did they ever find them?"

"No. I'm assisting Gamble Racing in the search."

"You?" Alicia raised her eyebrows.

He tried not to react to her apparent incredulity that he was capable of helping someone with a mystery. "Yes. I have a few contacts in the art world and I offered to help. Plus, it's an interesting puzzle, you know."

"It is. Nicking trophies is so weirdly personal. I can't imagine wanting to have someone else's Cups in my trophy cabinet."

He smiled. "Your trophy cabinet is probably impressive enough."

"That's not really the point though, is it? Why on earth would anyone want to have trophies won by someone else?

I don't understand the psychology behind that, unless it's some twisted fucking revenge plot."

Freddy hadn't considered that angle. "You know. It is very strange, and if it were just Socrates' trophies, then you'd probably be right."

"But there are others?" Alicia held up one finger. "Oh my God. Seb's trophy. Who the fuck would do that?"

"That's what I'm trying to help find out. I have a meeting with Jaxxon and Marcel later to talk about some developments."

"Oh, I spy gossip."

"You'll be the first to hear when there's something concrete to talk about." Freddy would have to tell Jaxxon about this conversation, but hopefully he'd headed off any rumours about the two of them before they'd grown into anything difficult.

"I don't understand the connection between Socrates' trophies and Seb's one..."

"Neither. They are different eras and drove for different teams."

Alicia shook her head. "Yeah, I've got nothing. You know it was weird that night at Gamble. There were people on the stage pretty much all the time and they just disappeared from under a sheet. How?"

"We aren't sure, so if you have any clues, I'm sure Socrates would appreciate the help."

Alicia frowned. "I mean, there was about ten minutes before we started when we turned the lights down on the stage, just before you and I walked on to do the introductions, but people were seated in front of the stage and they would've seen people moving about, even if it was just shadows."

She was right and in the mayhem of that night, no one had thought to ask the people seated at the front tables.

"I'll mention that in our meeting. Thank you."

"Anytime. It's a weird one, for sure."

His earpiece beeped. "Back to work first."

"Yes." Alicia slipped easily back into presenter mode, allowing him to follow. This trophy mystery was eating away at him, stealing his usual focus on the job, or perhaps it was just being with Jaxxon and all the sneaking around that bothered him. No, they were still working out this ... thing between them, it was too early to be making any declarations to anyone else about them. He glanced at the screen showing the current cars on the tracks and the times and settled in for the rest of the session.

CHAPTER 22

HUNGARY

After seven races in three months, Jaxxon desperately needed the summer break. He was shattered and so was his team. Everyone had a mandatory ten-day break before they met in the factory again. A month away from racing didn't mean a month away from work, but he could ensure that everyone in the team took some time to recuperate before the next part of the season.

Jaxxon stood in the line to board for business class on Monday afternoon, wearing a three-piece suit. The suit was a pre-emptive weapon that prevented any questions from racists about whether he was standing in the correct line. He'd much rather just wear his Gamble uniform or loose track pants like the white guy in front of him in the line, but this choice created less drama, and what he needed right now was to get home without interacting with other people. In less than three hours, he'd be back in England

and he could sleep for a week. The first half of the season was done, and the summer break was about to begin. It rattled around in his head like a promise—summer break, summer break. The snatched moments with Freddy between races could be replaced with actual time together. He wanted to curl up in Freddy's bed and do nothing for ages; well, a couple of days anyway, before he got bored with resting. Gamble Racing was fourth on the constructor's championship—a satisfying start to his first season as Team Principal—but with 187 points, they were quite far behind the third team who had 301 points and there was plenty to do to improve things. His drivers were currently sixth and eighth in the driver's standings; fair but not exactly where Jaxxon wanted the team to be. His phone dinged.

> **Freddy**
> You done?

Jaxxon didn't know what Freddy meant.

> **Jaxxon**
> I am about to board the plane for home.

> **Freddy**
> Oh. I figured you'd still be in the paddock.

> **Jaxxon**
> Why?

The race was over, and all the media analysis was complete. Pitlane had been packed up last night and everything was already on trucks heading home. He'd stayed in the hotel on Sunday night because they had a Team Principal meeting with the S1 board this morning, which had gone well. It was easy for him as his drivers both had multi-year contracts. No silly season dramatics for Gamble Racing. At the end of next season, Ondrej's contract would be up, and he hoped their results by this time next year would be good enough to re-sign him. Paulo came with sponsorship, so that tied up the issue of sponsorship and the second driver while Paulo's contract was still valid. The biggest threat there was other teams trying to poach him, but his results weren't quite good enough for that to be a tangible problem. Yet. He'd need to keep an eye on that. Money often talked louder than results in this sport.

> **Freddy**
> Didn't you have a meeting?

> **Jaxxon**
> It's done

> **Freddy**
> I'll meet you at Heathrow.

Jaxxon held out his ticket to scan and followed the other passengers onto the plane. He sent Freddy a quick thumbs up and his ETA before turning his phone off for the flight. Soon he'd be with Freddy—who'd flown home late last night—and they wouldn't have to sneak around like they had for most of the season so far. They'd had a near-miss back in Spain when Freddy's colleague, Alicia, had noticed they'd been spending a lot of time together, but they'd put her off with the trophy mystery. The spreadsheet of S1 memorabilia sales hadn't yielded any clues and with no further action, he'd given up on finding Socrates' trophies. During the season, he hadn't really had the headspace to think about it too much, but maybe he could put some effort into it during the summer break. Victor had an idea for some upgrades that he wanted to test in their wind tunnel, and he was going to visit Socrates and spend a day reviewing the season so far, going over the budgets, and planning the rest of the season. Other than those things, his summer break looked quite free. It'd been months since he'd seen his folks and he realised with a small catch of breath in his throat that he missed them. He talked to them on the phone every week, but nothing beat being there in person and getting a hug from his mum and an apple Danish from his dad. He made a mental note to add in a trip home to see them during the break, and he closed his eyes on the realisation that he wasn't going to get much resting done in the next month.

When the plane touched down, Jaxxon woke with a groan. His neck was all stiff from sleeping sitting up. The bigger business class seats were quite comfortable for a plane—and it was an upgrade from when he'd been Ondrej's race engineer and travelled in economy with the rest of the team—but his body still didn't appreciate being forced to snooze sitting up. He rubbed his eyes, half-listening to the captain's welcome message. Eventually he pulled out his phone to turn it on and he scanned his notifications. Among the several emails, there was an alert email letting him know that Freddy had published an article. He clicked the link, reading as he walked off the plane, dragging his carry-on suitcase. He always travelled light to race week-ends, so he didn't have to wait around for checked in luggage. It was a bonus of having a team; he could send most of his stuff with the logistics team.

The Silly Season Has Begun With a Blast, by Freddy Hiptonstall

With seven of the twenty S1 seats up for grabs as we head into the summer break, this promises to be an intriguing silly season. The shock announcement of Dwight Etrulius' retirement should create a few changes in driver line ups across the grid, while the rumour mill is already in overdrive surrounding the potential seat for S2's Letherbarrow who is leading the championship over there in a sensational debut season.

The rest of the article outlined all the information Jaxxon already knew, and he appreciated that Freddy buried Gamble Racing's unchanged driver line up in the middle of the article. He put his phone away to go through customs, and finally, he emerged into the arrivals section.

"Jaxxon." Freddy walked up to him, a smile on his face, and Jaxxon glanced around but he'd been the only Team Principal on his flight. One of the top teams was based in Italy, while the other two were in England—like Gamble Racing—but they had private jets, hence why he didn't expect to see those Team Principals today. Like many other mid-field teams, Gamble Racing used commercial flights to save on costs because Socrates preferred to spend money on winning races, not people's comfort or catering, and it was a philosophy Jaxxon agreed with. Budgeting and working out the best spend of funds were his strong point.

"Hello."

"You look exhausted." Freddy reached out for his hands.

"Not here. There's probably others on the plane." Others from the paddock.

"I'm done with hiding."

So was he, and there was no need for it, not really. They were two grown men and it was no one's business. He hadn't even intended to hide this, it'd just happened that way. "Yeah, same, but I'm also tired. Can we talk about it tomorrow?"

"Yes. It would be better to control the story. Come along." Freddy's fundamental understanding of S1 media was useful and helped calm the exhausted scrambled mess in his head. He followed Freddy who took him to the cab rank and he snoozed in the back while they were driven to Freddy's apartment. The idea of falling asleep in Freddy's amazing bed was absolutely what he needed; the perfect beginning to the summer break. Tomorrow would be for decisions, or whatever. He let himself be led out of the cab, into the elevator, and into Freddy's luxury apartment. If he thought of it as being just another fancy hotel room, then he was less likely to compare their upbringing. He was being a fool; so what if they had different childhoods, he'd been lucky with his loving parents. Money only mattered because it ruled his working life. He didn't have to let it rule the rest of his life too.

"You look sexy."

"What?" He was too tired for that. "How?"

"All rumpled in that suit, like you've been working all day and you need someone to take care of you."

"And that's going to be you?"

Freddy held his hand over his chest. "Don't wound me with such nonsense. Of course, it's going to be me." He undid Jaxxon's tie and slipped his jacket off his shoulders, shaking it out and draping it over a chair. With steady fingers, he undid Jaxxon's cuff links—Gamble Racing branded—and then undid the buttons down the middle of his chest. Slowly, carefully, Freddy undressed him, until he stood there in Freddy's lounge in boxer shorts and socks.

"Come and have a shower, then we'll order some food, and maybe watch a movie in bed."

He nodded. It sounded exactly like what he needed. "It's been a long season so far." He could've done with more guidance from Socrates in his first stint as Team Principal, however, it wasn't to be—Socrates had his own problems that needed focus—and he'd had to figure it out by himself as he went along. Having a good team helped, but ultimately, the final decisions lay with him. The intensity of being in the social media scrutiny had been new too; when he'd been a race engineer it'd been muted compared to the constant comments on his job as Team Principal.

"Come on." Freddy tugged him towards the shower, and soon enough he stood with his head bowed under the stream of hot water, as Freddy soaped him all over. He was so tired that he was worried that he'd got into the shower with his socks still on. A glance downwards confirmed that he wasn't.

"I've never seen your dick all soft like this. It's charming and beautiful."

Charming? "Sure, Freddy. After I've slept, I'll be back to normal programming."

"What? Hard and keen for me." Freddy washed his dick and it responded to his touch, hardening up quickly.

"Ignore that. I'm too tired."

"I would never push you, Jaxxon, and you are obviously nearly asleep on your feet. You really need this break." Freddy washed off the soap, then turned off the shower, and helped Jaxxon get dry in a warm fluffy towel.

"How is that towel so nice?"

"It's my secret."

"Okay." He let himself be led to bed, and the moment he lay on those soft high thread-count sheets with a pillow tucked under his head and the blankets around him, he drifted off into sleep. Months of travel and not sleeping well had accumulated and he was glad for the month off over summer. Not that he'd have the whole month off, there was still a lot to do to prepare for the rest of the season. He rolled onto his side, moaning as warm hands caressed his spine, gently pressing into the knots in his neck and shoulders. Best dream ever.

CHAPTER 23

Freddy ordered breakfast and coffee from his favourite place down the road; making sure he had a sweet pastry for Jaxxon to go with the eggs benedict. The whole summer break lay before them, a month where no one was watching them. Yes, he would have to do some work—mostly writing for Inoue Media about any driver contract changes—and Jaxxon probably had stacks to do. He wasn't sure what Team Principals did during the summer break, except they had a whole team to run, and the S1 machine didn't stop just because there was no racing happening.

"How much time do you have off?"

Jaxxon pulled the pillow over his head. He was so bad at mornings, and Freddy touched his chest at the adorable growl from Jaxxon. Sometimes he couldn't believe that he got to have this man in his bed.

"A few days, maybe a week if nothing happens." Jaxxon's voice was muffled.

"Let's go somewhere."

Jaxxon made a non-committal noise that Freddy chose to interpret in his own favour.

"No decisions before coffee?" He teased, even though it was true. During race weekends, when they shared a hotel —and often a bed—Freddy hated the mornings when they deliberately didn't eat breakfast together because watching Jaxxon stumble into the hotel breakfast room and fumble until he'd had coffee was the worst. All Freddy wanted to do was be there for him; bring him coffee and let him wake up on his own time.

"Abso-fucking-lutely." Jaxxon tossed the pillow aside and glanced at Freddy with a half-grin hovering on his lips.

"It's a good thing that I ordered you one already, then."

"Thanks." Jaxxon rolled over, once more buried under the covers.

"Get dressed. I'll go down to the foyer to meet the delivery person." Freddy needed the space, suddenly, rather than just letting some random person up here. By the time he'd gone down to the foyer and taken the order from the delivery person—and tipped them—his heart had settled down a bit. He really wanted to go somewhere with Jaxxon; somewhere they didn't have to worry about the response from the paddock if they were seen together too much. Damn, Alicia had gotten into his head with her questions back in Spain. It was seven races ago, and they'd both been so careful since then, and he wasn't even sure why they were sneaking around. He set the table and dished up the food, plating it so it looked nice.

"You look very domestic." Jaxxon leaned on the bedroom door, wearing a Gamble Racing polo shirt and blue jeans; too much like he did at work, but he'd come straight from Hungary, so it was probably all he had with him.

"If only I could claim to have cooked it myself."

Jaxxon grinned. "Can you cook?"

"Hell no. I suppose you can?"

Jaxxon sat and sipped his coffee, making a little moan of pleasure that shot right into Freddy's cock.

"Yes, I can cook. My mum believed that I need to learn the skills to be a self-sufficient adult."

"Hey, I'm a self-sufficient adult."

"Who uses money to make up for your lack of life skills." Jaxxon's teasing note was delightful, so he teased him back, clutching his chest, pretending to have been stabbed in the heart.

"Isn't that a life skill too?"

"Sure." Jaxxon picked up his cutlery and started eating the breakfast. Freddy slid onto his chair and started to eat too. It was amazing, the rich hollandaise sauce, the oozing yolk of the egg, and the tang of the perfectly baked sourdough, with a small sprinkling of chilli flakes to add a touch of heat to the meal. He missed this breakfast when he was travelling.

"We should probably talk."

"Sounds ominous." Jaxxon's retort made his chest tighten.

"It's not. We just need to figure out what we want to tell people."

Jaxxon put down his cutlery. "I know. I shouldn't have joked. I think it's only a big deal because people might think we are trading secrets between teams."

"We can't control what other people think. How about

we go on a holiday somewhere and just put pictures on social media?"

"What, like here we are on a queer beach, just hanging out like pals?" Jaxxon raised one eyebrow. "I work for Gamble Racing. No one is going to find that unusual at all."

"Yes, but with more kissing." He wanted to tell everyone that how amazing Jaxxon was and how fucking lucky he felt to be with him. Jaxxon's reticence to be openly with him made his heart ache. It shouldn't, because they'd barely discussed the topic, and they were both out as bisexual men, which meant it wasn't about that. Freddy's unhelpful brain immediately decided that it could only be possible if Jaxxon was ashamed to admit he was with Freddy, or perhaps it didn't matter to Jaxxon as much as it was starting to matter to Freddy. He gulped.

"I'm not kissing you for social media. I'd rather just send an email to all the other Team Principals—"

"Email? You want to announce us via email?" There was an unhinged sounding laugh and he realised it came from him; slightly wild and hysterical.

"No. You are right. I need to ring them."

Freddy's skin fluctuated cold and hot. What would he advise a colleague to do? "Actually, no, an email would be better because then they'll get the news at the same time. If you ring them, then there'll be a perceived priority order and it could create—"

"—unwanted tension. True. I don't want to have them ringing each other to boast that they heard it first. Fucking competitive assholes." Jaxxon grinned and the tension in Freddy's shoulders started to ease.

"As if you wouldn't think exactly the same thing."

"Yes. That's why I know you are right." Jaxxon shook his head. "Damn though. What do I say – hey, by the way, in case you didn't know, Freddy and I are fucking, so if that's awkward, let's chat?"

Freddy slapped his thigh to try and hide the prickle behind his eyes. Just fucking? Was all that Jaxxon thought they were?

"No. Jesus, Jaxxon. How about—" He breathed in deeply, not that it helped the tremor in his heart, and took a leap of faith. "In the interests of disclosure, I am in a relationship with Freddy Hiptonstall, and I realise that this might create a perception that I have access to media releases before they are public knowledge, please trust that Freddy is a professional and we both understand the bounds of our jobs."

"Freddy. I'm not going to tell them to worry." Jaxxon was frowning; about which part? Work or …

"No, you'd be telling them not to worry." He hoped it wasn't the 'in a relationship' part that Jaxxon was avoiding.

"By reminding them of the potential confidentiality problems?"

Freddy frowned. "Hmm. If it was one of your staff, what would you do?"

"We have an HR policy on relationships between staff and the disclosure of them."

"So do that. I know you are competitors with the other Team Principals, but they'd appreciate the heads up."

"Just a heads up, I'm fucking Freddy and I thought you'd all like to know that I intend to be professional about it."

Freddy closed his eyes. It hurt, with the weight of a massive G-force crash, to hear Jaxxon repeat that they were just fucking.

"What's the matter?" Now Jaxxon was asking that. Hell.

"I'm pretty sure they don't want to know that you are professionally fucking me." He glared at Jaxxon, needing to communicate that this joke was his way of being upset at the implication they were nothing to each other but a convenient body.

"What?" Jaxxon frowned. "Oh. Shit. I didn't mean it like that."

"I know, but that's why..." Freddy gasped for air; he wanted to laugh or cry and didn't know which. Both, probably. "Just tell them that I'm your boyfriend. Fuck."

"Are you?"

Freddy stared, as the hurt twisted inside him. "Yes. What kind of question is that? It's been months, Jaxxon."

Jaxxon swallowed. "Of course. I'm sorry."

"You are sorry? For assuming that we are just fuck buddies after all these months? That's what you are sorry for?" He couldn't stop himself and it all poured out.

"Yes. I hoped it meant more but we never really talked about it, and it was ... um."

"It was what?"

"Safe to assume it meant less to you than to me."

"Safer?"

Jaxxon closed his eyes and leaned his head back, before sitting up straight and focusing those dark eyes on him. "Yes. We made a plan, that this was chemistry and we had to be careful because the paddock can be an intense place, and I didn't want to deviate from it."

"You are your bloody plans. Come on holiday with me. Let's indulge ourselves without having to be careful or worry what the paddock thinks." He wanted to be with Jaxxon. Completely.

"What do you mean?"

"Fuck safe. I want to have all of you, Jaxxon." He was a risk taker by nature and it was time to chase after what he wanted. "I know I was the one who said no one from the paddock, but fuck, that was because my last boyfriend stalked me. It wasn't because of what anyone else would say about us." He was done with wasting so much time stressing about the past and what it might mean. This discussion and the way it made his chest hurt told him the truth. He wanted to be with Jaxxon. Properly.

"People aren't going to be happy though."

"And you know what... they can piss right off. I want to be happy. I want to be with someone who wants me, not my money, or the possibility that I'll be Duke one day, which I never will be, to be clear. I just want to be with someone who likes me." He swallowed. "Someone who values me."

Jaxxon stood up and walked around the table. He knelt beside Freddy, which ... fuck ... did some weird stuff to his body, like the anticipation of heat curling in this stomach.

"Jaxxon?"

"Freddy. You are a fascinating man and I adore you. I told myself to be content with this arrangement because it was what you wanted, and I'd take every little piece of you that you could give me. I didn't want to be too intense. I didn't want to scare you away if I cared too much."

Hell. Freddy kicked his chair out of the way and fell on top of Jaxxon. It was untidy, awkward, and their limbs splayed everywhere on the floor. He kissed Jaxxon with everything he had, like he was dying and he wanted the taste of Jaxxon to be his last meal.

"Please care for me. I want a relationship with you. This is more than chemistry. I like you." It might even be more than that, but it was all he could ask for in the same conversation as Jaxxon shifted from just fucking into wanting more. Freddy couldn't completely reveal feelings that he wasn't completely certain about yet, or he could just blurt them all out now and be damned with the consequences. Take a giant risk; like he used to do when he was driving. He'd forgotten how good that felt.

"Okay." Jaxxon's simple acceptance was enough, and when Jaxxon rolled them pressing Freddy into the hard floor, he groaned and wrapped his legs around Jaxxon's waist. They'd had a lot of sex over the past few months, but the desperate moans from Jaxxon as he held Freddy's cheeks and kissed him was hotter than anything so far. This was a kiss that conveyed a connection between them. He grabbed at Jaxxon's shirt, pushing it up, so he could hold his skin, warm and perfect under his palms, and he dug his heels into Jaxxon's ass. Jaxxon rocked his hips, grinding their hard cocks togethers through too many layers of clothes, and all the while, they kissed with tongues grappling.

"Too many clothes."

"Don't care." Jaxxon pressed the heel of hand to Freddy's throat, not hard, and when he blew hot air into Freddy's ear, he gasped.

"Jaxxon?"

"Come for me." Jaxxon's command enveloped him in sensation, like the rush of acceleration down the COTA straight.

"Now?"

"Yes. Desperate for me, on the floor of your apartment, completely debauched by me."

Oh God. His eyes rolled back in his head and heard an obscene noise emit from the depth of his throat.

"Yes. Like that."

"Fuck me." He needed Jaxxon's cock inside him. He needed more than this dry humping through clothes.

"No. I'm not your fuck buddy, Freddy. I'm here, kissing you because I like you and I want you to know it." Jaxxon had the audacity to smile before he kissed him again, shifting his hips just enough that the pressure was perfect. Freddy nearly burst, his heart was going to leap right out of his chest and cling to Jaxxon's words, and when Jaxxon stroked his cheek and pulled his hair, Freddy whimpered.

"Yes. Come for me. Be with me."

"Jaxxon." He came, making a mess of his clothes, crying out with relief. Jaxxon covered his mouth in one more giddy kiss, before his mouth slid across Freddy's cheek and his teeth sunk into Freddy's shoulder as Jaxxon came on a roar.

"Be my boyfriend. Let me tell everyone."

Freddy's head spun. "I'll write a press release."

Jaxxon buried his face against Freddy's neck, making

soft snorting noises that sent fresh shivers of heat across Freddy's abused skin. "Is that a yes?"

"Yes, Jaxxon. But I want—"

"A pre-nup?"

"No. Whatever. Take half my money if we break up. You will have already destroyed me if that happens, and I won't give a fuck about the money."

"Oh." Jaxxon lifted his head, a query in his beautiful brown eyes. "I'm not going to do that."

"I don't think you'll be able to stop yourself. I've already fallen harder than I ought."

"Freddy." This time his name was soft on Jaxxon's lips, a hopeful loving sound, and damn, he was a fool for wanting this. When they'd first been together, he'd known he would be fucked if it went further, and now he knew; this man held his heart in his palm and had all the power to destroy him. More than Chester who'd really just been a pain in the ass. More than his father's expectations. More than realising he couldn't drive competitively anymore. Jaxxon was going to break his heart one day, and he was going to let him because every day until then would be worth the future pain.

"Come on holiday with me. We could go anywhere."

"Or we could stay right here in your amazing bed."

Freddy smiled. "You say the sweetest things."

Jaxxon kissed him again, then rolled them to their sides, before he stood up. He held out his hand, and Freddy let Jaxxon pull him up.

"Come on, boyfriend. Let's get cleaned up."

"I haven't finished my coffee." Jaxxon frowned and Freddy grinned.

"Are you saying that I distracted you from your morning coffee?" He felt important in a way that words couldn't communicate.

"Yes. You owe me another one."

His smile grew of its own accord, and he tugged Jaxxon's hand. "I always pay my debts. There's an excellent café just around the corner; it's where I ordered breakfast from. But we both need clean clothes first." His cum had started to dry on his trackpants and it wasn't very pleasant.

"Okay. Let's get cleaned up, then you can treat me to coffee."

"And you'll email all the Team Principals with our news?"

"Absolutely. I only wish I'd said something yesterday when we were all in the same room, and I could see their expressions."

"Most of them would be fine." Freddy knew exactly who would sneer and make some whispered remark about Gamble Racing being the gay team. Fuckwits.

Jaxxon pulled Freddy into a hug. "It's not about them. I'm only telling them, so we don't have to pretend anymore. I want to be completely with you, even in the paddock, and a little bit of transparency will prevent any nasty gossip."

"I'm not naïve, Jaxxon. I know this will make some of them hesitant to talk to me." It was more likely to make his job harder, not Jaxxon's. He would have to tell Carol and Mr Inoue. Neither would care about who he was with, they weren't bigots, it would only be an issue if it impacted his job, and he would make sure that it didn't.

"People know you, Freddy. They'll accept this because they know how much you adore S1. Your passion for the sport resonates in everything you do." With only a few words, Jaxxon demonstrated why Socrates had chosen him as his replacement for Team Principal. More than that, Jaxxon had paid attention to him as a person, as a tv presenter, as someone who knew what was important to him. And it was those things that made him all warm and gooey inside.

"Thank you. Now, come on, let's get cleaned up." He bolted to the bathroom and stripped off, jumping in the shower, needing to shed himself and wash off all the old doubts. And when Jaxxon joined him, with his arms wrapped around him, hands on his cock, he was perfectly content. This was home.

"Again?" Jaxxon stroked him gently and Freddy leaned his head backwards, resting on Jaxxon's shoulder as he was guided into pleasure again by his incredible boyfriend. He was insatiable for this man.

CHAPTER 24

Two days later, Jaxxon was ready to go back to work. He'd sent his email and spoken to the other Team Principals who'd appreciated the heads up and their responses had reminded how much he needed to learn to be on their level. Some of them had a decade of experience over him. He had a lot of work to do to get on par with them.

"What has you so jittery this morning?" Freddy asked over bacon and eggs, delivered to their doorway.

"I have work to do."

"So do it."

He shook his head, suddenly aware that he was acting like a workaholic which had ruined all his past relationships. "I gave everyone ten days off, so there will be no one at Gamble's headquarters."

"And you don't think you deserve ten days off too?"

He probably needed them, but he was anxious about his career, and the list of things to do had started to run in his brain, and perhaps he was a little bit bored. He didn't cope with resting very well. "Deserve isn't the right word."

"Take the time off. Come somewhere fun with me. The Greek islands are always nice during the summer break. Let's not go to the Amalfi coast or French Riviera because half the paddock will be there, but Croatia is pretty and so is Sicily." Freddy sounded like an internet listicle; twenty cool places to visit before you die.

He didn't need anything so fancy. "I think I want to visit my folks."

"Oh, okay." Freddy's glow disappeared and he looked like a puppy that had been kicked; all sad and alone.

It took him a second to realise why. "Come with me." They'd already decided they were boyfriends; of course, Freddy would be welcome.

"Really?"

"Yes."

Freddy's face lit up. "You want me to meet your parents."

"We aren't young kids, Freddy. It's not that big a deal."

"How many other boyfriends have met your parents?"

Jaxxon rolled his eyes. "If you are hoping to be the first one and therefore special, I hate to break it to you. They've met everyone; Alec, Austin..."

"Alfred. Do you have a thing for people starting with A?" The nervous squeak underneath Freddy's teasing tone was unexpected.

"No. I had a girlfriend in high school called Maya, although I'm pretty sure she just liked me because I helped with her History homework." Jaxxon's phone rang, interrupting him. "I have to get this. It's Mike. ... Hold on a second, Mike." He waited, then touched Freddy on the shoulder. "Come with me, my folks would love to meet you."

Mike cackled in his ear. "I heard a rumour that you and Freddy are an item."

"Yes." Jaxxon had forgotten to tell his boss, so focused on other people's reactions, and now he felt like a damned fool.

"Damn, I owe Socrates a twenty."

"You two bet on us?" He was so accustomed to Socrates' antics that it didn't surprise him, and he realised he'd been avoiding telling Socrates because he knew he'd tease him. The words 'spectacular fuck' rang in his ears, and he really didn't want to answer that question. Bloody Socrates would assume a yes given his likely reaction. Well, it was true. He glanced at Freddy who was trying not to laugh.

"I told Socrates that Freddy wasn't your type."

"What made you think that?"

"He's not very ambitious. I figured you'd only want someone whose drive you respected."

Jaxxon frowned. He didn't think that was a very fair assessment of Freddy, who put in hours of preparation before each race weekend, to make sure he knew all the statistics and all the interesting things that had happened at each track, and all the drivers and engine mods...

"Then I guess you don't know me that well." Jaxxon deliberately used phrasing that could be interpreted in several different ways.

"Interesting. How long has it been going on?"

"Mike."

"Come on, Socrates will want to know."

Jaxxon chuckled. "You mean that you want to know, but you are blaming Socrates for your own curiosity."

"Ahh, you know me too well. Yes, share a few things."

"What a pair of nosy old queers you two are." His bosses were incorrigible.

Mike laughed. "Fine. I'll ring Freddy later and get all the details. He loves a good chat."

"How is Socrates?"

"He's doing well. It made a huge difference when you talked them into letting him watch all the races live."

"He's a racing driver at heart. You can't expect someone to heal when you don't let them have the one thing that's important to them." It was obvious to Jaxxon, and he was glad the rehab centre had agreed and it was helping Socrates.

"It's motivating. Every race he watches helps him remember why he's doing this."

Jaxxon swallowed. "Has it been very difficult?"

"Yes and no. Dealing with the alcohol addiction hasn't been that tricky, however, the rehabilitation after his stroke has been a lot of work. He still has a lot of nerve pain in his left hamstring and he's rebuilding his coordination slowly."

"And his reflexes?"

Mike sighed. "To be honest, age and the alcohol had slowly been robbing him of those, so it's been more of a grieving process to realise that he did that to himself."

"We don't have any news on his trophies." Jaxxon blurted it out. He really needed to put more energy into this over the summer break.

"It's okay. We are both resigned to never finding them. It's not your fault."

Jaxxon was about to protest that; it was literally his fault. He'd been the one who'd wanted to honour Socrates at the car launch. He'd taken them out of their secure storage and put them at risk. But just as he opened his mouth to say that, Freddy started waving his hands and jumping up and down.

"Excuse me, Mike." Jaxxon pulled the phone away from his head. "What?"

"Seb's trophy has been found."

"Holy shit." He lifted his phone again. "Mike. Mike. Seb's trophy has been found. Let me call you back when I know some more."

As soon as he hung up, Freddy started talking in rapid fire words all thrown together in a scramble of excitement. "They found it. Sonia texted me. There's apparently an art smuggling ring that was trying to export a bunch of items in a shipping container on the back of a train, and authorities in Sweden got a tip off on the arrival and they found the trophy. Well, a whole bunch of art and stuff like that too. Cliff is going to love this."

"Relax, Freddy. What about Socrates' trophies?"

"Sorry. Just Seb's one. But Sonia said they got fingerprints off it, so maybe there'll be a clue that'll help find the other ones."

Jaxxon breathed out. "Damn."

"Yeah. I wish they'd found all three."

"So do I." He flicked a quick text to Mike and sat heavily on the couch, weighed down by this news. It ought to be exciting, not disappointing.

"What's the matter?"

"It's the wrong trophy. I know that Seb will be thrilled, but it will only serve to remind Socrates that it's going to take a whole lot of luck to find his."

"True. I guess we wait for the police report now? I'll ring Cliff and see what he thinks." Freddy sat beside him, resting his hand on Jaxxon's thigh. "Hey. It's good news. It's a clue and it's more than we had before."

"Yes." He wanted to feel reassured by Freddy's confidence. "What now?"

"Let's go visit your parents today. It'll stop you thinking about this."

Jaxxon stared at Freddy. It was a good point; Jaxxon did need the distraction from work, but... "Today?"

"Yes. Where do they live?"

"Liverpool. It's not exactly practical to drive up there. It's a four-and-a-half-hour drive." Besides, Jaxxon's car was in Syresthorpe, the village near Pewett Downs, the estate owned by Socrates and where the Gamble Racing head-quarters were based. Even if they started now, they wouldn't get there until dinner time. He sighed. He was on holiday; he could take the day to go and see his parents for a few days.

"We will fly."

"Fly?"

"Yes. You are familiar with the concept?" Freddy nudged him.

"Yes. I suppose we could do that. If we book a flight soon, we'll be there for afternoon tea." Jaxxon could spend his life surrounded by rich people and never once think that the solution to a problem was just to fly somewhere. Doing it for work wasn't the same as deciding to do something that made his personal life easier.

"It'll be much faster to charter a helicopter."

Jaxxon choked. "Excuse me?"

"There's a service I use. They actually land on this building, so it's really convenient."

He breathed out slowly. *Just roll with it, Jaxxon.* "Okay."

Two hours later, he sat in the backseat of a helicopter, flying over Liverpool towards his childhood home. Freddy and the pilot chatted away over the radio as he watched his hometown span out underneath them. He'd only been in a helicopter once before, a couple of years ago when he'd first joined Gamble Racing, and Socrates had taken him for a spin in his tiny Robinson to show him Pewett Downs. This helicopter was bigger, and apparently much faster. As promised, they'd arrived here in just over an hour, only two hours after Freddy booked the flight. What a life. Being wealthy really did make everything easier. If he'd been driving, he'd barely be outside London, probably stuck in traffic and generally annoyed with the world.

"We are going to land soon." The pilot went through the procedures, which Jaxxon ignored because he'd never seen Liverpool from this angle. He pulled out his phone and took a bunch of photos to show his parents. The landing was incredibly smooth. The machine settled down on the ground with barely a thump, and soon enough they stood outside the hangar with Freddy booking a ride share on his phone.

"My folks would've come to get us."

"There's no need for them to go to any bother when ..." Freddy glanced at his phone. "Susie in her Honda Civic can do it."

"Okay."

"Should I bring them a gift?"

Jaxxon paused and stared at Freddy. "Susie?"

"No. Your parents. Should I bring something?" Freddy shifted from one foot to another.

"No." He wasn't sure what Freddy was worried about.

"Isn't it rude?" Maybe it was a rich person thing?

"No. They value time and presence more than presents. Being here is enough of a gift." He'd heard it so many times as a child; today is a gift, that's why they call it the present.

"Still, it seems odd to turn up empty handed."

"I usually take them to the pub for dinner. You can pay if you really want."

Freddy did that shift from one foot to another again. "Thanks."

"You don't need to be nervous. It's really no big deal." He rested his hand on Freddy's lower back, just for a moment, before removing it. He wanted to reassure Freddy that he didn't need to be nervous, and he wasn't quite sure how to communicate that effectively. Especially here, in public, and while it should be safe, it was best to be careful. Freddy glanced at him, still with that wary look in his eye. The car pulled up and they got in. Freddy's leg jiggled the whole way and Jaxxon knew there would be no reassuring him with words.

The resolution came quickly as they pulled up outside the bakery and Jaxxon's father stood in the doorway.

"Papa." He jumped out of the car and hugged his father. Or his father hugged him. It'd been too long. He hadn't seen his folks since he'd been given this promotion back at the start of the year, although he called his mother every week religiously, and usually spoke to his father too. Naturally, they'd heard the entire saga of how Freddy had ended up in his life and he'd sent them a text before they'd left London to inform them of their arrival.

"Jaxxon. Your Ma is inside."

"This is my Freddy." He stepped back and waved in Freddy's direction.

"Sir." Freddy held out his hand for Papa to shake. Papa, of course, grabbed Freddy's hand, shook it once, then pulled Freddy into a hug.

"Boy. You might be Jaxxon's Freddy but is he your Jaxxon?"

"Yes, sir."

"I like this one, Jaxxon. He is very polite."

"Manners don't make the man."

Papa grinned. "They are a behaviour learned to demonstrate class not the quality of a person." It was one of Papa's favourite sayings. Papa clapped Freddy on the back, and he hardly flinched. "Come inside and meet my beautiful wife, Rosie, Jaxxon's mother."

"Yes, sir."

"Call me Jack." Papa walked back into the shop, leaving Freddy on the street.

"Come on. You'll be fine." Jaxxon guided Freddy inside.

"Oh good, Jaxxon, you are here. We are all out of apples. Would you be so good as to head out and grab me some?" Ma threw the keys to her van in his direction, and he caught them.

"Ma. Are you going to say hello to Freddy first?"

"Hello Freddy. Now you boys get me some apples. I'd do it myself, but I heard that this Freddy of yours was a good driver, so he can do the errand."

Jaxxon knew that his mother approved of Freddy, right there in that moment, because she'd never teased any of his other lovers like that. The peppering of questions about Freddy's intentions would likely come later. He'd always been able to tell how much Ma approved of someone, based on her questions—the more, the better—but she'd never given the keys to her precious delivery van to someone before. It was a huge act of trust.

"I have also heard that Freddy can drive." Papa's eyes glinted as he grinned at Ma. Jaxxon shook his head at this happy foolishness.

"Yeah, he's alright." Jaxxon wrapped his arm around Freddy's waist and grinned. "Come on then."

"Um..." The blank stare on Freddy's face made Jaxxon gulp.

"Ma, remember what you told me about how it's only a joke if everyone is laughing?"

Ma grinned. "Freddy. Welcome to the family. I do need apples, so if you would be so good as to take my darling husband for a drive, he would be most appreciative."

"Shit." Freddy's whispered expletive wasn't at all what Jaxxon was expecting.

CHAPTER 25

Freddy didn't want to admit the problem to these fabulous people. They'd welcomed him without question, to the point of teasing him, which felt like a love language. And damn, his heart was fit to burst at the way Jaxxon's father—Jack—pulled him into a hug, and Jaxxon called him 'my Freddy' and Jaxxon's mother, Rosie, called him 'this Freddy of yours'. If it wasn't about driving, he'd have laughed along with them, but they wanted him to drive their vehicle. There was some sense in it; he used to be a famous race car driver and he talked about car racing for a job. It was probably the only vehicle they owned, and while he didn't care for any fines—he could afford them—but he didn't want his name in the press for the wrong reasons. Mostly, it was an embarrassing reminder of the privilege of his birth, something that he felt starkly—a cactus dragged over his skin—while standing in their humble, much loved, small business. The whole place was homely, filled with handwritten signs and several photos of Jaxxon including one of him standing next to a Subaru rally car with the driver holding a trophy, and the smell of freshly baked bread.

"There's one small problem, ma'am."

"It's going to be alright, Freddy. It's just a delivery van." Jaxxon's confidence was misplaced. He could drive anything mechanical, but this technicality meant he couldn't.

He shook his head. It must be a record, to fuck up meeting wonderful people in such a small time. "I can't."

"You can't drive?" Jack had his face all screwed up.

"Obviously I know how to drive, but I can't drive your vehicle. Not legally." He didn't have a licence.

"Freddy?" Jaxxon's question invoked a sigh.

"I don't have a standard road driver's licence. I never have."

"But how do you get around the place?" Rosie had an incredulous expression as if his life made zero sense to her and she couldn't figure out someone so useless could be with her son. Fair enough too.

"Ride shares, cabs, the Tube. I just never needed to get it." He had only just met these people and now he had to explain. "It never happened. I had my super licence, obviously, but I've just never found the time or the need to get a standard one."

Jaxxon started laughing, then clapped his hand over his mouth, mumbling something that was probably an apology.

"Fine, yes, laugh at me. I must be the only person in the world with a super licence and no normal driver's licence. It's more paperwork." A super licence was purely for driving in S1 and they had to be renewed every three years with strict racing qualification standards. Most people had to have a standard driving licence too, but his team had gotten an exemption from that rule given his age at the time.

"What is this super licence? Can't you just use that?" Jaxxon's father asked.

"It's a racing licence for S1 cars only. While it might impress a cop, depending on the cop, it's not technically legal outside that one particular class of car on a racetrack, and besides, mine expired years ago."

"This is all very interesting, but I still need apples." Jaxxon's mother waved her hands.

"Yes, we are going. I will drive the van." Jaxxon jangled the keys. "Papa, do you still want to come?"

"Only if your Freddy drives in the carpark, where it's not a legal road. I want to be driven by a famous driver." Jaxxon's father winked and Jaxxon laughed. This family were so bloody adorable.

"Absolutely I can do that, sir." His expired super licence was in his wallet, a reminder of a life he didn't have any more. A funny little prickle clung to the back of his neck. Weird. He didn't like the idea that he had no licence at all, and now he'd have to start at the very beginning if he wanted to regain any of the racing class licences too. He wasn't important enough anymore to get any exemptions and he didn't want to ask for them either.

Jaxxon dangled the keys again, then whispered in Freddy's ear. "I can't believe I never noticed that I'd never seen you drive."

"It's a bit embarrassing, but by the time I thought I probably should get my standard licence, I was famous and

I didn't want to turn up at the licencing place and end up going viral."

"And I suppose you never really needed it, either."

"No."

"Well, come on. Let's get some apples." Jaxxon paused, then leaned in close and whispered. "I assume Ma is making the excuse just to put you and my father in a closed space together for a while."

"I assumed as much. It's sweet, you know, that they care so much for you." He wanted to be quizzed by them. Wasn't that a rite of passage when meeting someone's family? His own family certainly didn't give a shit about any of his partners; they'd been zero help during the Chester drama with his father pointing out that he'd better not drag the family name through the press. As if it were his fault.

"Come on boys, let's get moving." Jack called out, and they both trotted after him. The Renault van had a well-maintained, if well-used and slightly battered, look about it.

"I keep offering to get them a new one."

"They won't let you?" Freddy didn't understand that mentality.

"I already bought the bakery for them a few years ago. Apparently, that's enough of a gift." Jaxxon ducked his head.

"What is keeping you boys?" Jack leaned out of the passenger window.

"We are coming." Jaxxon walked around the van and climbed into the driver's seat, and Jack shuffled across into the middle of the bench seat, leaving a small spot for Freddy.

"It's good that you are a slender man." Jack patted him on the knee in a vaguely fatherly tone, if a touch had a tone. Jack had the same body shape as his son, and Freddy was filled with the settled notion that Jaxxon wouldn't change much as he aged. There was no chemistry from Jack's touch —he was similar to his son but an entirely different person obviously—only a steady sense of peaceful acceptance into the family. Would it be weird to call Jack Papa? Maybe one day.

"I have to stay thin for my job." He probably didn't, not now that he'd done this job for five seasons and was part of the team, but he liked being fit.

"And you are an athlete."

"Retired."

"All those drivers do seem very fit."

Freddy grinned and turned towards Jack. "It's necessary. Driving a race car is more than sitting down and steering."

"You sound like you've had that argument a few times."

He nodded. His father refused to understand that it took physical strength to have the stamina to concentrate for a whole race. "An S1 race takes a couple of hours, it's a long time to stay at the limit."

"You don't need to convince me." Jack directed Jaxxon along a street and into a driveway between huge warehouse buildings.

"Ray, the fruit guy is at the end."

"He's still there?" Jaxxon asked.

"You know Ray. He's going die on that stall." Fondness filled Jack's tone, and Freddy felt like he was being introduced to a whole new world, where people liked each other and did business without being assholes to each other.

"Papa. Did you want Freddy to drive you here because Ray is an S1 fan?"

"Of course."

"Does Ma even need apples?"

"She always needs apples for your favourite apple Danish." Jack winked, his wide grin so similar to his son's that it floored Freddy for a moment. He could see where Jaxxon got his ability to tease so well. Freddy swallowed. They didn't need to trick him. He would happily have driven—to let himself be shown off—for this family who welcomed him in so easily.

"Stop the van. I'll drive from here." Hopefully he wouldn't stall. It'd been years since he'd driven a standard manual transmission. Jaxxon stopped the van in the middle of the driveway and they both hopped out, swapping seats. Only Jack's massive grin stopped Freddy from overthinking this. It was a vehicle. He used to be one of the world's twenty best drivers. This should be simple.

He stalled the van with a lurch. "Fuck."

"Maybe Jaxxon needs to give you some lessons and help you get your licence?" Jack elbowed him, and damn if it didn't make Freddy feel like he was actually part of their loving family. He was going to melt with the niceness of being teased as if he belonged here. He had another go, and this time he managed to drive smoothly forward. Jack gave him directions and after a couple of hundred metres, they pulled up outside an open warehouse door with an older Black guy leaning against the doorframe. Freddy parked the van, and everyone piled out.

"Ray. I have a little surprise for you." Jack waved in Freddy's direction, and he walked around the van towards them. "This is Jaxxon's Freddy."

Holy hell. He'd never get tired of being introduced like that. Forever. Having someone say that he belonged to Jaxxon was absolute perfection. If his heart swelled any more today, it was going to explode out the front of his chest like a big loving alien. He held out his hand to Ray.

"Hi, I'm Freddy Hiptonstall. Pleased to meet you."

Ray shook his hand. "I had your poster back in the day. Always hoped you'd win a championship."

"So did I, Ray." He shook his head. "Not the poster, obviously. That'd be vain even for me."

Everyone's laughter surrounded him like a warm hug, and he wished he could say how good it felt to be welcomed, and not because he was famous either.

"Will you take me for a drive?" Ray asked.

"Sure. What car do you have?" Freddy could drive him around this warehouse complex since it wasn't technically a road.

"An ancient Mini."

"One of the originals? Built here?"

"Yes."

Freddy smiled. "It always makes me laugh that the guy who commissioned the Mini, the Chairman of the British Motor Company, was called Leonard Lord." The British Motor Company was a merger between Austin and Morris in the fifties, but he was pretty sure Jaxxon's family friend didn't care for all that information on the history of his car.

"Why is that funny?" Jaxxon asked.

"He's Chairman Lord, like title title." Everyone looked at him oddly. "Never mind. Let's see the car. What year?"

"1967 Mini Cooper S."

"Oh, the rally model? This should be fun. Shall we squeeze these two in the back seat?"

Ray clapped him on the shoulder. "Well, the engine isn't going to like it."

"No, but I can make it fun without wrecking your car." Freddy had driven a Mini once as promotion for Silverstone and the tiny car had loads of manoeuvrability, so it'd be fun to haul it around this carpark.

"Okay, but let's get Ma's apples first." Jaxxon's practicality grounded him.

"Apples first, then racing." Ray laughed, and Freddy helped load the box of apples into the van.

Driving the car had been fun—especially the way Ray had cackled as he'd flung the car around a corner, tyres squealing—but dinner in the pub with Jaxxon's parents was better. The four of them had a booth in the corner of the slightly run-down place with 1980s pop on the speaker system and paper coasters that had been reused too many times, all curled up at the edges with water stains on them. They'd ordered standard pub food, fish and chips with a pathetically small side salad. It was cosy. Jaxxon answered all his parent's questions about work, and it gave Freddy a strong insight into where he'd gained his business acumen. Jaxxon's parents had run a successful small business all their lives. Jaxxon's job might be on a different scale with six hundred staff members and a multi-million-dollar budget, but the principles of business didn't really change. When they all quizzed him about his job and his life and intentions with Jaxxon, his sense of belonging grew and grew, like a giant soap bubble that would burst one day leaving a film over everything.

"Thank you for taking Ray for a drive today. You will have made his year." Jack opened the door to their flat above the bakery. He wasn't sure how to answer; driving someone else's car was a pretty easy way to make someone happy.

"I enjoyed it too."

Rosie walked up the stairs first, welcoming Freddy into her house with a big grin. "You boys want to stay up with us and watch some telly?" The difference between Rosie and the vague memories of his tense, elegant, mother couldn't be starker. His mother lived in America now, trading on her social status as a Duchess, with the need to be bothered with her children. He didn't blame her for leaving his father; he wasn't exactly pleasant. Freddy had been brought up by nannies, a situation that likely wouldn't have been any different if she'd stayed. He'd much rather she wasn't miserable, even if he had occasionally wished that she'd been there to step in between him and father when he was younger. The reality was such that she couldn't have done much anyway.

"Okay." Freddy shook off those old thoughts—he was a grown man now—just wanting to just hang out with this family forever and absorb the cosiness of them. He'd never imagined that a family could be like this with their adult son.

"Jaxxon, you bring your Papa a beer, he's been working all day."

"Yes Ma. You want your usual too?"

"Yes please."

Freddy followed Jaxxon into the small kitchen. It was impeccably clean, but ancient, a 1950s relic but with a shiny new stove and dishwasher.

"I bought them new appliances when I got this promotion."

"I'm surprised they let you."

"I ordered them online and had them delivered so they had no choice."

"Sneaky. Your parents are—"

"Proud. And I understand it too, but I wouldn't have this job with all this money ... not like your amount of money ... but it's a big amount for me, um, I wouldn't have any of this if they hadn't encouraged me to be my best. And a few nice appliances seem like nothing compared to that."

"I understand. Your parents are amazing people. I've had the best day."

Jaxxon flicked his head up, as if surprised by that, and bundled Freddy into a tight hug. "I'm so glad."

"Just don't expect the same warmth if you ever meet my family. AA tries but he's a product of the system, you know, and His Grace is a distant fucker at best." He buried his face against Jaxxon's warm chest, wanting to hide there, before he lifted his head to look at Jaxxon's soft expression. "Actually, let's not think of them today. I don't want to sully how great this has been by thinking about that."

"Then stop thinking. Come and watch television with my parents." Jaxxon didn't let him go, though. He tucked his head under Jaxxon's chin, breathing in the warm buttery familiar scent of his skin. Jaxxon always smelled a little bit like the bakery; like fresh bread and butter and sugar and spice. And now that he'd been here, he wanted to soak it all in, absorb Jaxxon and his family like a weirdo who wanted the one thing he'd never had. Family who loved him and accepted him, flaws and all. He knew he'd never have to perform for these people to be granted a grudging acceptance.

"Come on. Stop thinking." Jaxxon stroked his back, and then handed him a small glass of spirits. "This is for Ma." They walked into the small lounge, handing over the drinks to Jaxxon's parents. Rosie patted the couch and he settled down beside her to watch whatever football game was on tonight. He didn't even care what the game was, just snuggling in against her as if he were a child, and he bloody loved it.

CHAPTER 26

"Games over, lad. Bedtime." Papa shook Jaxxon's shoulder, and he woke with a funny snort that hopefully no one notice. Freddy was tucked up against Ma with a blanket thrown over his legs. He had his arms outstretched as if he were in the middle of a story and he'd paused, stuck.

"Let Freddy finish his story. I want to know about the milk story. He promised me embarrassment."

Freddy chuckled. "I did not. I said it was ridiculous."

"Come on then." Jaxxon stretched out his legs.

"And yet you'd hardly started. Something boring about doing a promotion for a car, as if that wasn't your whole job as a driver." Ma teasing Freddy was beginning to be Jaxxon's favourite part of this visit. The two of them were having so much fun together; he loved the way Freddy slotted right into his family with no judgement of their small house or anything that Jaxxon had been worried about. Having Freddy like his parents and their life meant more than he knew how to articulate. It wrapped around him like the blanket covering Freddy's legs.

"Basically, someone in the social media team—"

"Sonia?" What he'd really wanted to ask was if it was Freddy's stalker, but he couldn't bring that up without derailing the whole conversation or breaking the confidence and trust Freddy had placed in him by telling him about the ordeal.

"Probably one of her team." Freddy waved his hand as if to say it didn't matter. "Anyway, we had to drive this car up and down pitlane between cones while holding a bowl of milk."

"Milk?" Jaxxon asked.

"Yeah. And the film crew added a thickener to the milk, so it would look cooler when it slopped out of the bowl, you know, with the droplets sticking together and hanging in the air for a slow-mo shot before they landed on us."

"Messy."

"It was very messy. And basically pointless. If I'd been able to win by going fastest or keeping the most milk in the bowl, then it would've been more fun."

"Are you that competitive for everything?" Jack asked.

Jaxxon laughed. "He's a driver. Competition is the baseline setting."

"I can't argue with that." He shrugged, then pulled out his phone and clicked through to something. "This is the final ad that they made."

Jaxxon leaned over the back of the couch, next to his father, as the four of them stared at Freddy's screen. Freddy sat in the passenger seat holding a bowl of milky liquid, while his teammate, Ricky Dee, drove. At first, Freddy held the bowl so it swayed with the cornering of the car, but when Ricky flicked the back end out to swing around the last cone, milk went everywhere. Freddy and Ricky's laughter was a soundtrack underneath the narrator talking about the car's handling.

"Oh, that's gross." Ma shook her head. "The poor cleaner. Imagine trying to get all that milk out of the fabric in those seats."

Freddy's face paled. "I never thought of that. I just thought you'd think it was funny to see me covered in milk splats."

"It's fine. We used to do stunts like this when I was in rally, and the people who detailed the cars afterwards were paid very well." Jaxxon jumped in before Freddy—his Freddy—could castigate himself about his privilege. While it was gratifying to see him understand it, it didn't need all the constant guilt. "Don't feel guilty for doing your job; which was to sell the car."

"Says someone who has never tried to clean milk out of fabric." Ma grinned.

"Are you kidding me? Remember that time Jaxxon dropped his milkshake all over the carpet."

Jaxxon glanced at his father. "Yeah, and all three of us cleaned it up because we are family, and Freddy is family too, so we can watch his video of being covered in milk and find it funny."

"Darling boy. I'm only teasing him."

"It's okay, Jaxxon. I like being teased." Freddy stood up, walked around the couch, and touched him on the spine. He wanted to lean into Freddy's hand. "Let's get your sleepy head to bed."

"Good idea. Look after my boy, will you?" Ma grinned up at Freddy.

"I can't believe you slept through most of the game!"

"It's been a long season so far. I am quite tired." He didn't mean to justify himself to his parents.

Papa elbowed Freddy. "You should've seen Jaxxon when he was a small boy. He used to get so surly when he was tired. It was the cutest thing."

"I'm sure Freddy doesn't want to hear about me as a kid. Good night, Papa. Good night, Ma." Jaxxon stood up straight, and Freddy pressed his hand harder against his spine.

"Maybe tomorrow." Freddy traced a circle on his waist. "Come on, time for sleeping."

Everyone said their good nights, and he walked the few steps down the hallway to his childhood bedroom. He always stayed here when he visited, but it wasn't until he pushed open the door to see his single bed and poster-covered walls, that he wondered how this was going to work.

"Cosy." Freddy wrapped his arms around Jaxxon's waist and nudged him until they were in the room.

"I barely fit on my old bed. We aren't going to ... how is this going to work?"

"It's fine. We'll make it work. Your parents are so nice. I wouldn't want to insult them by going somewhere else." Freddy stripped off his clothes and slid under the covers. He lay carefully on one edge of the slim bed, then patted the spot beside him. "Come on. There's heaps of room."

"If we cuddle up tight."

Freddy's grin was obscene. "You say that like it's a bad

thing. Come here to me. I've had the absolute best day and I want to share it with you." Freddy's joy infused the air with a happiness that wrapped around Jaxxon and pushed away his tiredness. He stripped off and slid into bed with Freddy, lying on his back. His arm fell off the side of the bed, and Freddy had almost no room, so he rolled onto his side. "How's that?"

"Incredibly cosy. We are going to be far too hot."

"It is summer."

"And you are a thermal emitter."

Jaxxon grabbed the blankets and pulled them off, leaving only a sheet covering them. "This will be fine."

"Yes, you'll keep me warm." Freddy burrowed up against him and the roar of desire was tempered by the fact that he was in his parent's house.

"God, I feel like a teenager, sneaking around."

Freddy laughed. "It does have the feel to it, especially with the posters of cars all over the walls."

"Ergh." Jaxxon plucked Freddy's hands off his waist and got out of bed to turn off the light, then slid back inside. The dark of night was softened by the sole street-light outside his window. Artificial yellow light snuck between the edges of the old curtains and the window frame, casting a warm glow over everything.

"This is nice." Freddy stroked his hands all down Jaxxon's side, then squeezed his hip. He growled under his breath.

"We can't."

"Oh?"

"Aside from the logistics on this small bed, this is my parent's house and the walls are quite thin."

Freddy reached up and placed his palm gently over Jaxxon's mouth and whispered, "then we will have to be very quiet."

Desire roared to life, threading in his veins, and centred in his cock. The pressure of Freddy's hand on his lips added to the sense of rebellion at doing this with Freddy in his parent's house. He was an adult. His parents adored and accepted Freddy. Logically, he wasn't getting away with anything—and didn't need his parent's permission either—but his body had already decided that it was hotter to let Freddy keep him quiet in case someone overheard them.

"We wouldn't want your wonderful parents to think that I'm taking advantage of their son." Freddy's whisper sent a shiver across his skin, and he gasped as Freddy dragged his fingernails down Jaxxon's chest. Suddenly his lungs felt airless, and he sucked in a breath but that only pulled Freddy's palm tighter against his mouth.

"Shhh."

He licked Freddy's palm, loving the way his nostrils flared as he tried not to make any noise either. Freddy responded by curling his fingers around Jaxxon's hard cock and stroking. Too lightly. Jaxxon wanted more and he shifted his hips. Freddy tightened his grip, then slid his thumb over the end of Jaxxon's cock. He hissed.

"Quiet." And then Freddy shifted his other hand away from Jaxxon's mouth, leaving him free to make noise, making his choice to stay quiet. Freddy slid his hand down his throat, drawing out ragged breaths from Jaxxon, and just as he wasn't sure he could hold back a growl, Freddy kissed him. Jaxxon grabbed onto Freddy, letting his hands do the talking that he couldn't, needing to touch every piece of him. They rolled together into the middle of the tiny bed, with Freddy covering Jaxxon. Not being able to make noise made it feel more frantic, and he poured every pent-up moan into their kiss until he was going to explode with the need to cry out. The streetlight touched Freddy's brown hair with a golden glow, like gold paint on dark polished wood.

"Come for me." Freddy used his knees to create enough space between them for his hand, holding their hard cocks together. It was dry and too rough. He needed relief not this desperate delicious agony. He spat in his hand, and pushed Freddy's hand out of the way, using the wetness to make it more comfortable for them both. Freddy covered his hand with his own and he had to pinch his lips together to strangle the groan that wanted to escape.

"Shh. You can come quietly."

A desperate little laugh escaped. Freddy couldn't even stop talking when he was trying to be silent.

"I can, but can you?" He wasn't certain he could, but he knew Freddy would thrive with the competition. Sure enough, Freddy buried his face against Jaxxon's neck and let out of breathy cry, muffled by Jaxxon's skin, as he came. It was all it took for Jaxxon to follow, his body shaking. Stars shone behind his eyes with the joint pressure of release while withholding any sound. His throat felt full of air and he tried to ease it slowly, closing his eyes to focus on the task.

"Do you think they heard?" Freddy asked, after a while.

He opened his eyes to see Freddy's cheeky grin and glowing expression. "I hope not, but probably."

"Did you lose your virginity in this bed?"

"Freddy."

Freddy's grin grew. "I love it when you say my name like that."

The happy buzz in his ears got a little louder. "Did you just ask me that question, so I'd say your name with reproach?"

"Yes."

"Freddy." He was rewarded with a kiss. A kiss that tasted like Freddy and home and everything he had ever have wanted and had been afraid to hope for. He'd assumed he'd never find someone as obsessed with his work as him, that his relationships would forever be doomed to fail because he was always travelling, always thinking about work, and now he had Freddy who was equally as obsessed with racing as him.

"Let me clean us up." Freddy shifted off him and he missed his weight.

"Okay. But come right back." He shifted the sheet, so it didn't land in any of the mess; cum painted on his stomach, and when Freddy wiped him clean with a soft dry piece of cloth he let his eyes close slowly. Freddy slid back onto the bed, curled up against him and the possibility of doing this forever with Freddy was Jaxxon's final happy thought before he drifted off to sleep.

CHAPTER 27

Freddy wanted the summer break to go on forever. He'd gone online and applied for his provisional driver's licence and now just had to sit the tests for the next stage, but he was allowed to do driving practice immediately, so he'd spent a week helping out in the bakery. When he'd put a message on his social media that he'd be driving the delivery van for a week, they'd been inundated with orders, which resulted in Jaxxon directing him around Liverpool as he delivered baked goods to people and let them take photos of him, always making sure the van's logo was in the background. What was the point of having millions of followers online if he didn't use it for helping the people who'd so easily included him in their family?

"What time is our flight?" Jaxxon had to be back at Gamble Racing headquarters tomorrow.

"The chopper will be ready in an hour." They stood in Jaxxon's bedroom, packing up after an amazing lunch with Jaxxon's parents. He'd wanted to take them out for lunch today, as a thank you for their hospitality this week, and they'd gone to a brilliant restaurant. Jaxxon kissed him on the forehead, and together they gathered up their stuff before walking down the steps to the van. Freddy had wanted to book a ride share, and not take up more of Jack and Rosie's time, but Jack had declared that he could take them in his van.

"What took you both so long?"

"I think they were kissing again. Look, our Freddy is all flushed."

Freddy wanted to bottle up Rosie's laugh and take it with him. "Thank you for having me this week. I've had the best time."

"My sons are welcome anytime." Rosie wrapped him in a hug and he breathed in deep. She was so warm and motherly and he was so grateful that this could be his family now that it took him a few minutes to realise that she'd used a plural.

"Sons?"

"Yes. Jaxxon obviously loves you and I can see why. You are my son too, for as long as you want to be."

His chest was going to burst. "Thank you. That means a lot to me."

Jaxxon joined their hug, squishing Freddy between him and his mother. "It's true. I do love you, Freddy."

He choked on his tongue. "Why did you have to declare that now? In the middle of the street?" In front of Jaxxon's parents. Freddy could hardly respond in the way he desperately wanted to with Jaxxon's parents watching.

"I'm not taking it back."

He wriggled out of their hug. "Don't you dare. I love you too Jaxxon and your incredible family and as soon as we get somewhere private, I'm going to show you exactly how much." He refused to look at Rosie, partly wanting to suck that comment right back into his head where it belonged, and partly content with blurting out his feelings in an oddly sexual way for this situation.

Jaxxon winked. "Promises."

"Boys." Jack cleared his throat. "Come on, you'll miss your flight."

"Thanks, Papa. Ma, I'll text as soon as we land."

After a few more hugs from Rosie, they finally got into the van. Freddy settled into the seat, letting the happy buzz float around him, like that one time Nanny Belle had cleaned up his knees when he'd fallen off his bike and made him feel like someone cared about him. Jaxxon's family gave him that same feeling and they weren't even being paid to do it. It just was, which made it even better.

It was only mid-afternoon when they landed at the Gamble Racing headquarters. The last time Freddy had been here was late at night last winter. Lucien Grenville had collected him from the hangar, and he'd walked into absolute chaos to discover that Lucien had punched Gamble Racing's old engineer's son, because he'd been sabotaging their cars. Curiosity had ruled that night, which was all journalistic instinct and chasing down a story. It couldn't be more different to today, where he wanted to go home with Jaxxon and share this incredible sense of belonging with him. He wanted to belong to Jaxxon. He glanced over at Jaxxon, who was staring out across the test track at the massive workshop.

"You aren't going in there." Freddy nudged Jaxxon. The

helicopter took off again, temporarily filling the air with noise.

When it faded, Jaxxon turned to him with a frown. "Work?"

"No work until tomorrow. I have plans for you."

Jaxxon kissed him on the cheek. "Oh no. I already made plans for tonight."

"You did?" He held his breath.

"Yes. I planned to take my boyfriend to dinner, then show him exactly how much I love him."

Laughter bubbled out of him, with a tiny bit of relief. After a week with Jaxxon's family, he ought to have known he was teasing.

"Hey. You stole my plan." He reached out and held Jaxxon's hand as they walked down the driveway from the hangar.

"Where are you taking me? I thought I said no work tonight."

"My car is parked outside the workshop. I travelled with the team to Hungary from here."

"In a truck?"

"Yes. With the logistics team."

"Do you do that often?"

Jaxxon blew out a noisy breath and Freddy curled his little finger around Jaxxon's finger. "Yes."

"Because of the sabotage issue?"

"Yes and no. Not because I think it will happen again. I try to spend time with all the different parts of the team as often as I can. It helps me understand their jobs and discover any potential problems before they arise. We have around six hundred people on the staff here at Gamble Racing."

"It's a lot to keep track of."

"Yes. The sabotage was a unique problem; I honestly don't think we'll encounter something like that again." It went unsaid that the sabotage had been caused by someone closely connected to Socrates, whose loyalty was legendary, but sometimes had consequences.

He tightened his grip on Jaxxon's hand, threading his fingers between Jaxxon's. "You are allowed to criticise Socrates."

"It's not about that at all. The sabotage wasn't the fault of his leadership; Reggie's son made his own poor decisions. It's more that Socrates and I have different strengths as leaders and different styles, and I didn't mean to criticise him when I said that I spend time with all the members of our team."

"Socrates is certainly a unique person."

Jaxxon shook his head. "Very true." He breathed out heavily and Freddy wanted to reassure him, but he didn't have time as Jaxxon continued.

"I've been thrown into this role without as much preparation as I planned. I thought I'd be race engineer for a couple more seasons, then perhaps another management role, before becoming Team Principal. Now I have to learn the business quickly, and by spending time with each division, it helps me get up to speed faster."

"Your promotion certainly surprised everyone in the paddock." It had come out of nowhere and he recalled how he'd struggled to write the profile on Jaxxon.

"It couldn't be helped. No one could have predicted that Socrates would have a stroke, or why."

"In the context, it made sense that he would promote someone internal."

"Yes. I'm not complaining about it; it's just been a huge learning curve. Lately Socrates has tended to promote people slightly before they are ready... Victor started the trend."

"Do you think it's a bit of a hangover from clinging onto Reggie for too long?" Freddy admired Socrates loyalty to his old engineer but it hadn't been good for the team and the whole paddock had been speculating about when Reggie would get replaced for a few years.

"Perhaps. I think Socrates believes in people's potential, and his loyalty to Reggie was about that more than clinging to the past."

Freddy wanted to know more but his phone rang. "Hold that thought. It's Georgia." He answered the phone.

"Freddy. Oh my God. Um, first a trigger warning, but you need to look at the photo I've just emailed you."

"Okay?" What the hell kind of photo was Georgia sending him if it needed a trigger warning.

"Now. Put me on speaker and do it now."

He swallowed and hit the button, holding his phone out so Jaxxon could hear too. "Hold up. What's the trigger warning?"

"It's a photo of Chester."

"Why do should I care about that?" He didn't want to see that smug face.

Georgia clicked her tongue. "This is important and

that's why I gave you the trigger warning. You don't have to look at it. I can just tell you what I saw."

"Why are you looking at photos of him anyway?"

"I check out his social media once a week to make sure he's fulfilling the conditions of his restraining order." Georgia doing her job with such competent focus on the details was why he employed her, and he breathed out slowly, rolling his shoulders to ease the sudden tension in them.

"And you saw something?"

"Yes. Take a look."

Jaxxon frowned. "Why not just tell him?"

"Indulge me. Trust me. You want to see this for yourself. My description will not do it justice."

"Fine." He slid his thumb up to switch apps and had a look at his emails, opening the one from Georgia and clicking on the jpg attachment. The photo showed Chester standing in a nice room with white walls, grinning at the camera. He wore one of those Henley shirts that he favoured. Freddy shuddered and was about to growl at Georgia and ask why she was wasting her time when he spied ... His gasp whistled as he pointed at the background of the photo.

"Is that Socrates' trophies on the cabinet behind him?"

"Yes." Georgia's enthusiasm rang clearly through the tinny speakers of the phone.

"Chester has Socrates' trophies? And he just put them on his social media for everyone to see?"

Georgia cackled. "I imagine he forgot they were there. This is such a thirst photo." He could hear her eyes rolling.

"Congratulations on finding the missing trophies." He

would never have suspected Chester, except... "Do you think he picked these because of me?"

"Yes. Absolutely. All three missing trophies have a connection to you, and I think he wanted you to pay him attention by trying to find them."

"It makes sense. You were the presenter at our car reveal and Seb drives for your old team." Jaxxon mimed slapping his forehead.

"What do we do now? Freddy fought the instinct to make it all go away—that was his privileged upbringing talking—and tried to quiet his breathing until he could help.

"Gamble Racing needs to take that image to the detective working the case."

Freddy nodded and forwarded it to Jaxxon. "I've forwarded Georgia's email to you."

"Go get him, Freddy."

"Thanks for this, Georgia. I really appreciate how you've always got my back."

"It's my job."

"You know it's more than that."

"Yeah, but let's not get too sappy until we have the trophies returned to their rightful owner."

Freddy glanced over at Jaxxon who had one eyebrow raised. "That's fair. We will get right on to it."

"Good luck." Georgia hung up.

"I think this will ruin our plans for dinner." Freddy just wanted to hang out with Jaxxon with all the happy feelings of the last week.

"Don't say that. Let's duck into the workshop, sort this

out, and then we will continue with our plans. Only one question remains."

"What's that?"

"Should I tell Socrates or wait until we have the trophies in our hands?"

"I don't know. All I know is that I want to help fix this. If it's really Chester continuing to target me by hurting the people around me, then I can't keep paying other people, like Georgia, to keep sorting it out for me."

Jaxxon spun Freddy around and hugged him. "It's okay to ask for help when someone is stalking you."

"I'm not just using my privilege to avoid dealing with it?" He knew Jaxxon would tell him the truth.

"There's two pieces to that question. Yes, you have privilege in that you can afford to pay someone to help you. No, you aren't avoiding dealing with it. You are looking after yourself."

He rested his head on Jaxxon's shoulder for a while before standing upright. "Thank you."

"Now, let's get this sorted quickly so we can go to dinner. I want you to spoil me." Jaxxon kissed him on the forehead and all those good fluttery feelings of belonging returned. But first, they had some work to do...

CHAPTER 28

Two weeks later, Jaxxon parked his Jag outside his cottage in Syresthorpe and walked inside, breathing in deeply.

"Freddy. That smells amazing." Like charred chilli and fresh tortillas and something a bit sweet too. His sweet tooth could always pick out those notes in anything.

"I made pork tortillas."

"From scratch?"

Freddy laughed and pulled Jaxxon in for a hug. "Don't be silly. The supermarket had a kit for sale, with marinated pork, and tortillas, and everything else. I just had to follow the instructions."

"You've done a great job."

"Perhaps you should eat before you make that declaration." As if Freddy hadn't spent the last two weeks learning how to cook because he wanted to learn a new skill while Jaxxon had to work. "I thought we'd sit outside." Freddy loved to sit on Jaxxon's deck and watch the sun set over his little backyard.

"Good plan." He kissed Freddy who kissed him back with great enthusiasm, then laughed as Freddy wriggled free.

"Pour us a beer each and I'll bring them outside."

"Sure." They'd worked out a routine where they spoiled each other in equal measures. Jaxxon had always loved this part of a relationship; having someone to come home to after work, and it was even better knowing that in a week's time, they'd be back on the road together. Leaving someone behind had always caused problems. With Freddy they'd be living together all year—just in different hotels every race—supporting each other's work and life. He sorted out the drinks while Freddy fussed with the food, plating it up. Soon enough they sat down outside.

"How was work?" Freddy asked. He fussed with his napkin and Jaxxon reached out to hold his hand because he only ever fidgeted when he had a problem that he wasn't sure how to discuss.

"Work was fine. We did some wind tunnel testing."

Freddy perked up.

"You know I can't tell you about that yet. I'm more interested in why you are destroying that poor napkin. What's the matter?"

"They arrested Carol today."

Jaxxon stopped breathing. He'd been expecting an announcement about Chester, now the trophies had been recovered, not this. "What? Your producer. When?"

Freddy held up both hands. "Hey."

"Sorry."

"Um, yeah, that was my reaction too. I only found out

an hour ago and I've been struggling to work out how I feel."

Jaxxon nodded. He didn't mind that Freddy hadn't told him immediately. It was quite shocking news and sometimes things like that took people a while to process, which was pretty much what Freddy had said. He breathed out slowly.

"Carol?"

"Yes. Chester offered her money to take the trophies."

He rubbed his eyes. "I don't understand."

Freddy pulled his hand away from Jaxxon and ran both hands through his hair. "Neither. Why didn't she just ask me?"

"For the trophies?"

"No. For the money."

"I don't understand."

Freddy growled. "You said that."

He waited. He trusted Freddy to tell him the story when he was ready.

"Carol's brother is in America and needs a heart transplant, so she needed money. That's why she stole the trophies for Chester. But she could've just asked me for the money. I would've sorted it out. I have plenty."

"Perhaps she was embarrassed?" He couldn't make it make sense either. "She's risked her whole job for her brother." It was admirable in some ways but also desperately sad.

"And now she's been arrested and lost her job. She may not have been a fan of S1 but I liked working with her. She was a great producer, and she's thrown it all away."

"For her brother."

"Okay, but I could've given her the money."

"What a fucking mess."

Freddy breathed out slowly. "Yes. I don't understand how Chester even knew that about her to ask."

"Obsession knows no bounds, I suppose."

This time Freddy did growl. "That fucker. The audacity of him to stalk my colleagues so he can find someone desperate enough to do this for him. I hope he rots."

"Now that's something I do understand."

"What?"

"The urge to see Chester pay for the pain he's caused people." He stood up and walked around the table towards Freddy. "Come here."

Freddy stood up and stepped into Jaxxon's outstretched arms. "Thank you. I hate Chester has dragged other people into this."

"Poor Carol and her brother, dealing with this on top of the dreadful American medical system. From what I've read about it, their system would drive any rational person to desperate measures. Our insurance for the American races is such a nightmare of paperwork." The Gamble Racing administration team employed someone to deal with it, and it took an entire full-time position to ensure that all the forms were correct for their team and that they ended up with the best price package for the whole team. And that was only for two races a year.

Freddy was still tense and stiff against Jaxxon's body, so he gently rubbed his back. Freddy needed comfort, not a lesson on insurance and the dramas around it, although he'd probably love to know all the details and interview Jodie for one of his behind the scenes pieces.

"I don't blame Carol. I'm mostly hurt that she would rather steal from Socrates and Seb than ask me for help."

"It's not really about you."

Freddy tipped his head backwards and laughed manically. "It's completely about me."

"Technically, yes. But not in a selfish way. Other people have made some bad choices because they wanted to have a negative impact on you."

"Yeah, thanks." Freddy sighed. His arms had been hanging lax at his sides, and now he lifted them to rest on Jaxxon's hips.

"It's going to be fine. The trophies have been returned. Chester is in jail. Carol made a desperate choice in a desperate circumstance, but that's not your responsibility. Georgia has your back, and I'm here. Everything will be fine." He meant it.

"I love you, Jaxxon. I'm not sure that you are right but with you here, it's enough."

He kissed Freddy, a gentle kiss that tasted like hops and chilli and Freddy. "Together we can face whatever the world throws at us. Look at us."

Freddy's smile was his whole world and it warmed him all the way through. "We can."

"Tomorrow we'll go to Spa and show the paddock that we are better together. I love you."

"I promise I'll ask some curly questions just so people don't think I'm being soft on you." Freddy's voice was still a little shaky, but Jaxxon could tell the shock was wearing off now. If Freddy was ready to tease, Jaxxon could play that game too. He thrust his hips to grind their cocks together.

"Soft is not how I'd describe you."

"Ha." Freddy's face flushed. "Just as long as you let me rescue you as often as you've rescued me."

"I haven't rescued you at all. You did this yourself and before you say that Georgia did a lot of it, you were the one who employed her knowing that you'd need a team around you."

Freddy's eyes glinted and that was the moment Jaxxon knew everything would be okay. "Socrates did say I was great in bed."

"Freddy." Jaxxon used Freddy's favourite tone, because he knew what it did for him, and was rewarded with a little growl and Freddy's hands slipping down his spine to grip his ass.

Freddy frowned. "Technically Socrates only knows that because Chester said it."

"Yeah, I'm sorry."

"Hey, I was the one who mentioned it. I do enjoy that rumour." Freddy winked. "Socrates was wrong about one thing thought."

"Oh?"

"My lack of commitment. I just hadn't found the right person yet."

Jaxxon leaned his forehead against Freddy's. "I can't even be annoyed at him. His meddling resulted in us spending time together."

"Bloody Socrates."

"Yeah but his scheming has always worked out well for me, so I think I'll let him keep doing it." Jaxxon kissed Freddy again, letting himself get lost in the taste of Freddy and their kiss. He loved this man, who talked too much and loved car racing, and was a lot more anxious than he let on to the world, and who overthought everything. They kissed until Jaxxon's stomach grumbled.

"We'd better eat this food before it gets cold." He kissed Freddy on the forehead and returned to his chair.

"Eat quickly. I have plans for you."

Jaxxon smiled. "You know how much I like plans."

An hour later, they'd finished eating and had washed up. It was incredibly domestic. Jaxxon could live like this forever, comfortable with Freddy in his space. He loved the way Freddy wasn't bothered by his small cottage. When he'd bought this place, it'd reminded him of his childhood home. Cosy and comfortable. The type of home his parents would be able to relax in, not like Freddy's London apartment that was all glass and luxury. Freddy's apartment had many advantages too and he could just as easily see the two of them spending time there, enjoying a London lifestyle when they wanted to.

"Want to go for a walk?" Freddy asked.

"If that's what you want."

"Yes. Walk with me to the lounge."

Jaxxon laughed. "So far?"

Freddy trailed his fingers across Jaxxon's throat and down over his shoulder as he walked past. "Come on."

He jogged after Freddy and was about to ask what his plans were when Freddy cut off any words with a kiss. A hungry, tender, kiss that said all the things they'd already said in words. This was love. Freddy caressed his mouth with his tongue, slipping his hands under Jaxxon's work shirt, warm hands on his skin.

"Fuck I love the way you feel." Freddy's breathless confession sent shivers along his spine, concentrating in his hard cock.

"I love everything about you."

Freddy laughed with his mouth against Jaxxon's neck, muffling the sound. "Aren't we competitive?"

"Says the driver."

"I excel at everything I do." Freddy sank to his knees, dragging his body down over Jaxxon as he sank. Jaxxon gripped Freddy's shoulders, needing something to anchor him, as Freddy undid his pants and slid them down his legs. He licked all the way up Jaxxon's cock. Jaxxon shivered as Freddy savoured him, heat coursing through his veins, and a gasp tangling in his throat.

"Please." Jaxxon threaded one hand through Freddy's hair, trying to stay upright and not let his knees buckle as Freddy sucked him deep. His hot wet mouth was fucking perfect. This beautiful man and his competitive desire to be the best at everything he did currently had incredible benefits as he sucked and licked and took Jaxxon right to the edge.

"Not yet. I have plans for you." Freddy's voice was hoarse; his throat well fucked.

"Do those plans include you fucking me?"

"You want that?"

Absolutely. He loved being taken apart by Freddy. "Yes. I want you to lose yourself in me." And he knew that Freddy needed that too after today's news about his boss. Seeing Freddy close his eyes and shake his head made Jaxxon's balls tighten even more.

"I can do that."

Jaxxon lowered himself to the ground, grateful for the soft rug he had on the floor. They kissed for a while with Freddy holding Jaxxon's cock in his hand, far too softly, just stroking lightly to match the movements of his tongue. Hell, he wasn't going to last at this rate.

"Freddy."

"Yes?"

"Can you?" He couldn't really form words anymore. His body was on fire and he needed to be covered by Freddy. "I want your weight on me."

"You'd better get naked and kneel on the couch then."

He scrambled to his feet and tore off his clothes, desperate for Freddy. "Like this?" He wriggled his backside and was rewarded with a small tap from Freddy.

"Perfect."

He couldn't help it and turned to watch Freddy as he undressed. "All the work you put into that body is worth it."

"Thank you." Freddy winked as he slowly removed his boxers.

"You know I'll still love you no matter what you look like."

Freddy's grin widened. "I know. I look like this for me and my job, you just—"

"Get to benefit."

"Absolutely. Now stop distracting me by waving that gorgeous cock of yours around."

"Like this?" He rolled onto his back and grabbed his cock. The flush across Freddy's skin was fucking beautiful and the way he choked was even better. Freddy grabbed some lube and a condom and got himself ready, and the showy way he did that was all the anticipation Jaxxon could deal with. He moved back onto his knees, just as Freddy had requested, and waited. Freddy leaned over his back, all warmth and hard muscles pressed on his spine, and breathed against Jaxxon's neck.

"My Jaxxon." Freddy took his sweet time getting Jaxxon open and relaxed and he hovered on the edge of satisfaction for what felt like hours until Freddy pressed inside.

"Home." It came out spontaneously, the description of how this felt, and Freddy growled deep and rumbling through his chest against Jaxxon's body. Freddy filled him, thrusting deep with every stroke touching his prostate and sending him spiralling closer and closer to release. The room filled with the sounds of flesh against flesh and their collective moans. When Freddy reached around and stroked Jaxxon's cock and whispered his love against the back of Jaxxon's ear, he came hard, pleasure tearing through him.

"Freddy." He cried out and Freddy came with a deep thrust, shuddering inside him. They collapsed together into an untidy hug, cleaning up with thanks to the supplies Jaxxon kept in the lounge for that purpose.

"Summer break is almost over. I'm going to miss coming home to you."

Freddy kissed him on the cheek. "We are sharing a room at Spa. It'll be pretty much the same."

"We really do need a plan for the rest of the season."

"You and your plans." Freddy nuzzled in closer. "It'll be fine."

"Not if Gamble Racing are paying for all your hotel rooms."

"How about we do a little contract? Gamble pays for

the hotel room and Inoue Media can pay for our food and all the little adventures I want to take you on."

He nodded. "That sounds fair. Want to watch a replay of last year's race?"

"Absolutely."

He stood up and get the remotes. Freddy wandered off to the kitchen to grab a couple of drinks, and soon enough they were cuddled up, naked, under a blanket watching telly. He could get used to a life lived like this.

CHAPTER 29

SPA

Freddy pushed through the crowd of journalists and shoved his microphone in Jaxxon's face, unsurprised to see Socrates standing beside him. Having the Gamble Racing team owner back at the track had helped prevent all the gossip being about him and Jaxxon.

"Let's grab Jaxxon Loharani-Jones, Team Principal for Gamble Racing. Jaxxon, what a way to start the second half of the season." Gamble Racing had just finished one-two on the podium at Spa; the team's best result for years, and a brilliant way to begin the second half of the season.

"Yes. I always had faith in this team and in Jaxxon's leadership." Socrates didn't give Jaxxon a chance to answer, and from the glint in Jaxxon's eyes, he didn't mind one bit.

"Welcome back to the paddock Socrates. Everyone has been worried about you as you've been away all year battling a health condition. It's so good to see you back."

Okay, he was rambling now, but it really was true. They'd already interviewed him a couple of times during the weekend, however, it was worth saying again since the viewership data showed that some people only watched the race, not the entirety of the weekend's build-up.

"We wanted to welcome Socrates back to the paddock in style and our cars and drivers certainly delivered today." Jaxxon did Freddy's job for him and kept the interview on the thing that mattered.

"One-two on the podium certainly makes a statement for the rest of the season."

"We are thrilled to see Paulo Sanchez get his first race win, and the one-two is a great achievement for our hard-working team. We'd expected big things this weekend because the cars showed a lot of pace in the early practice sessions although I wouldn't have put money on us finishing with both cars on the podium."

"It is impressive for a mid-field team."

"The teams at the top are highly competitive and we had to have a few things go our way—" Jaxxon alluded to the skirmish that had taken out the three leading drivers, leaving room for Paulo to take the lead at the half-way point. Ondrej tracked him throughout the rest of the race, slowly making his way from fourth into second, but Paulo kept his ten second lead to the end of the race to get his first S1 win in only his second season at the top level.

"It's one thing to take the lead of a race like this after an incident, and quite another to keep it. Both Paulo and Ondrej drove their hearts out for us today and the team is incredibly proud. I'm so thrilled." Socrates' big smile would be centre of the shot Maddock was getting and Freddy loved it.

"This is the culmination of the work we have done with the team over the past year and half since Victor and Paulo came on board, and today we are reaping the benefits. We've had confidence in this car, and in both Ondrej and Paulo, and we know they are both capable of winning more races for us. Hopefully we'll be able to keep the momentum going into Zandvoort and for rest of the season."

Freddy hadn't been to a team party for years, not since he'd been a driver, and now he was attending Paulo's victory party as Jaxxon's plus one. He fussed with his shirt until Jaxxon clucked his tongue at him.

"It'll be fine." Jaxxon kissed him on the cheek, then grabbed his phone and hotel key card. They walked together to the elevator and down to the ride share that would take them to the restaurant Gamble Racing had booked for their winner's celebration. He spent the ride babbling about the race, the drama surrounding the incident at turn four and who had had the racing line and whether the five second penalty had been consistent with other similar incidents this year. Jaxxon let him talk, simply resting his hand on Freddy's thigh. The ready comfort was absolutely what he needed.

"Relax, Freddy. No one is going to notice us."

"We've been the talk of the paddock all race weekend."

"Yeah, no. We haven't. It just feels like that. Everyone is caught up in the latest silly season dramas, especially with Letherbarrow tweeting out that he's in talks with four different teams." Jaxxon knew exactly how to stop him stressing.

"Letherbarrow... He's quick, but he's an asshole. I'm not sure I'm keen to see him step up from F2 just yet." Freddy breathed out and followed Jaxxon out of the ride share and into the restaurant.

"Hey, it's my new favourite couple." Socrates greeted them both.

"You damned old match maker." Freddy grinned as he shook Socrates' hand, while Jaxxon rolled his eyes.

"Let's keep the focus tonight on our race winner." Freddy glanced around the room but couldn't see Paulo among the hoards of people.

"Yes. Come on. Time to toast Paulo; and yes, I'm not drinking tonight." Socrates' face fell for a second.

"Good for you. I've been cutting back since your accident too." Freddy gave Jaxxon a gentle nudge to send him off to do his job. Before Jaxxon could move, there was a huge commotion at the front door of the restaurant. Paulo walked inside accompanied by a stunningly beautiful young woman.

"Is that Dalynda Cardoso?" Socrates asked.

"Who?"

"She's a supermodel. Don't you follow fashion?"

Jaxxon chuckled. "Freddy only cares about racing. I didn't pick you for a fan of fashion, Socrates."

"Are you kidding me? I have a certain dress standard to uphold. Besides, we have a sponsorship deal with the same fashion brand that she is an ambassador for. They do all our merchandise."

"Paulo, come over here." Jaxxon turned to his driver

and stuck out his hand. "Congratulations. Again. Well deserved win."

The soft blush made Paulo look even younger, and damned if that didn't make Freddy feel old. He remembered being that young, the thrill of his first win, and the validation of being in the select group of S1 drivers who won a race. Socrates nudged him in the side.

"Congratulations Paulo. It was a solid drive."

Paulo shook his head. "Not really. We gained the position through an undercut, taking the punt on tyres, then the leaders crashed. All I had to do was hold my position."

"For over thirty percent of the race. Don't underestimate how hard it is to defend for that long." Freddy knew. He'd been in that exact circumstance. "Trust me. I know."

"Thank you." Paulo glanced between Freddy and Jaxxon. Was he uncomfortable with them as a couple? If so, he was in the wrong team. Gamble Racing was the most openly queer team on the grid.

"And are you going to introduce us?"

"Yeah. This is Delynda Cardoso. She's a friend of my sister and we had a thing to do after the race, so I invited her to come with me." It was an odd way to phrase having winner's celebration sex, and Freddy hoped that Socrates didn't...

"A thing? Like sex?"

Paulo's blush made Freddy feel sorry for him. "No. Um, no one expected me to win today, or ever, I guess, so my father had booked a photo shoot for after the race while we were both in the same country."

Delynda stopped looking around the room and paid attention to them. "Mr Sanchez has a new range of clothes that he needed us to model, and this was the only night my schedule aligned with Paulo." She was dismissive and aloof, but not unpleasant.

"And now you get to spend the evening with a bunch of car racing enthusiasts." Socrates winked.

"Arriving here for the celebration of Paulo's win is good publicity for both of us." Delynda shrugged one shoulder as if to say she'd rather be anywhere else than hang out with Paulo. Poor kid.

"I understand." Freddy had done plenty of those types of publicity stunts during his own driving career. "Welcome and I hope you enjoy the evening, regardless. We'll get some good photos of you and Paulo with the trophy that look—"

"Casual. Yes, that would be useful. Being seen with Paulo helps both of us." Delynda's statement showed a depth of understanding about celebrity life. Freddy would've said as much but Paulo cleared his throat.

"Is the trophy here?"

"You don't have it?" Socrates asked in a tone that reminded Freddy of how long it'd taken him to find the missing trophies; and how he couldn't have done it without a team.

"No. I gave it Monica to keep safe while I was working with Delynda." Paulo's race engineer was over by the bar, chatting to Theron and Ondrej and a few of the mechanics.

Jaxxon waved his hand. "It's on the bar near her."

"Come on, Delynda. I'll show it to you."

The model smiled—what a knock-out smile—and followed Paulo across the room. As she moved, almost everyone in the room turned to stare at her.

"She's got real star power." Freddy was impressed, not many people had the ability to turn heads like that.

"Yes. Nothing like Paulo, who still doesn't seem to believe he belongs here. Even after a stunning race win like today."

Jaxxon sighed. "It's hard not to internalise the incessant comments on social media about how he bought his seat and how he's the second driver for us. We don't believe that. I'm just not sure how to make him understand our position."

"It will come once he holds the trophy for longer. Now he has his first win, and he's here with a beautiful woman, things will change. You'll see." Socrates said. "You two must be pleased with the result too."

"Of course we are." Jaxxon glanced sideways at Freddy with a 'what is Socrates going to say now?' look in his eye.

"A one-two for the team and having Paulo take all the attention by bringing a supermodel to dinner means almost no attention on S1 latest hot couple."

"I didn't plan for that, but I am happy not to be the centre of all the gossip." Jaxxon smiled. "The focus should be on the team and our results, not our personal life. It's called personal for a reason." And just as Freddy's doubt tried to seep in, Jaxxon slung his arm over Freddy's shoulder and kissed him on the cheek. "I'm perfectly happy being Freddy's boyfriend and I don't need to hide my love for him."

"I always knew you two would make a cute couple." Socrates smiled widely.

Freddy laughed. "If I didn't know better, I would've

said you'd stolen your own trophies, just to push us together."

Socrates shook his head. "I would never. I am smugly pleased that it all worked out, and that everyone is getting exactly what they've earned." His quiet reference to Chester being denied bail didn't make Freddy feel anything. Not even the slightest twinge of pettiness. Was that growth?

He leaned his head on Jaxxon's shoulder. "Should we invite your boss to our wedding? Or will he be too smug?"

"That's really up to him, isn't it?" Jaxxon didn't scare at Freddy's mention of a wedding, although it wasn't in their plan and they hadn't discussed it.

Socrates cackled with laughter. "When you are ready... Let's get tonight's party started first."

If you enjoyed this book, the next book in the series is DRIVEN TO PROTECT, featuring Gamble Racing's other driver, Paulo Sanchez.

Paid to protect him ... But at what cost?

Paulo's father's money bought him a seat in a Series One car, and now he needs to prove himself. Unfortunately, after a spectacular crash he finds it hard not to believe all the bad press about him. He escapes hospital to go to a dodgy bar, thinking a secret hook-up might get this all out of his system. Then he meets Cohen.

Working as a security guard in a run-down gay bar as a trans man has meant Cohen has seen a lot of things. But none as shocking as when rich and famous Paulo offers him a new job. He can take the money and protect his boss without getting emotionally involved. Can't he?

As the racing season progresses, they have everything to prove. Paulo needs to be the driver he knows he can be, and Cohen needs to show that he can protect the man he's falling in love with.

———

Want a bit more sexy romance? Sign up to my newsletter to read the free series prequel: http://www.reneedahlia.com/books/gamble-racing/news/

ACKNOWLEDGMENTS

I pay my respects to the Wangal people of the Eora Nation, who are the traditional owners of the land on which this book was written.

My kids, who are huge F1 fans, for working out the fake race season results for my drivers in this series and helping with other technical details. If you want to see the full spreadsheet, it's an extra on my Patreon.

Thank you to Lina, the Word Makers, Rachel Reid and the Carina discord. You've all championed this series and your support has kept me writing during a difficult year in personal life.

AUTHOR NOTES

The average cost of a heart transplant in the USA in 2019 was $1,382,400. In Australia, the cost to the individual at a public hospital is $0 (plus parking), and the average cost paid via insurance at a private hospital in Australia was A$150,000 in 2020. In the UK, a heart transplant done by the NHS costs $0 (plus parking) to the individual, and the average cost paid via insurance at a private hospital is £40,000 plus around £100,000 for the pre-surgery and post-surgery time in 2020.

McLaren drivers Ayrton Senna and Alain Prost won the 1988 and 1989 F1 World Championship. In my fictional world, these two years went to Socrates Drayton. Senna won again in 1990 and 1991, while Prost also won in 85, 86, and 1993.

On average F1 drivers' reaction speed is three times faster than the ordinary person. At the end of the 2021 season, there had been 770 drivers who had started an F1 race and only 111 (14.4%) had achieved a race win.

ALL BOOKS BY RENÉE DAHLIA

Thanks for reading DRIVEN BY AMBITION. I hope you enjoyed it. Reviews can help readers find books, and I am grateful for all honest reviews. Thank you for taking the time to let others know what you've read, and what you thought. If you write a review for DRIVEN BY AMBITION and email me (renee at reneedahlia dot com) with the link, I will send you a free copy of one of my books of your choice.

If you'd like to know more about me, my books, or to connect with me online, you can visit my webpage www.reneedahlia.com and if you sign up to my newsletter, you can grab a free book.

Twitter https://twitter.com/dekabat

Facebook https://www.facebook.com/reneedahliawriter/

Instagram https://www.instagram.com/reneedahlia_author/

Patreon https://www.patreon.com/reneedahlia
BookBub   https://www.bookbub.com/authors/renee-dahlia

You've just read a book in my Gamble Racing Series.
Contemporary Series: Gamble Racing

1. Driven to Distraction (mm)
2. Driven by Passion (mm)
3. Driven by Ambition (mm)
4. Driven to Protect (mm)

Contemporary Series: Seraph's Burlesque Club

1. Show Up (ff with bisexual heroine)
2. Show Off (ff with bisexual heroines)
3. Show Queen (ff)
4. Show Time (mm)
5. Show Dance (mm)

Contemporary Series: Kapow!

1. Out of Her League (fm with bisexual characters)
2. His Buxom Beauty (fm)
3. Craving His Spotlight (mm)
4. Her Pregnant Rival (ff)

Contemporary Series: Farrellton Foster Family

1. Betrayed (fm)

2. Forbidden (fm with bisexual characters)
3. Liability (ff)

Contemporary Series: Margaret River TV: Boxed Set

- Homage (fm with bisexual heroine)
- Uplift (ff with bisexual heroines)

Contemporary Series: Merindah Park

1. Merindah Park (fm)
2. Making Her Mark (fm with bisexual heroine)
3. Two Hearts Healing (fm)
4. Racetrack Royalty (fm)

Contemporary Series: Rainbow Cove

1. His Christmas Pearl (fm)
2. His Christmas Pride (mm)

Historical Series: Great War

1. Her Lady's Melody (ff)
2. Her Lady's Fortune (ff)
3. Her Lady's Honor (ff)
4. His Lord's Soldier (mm)

Historical Series: Bluestockings

Prequel: The Shipwrecked Earl's Bride (fm with bisexual hero)

1. To Charm a Bluestocking (fm with bisexual hero)
2. In Pursuit of a Bluestocking (fm)
3. The Heart of a Bluestocking (fm)